THE SWEETEST THING
YOU CAN SING

THE SWEETEST THING
YOU CAN SING

C.K. Kelly Martin

The publisher gratefully acknowledges the support of the Canada Council for the Arts and the Ontario Arts Council for its publishing program. We acknowledge the financial support of the Government of Canada through the Canada Book Fund (CBF) for our publishing activities, and the Government of Ontario through the Ontario Media Development Corporation, an agency of the Ontario Ministry of Culture, and the Ontario Book Publishing Tax Credit Program.

LIBRARY AND ARCHIVES CANADA CATALOGUING IN PUBLICATION

Martin, C. K. Kelly, author
The sweetest thing you can sing / C.K. Kelly Martin.

Issued in print and electronic formats.
ISBN 978-1-77086-411-5 (pbk.). — ISBN 978-1-77086-412-2 (html)

I. Title.

PS8626.A76922S94 2014   JC813'.6   C2014-905116-6
                                          C2014-905117-4

Cover photo and design: Angel Guerra/Archetype
Interior text design: Tannice Goddard, Soul Oasis Networking
Printer: Trigraphik LBF

Printed and bound in Canada.

The interior of this book is printed on 30% post-consumer waste recycled paper.

DANCING CAT BOOKS
AN IMPRINT OF CORMORANT BOOKS INC.
10 ST. MARY STREET, SUITE 615, TORONTO, ONTARIO, M4Y 1P9
www.dancingcatbooks.com
www.cormorantbooks.com

Rage on

CHAPTER ONE

❧

EVERYONE DISAPPOINTS YOU EVENTUALLY; it just comes as a bigger surprise when your favourite people do it. My brother Devin taught me that.

It was my other brother, Morgan, who showed me the power of second-hand stardust. The minute he appeared as a reality TV contestant on one of those claustrophobic shows that lock a group of pretty people into a house together, the popular tier at school started smiling at me and saying hi, as though my chubbiness was suddenly okay.

Don't think I overlooked the difference between ninth and tenth grade. It would be hard for me to miss how invisible my freshman self was first semester, except to my old middle school friends, Marguerite and Izzy. Then Morgan became a TV hit, making such a splash that mere days after his elimination, MuchMusic phoned him up and asked him to be their newest VJ.

At first the attention made me feel like maybe it didn't matter how much I weighed, but it turned out that most of the guys I was interested in still weren't interested back. They'd tell me about their weekends and kid around with me during class, but I can count on two fingers the times I made out with one of them at a party. The first guy pretended it'd never happened and bragged about the hot lifeguard girl he'd hooked up with at the community centre pool (which sounded more like a daydream he'd had while thumbing through Maxim than reality). The second guy apologized to me before math class, explaining that he was so plastered the night it'd happened that he'd fallen asleep over the toilet in between puke attacks.

Marguerite and Izzy told me I'd just chosen the wrong guys, but how could I choose the *right* guy when no one with a Y chromosome (except old creeps who leered from moving cars) looked at me with lust in their eyes? The truth is that no high school guy ever likes you for yourself. Being thin is prerequisite number one for being sexy. Other prerequisites include having skin that doesn't look like a biblical punishment, laughing at stuff guys say even when they're not as funny as they seem to think they are, and not acting like a complete loser (by doing things like wearing loser clothes, stuttering, or walking around like there's a "kick me" sign attached to your spine).

I had most of the prerequisites covered. I wasn't very good at approaching people I didn't know, but I could speak to them in a way that assured them I wasn't an absolute geek when *they* came up to *me*. Being Morgan LeBlanc's sister awarded me bonus cool points (and I already had clear skin), but unfortunately not even those could magically make me skinny.

One day last spring Izzy and I stayed at school late to talk over a geography assignment with Mrs. McClaren, and Izzy bumped into a guy from the junior basketball team as he was coming out of the gym. Two of his friends were with him, and as they were sauntering off we overheard one of them say, "Man, this year's freshman crop has been sad."

Izzy and I frowned at each other. Then the guy who'd collided with her seconds before added, "Isn't Serena supposed to be a hot girl's name?"

I frowned deeper and looked at my shoes. "They don't even *know* my name," Izzy said, like that was supposed to make me feel better. "Anyway, everyone knows the junior basketball team sucks."

She was right. The team did suck. Except for hotshot point guard Jacob Westermark, my current (and only) boyfriend, whom I acquired after shedding twenty-nine pounds of chunk. I convinced myself months ago that Jacob's presence in the hallway that day didn't matter because he'd been the innocent by virtue of his silence third guy.

Having such asshole friends should've been enough to reveal the asshole within and warn me that he'd let me down in a big way. It definitely shouldn't have come to this — Aya Yamamoto, sweaty from grinding with Wyatt and Orlando, one of her hands clasped on my knee, blinking at me like her eyelashes are butterfly's wings as Chaz howls in the background and Jacob urges me to, "Kiss her, Serena. *Damn*, you two are so hot right now. Give us some girl on girl action."

Aya's clammy hand smoothes over my kneecap. Slinky. Skanky. The same way she'd touch a guy to get his attention. Normally there'd be more people crowded around watching, but Wyatt caught major parental interference for the property damages from his last party and only invited a select few of us over to celebrate his birthday with him. As it is, all the guys in the room are ogling Aya and me like we've already pulled out our boobs and are seconds away from getting it on full-scale. A couple of the girls are watching too, and my heart's beating in a sickening, scary movie kind of way. My legs fuse to the couch fabric and my throat constricts, making it hard to breathe, when what I really want to do is knee Jacob, Wyatt, and Chaz in the balls and then make their noses bleed.

"You know I don't like girls like that," I tell Jacob in a scratchy voice. "It's like asking you to kiss Wyatt."

Jacob grimaces and tosses his head back. "That's not the same. Everyone likes watching girls together. It's hot."

"She'll never do it, bro," Wyatt yells from across the room. His crooked smile bites into his cheekbones. "She's more uptight than the state of Kentucky."

Aya herself says nothing, her hand still on my knee. We're all so bottomed-out drunk right now that it's not supposed to matter what we do, but it still does, at least to me.

Chaz starts howling again in the background, and the music's giving me what my brother Devin would call a superturbo headache — the kind he used to be hit with if he went too long without coffee. "It's just a kiss," Jacob says in the pleading, sexy voice he always uses to get me to do something I'm not sure about. "C'mon, for me. Just this once. Live a little, Serena." He sits forward on the couch so he can get a better look at Aya on my other side. "Look at those lips. Damn. If you don't do it I might have to take a shot myself."

Aya's stinky beer breath is in my face, and let me tell you, there's nothing appealing about it. Her butterfly blinks are growing longer and longer and I'm thinking that she could pass out cold any second now and probably not remember a thing. "What'd I tell you?" Wyatt shouts, pointing at me with a condescending look. "She's a good girl to the core."

My heart's racing worse and I hate how everyone's staring at me like no matter what I do it will be wrong. I can't win. Being fat or thin, being nobody or soaking up hand-me-down limelight, none of it makes any difference because people will only let you down in the end. That's what they do.

I push Aya's hand off my knee, and her unfocused eyes hang on me for a few seconds. Her newly freed hand races up to her mouth as she gags. Then the beer smell's worse, like a preview of its appearance on the couch and the plush beige carpet. I shoot up, edge my way past Jacob and away from the couch, my feet tangling up in each other momentarily along the way. The music's pounding inside my skull so I can't hear Aya puking, but everyone's looking over in her direction, either grossed out or choking up drunken laughs. Izzy and Marguerite would be horrified by the amount of stupidity inside this room right now, but of course they're not around.

Did they downgrade our friendship when I started going out with Jacob, or did I do that myself? Hard to say. Up till now I've been paying too much attention to my *oh so fabulous* boyfriend to really notice what's been going on with anyone else.

I'm not crying, that would just be dumb and dramatic, but my eyes hurt and I'm moving like there's a "kick me" sign permanently engraved on my back. It doesn't matter that it's invisible, I can sense it all the same, and so would everyone else if only they were looking at me.

Nobody follows me out into the hall where I wrestle my wool coat from the closet. Nobody sees me slip out the front door and into a dark November night. I don't really matter to anyone at this party, certainly not Jacob. Between that thought and the cold, I'm dead sober again.

With my short skirt and bare legs I'll be lucky if I don't transform into a human popsicle before I get home. Devin once told me that if I ever have to walk alone at night I should project the air of a girl who would claw a guy's eyes out if he tried anything. It's hard to do that when you're feeling disappointed, but I'm mad too and I concentrate on that as I stalk along the sidewalk, ready to shoot a lethal look at the first creep who dares to pull up next to me.

No one so much as honks at me the whole way home, but I don't doubt a castrating stare would protect me. If Devin said it, it must be true. Morgan might be the one everyone likes — the one who can make losing look like winning and challenges seem like fun — but Devin's the one who usually knows the right thing to say to me. Usually *did* know the right thing to say to me. Not anymore.

Didn't I say that everyone lets you down? Why should there be any exceptions to the rule?

CHAPTER TWO

IT TOOK ME A while to realize I wasn't chubby Serena anymore. If I'd tried to slim down it never would've worked. I like to eat. I mean, I was never all-out enormous, but I like second helpings, cupcakes at lunch, and soft drinks with real sugar. My brother Devin was the same way, and my parents never made us feel bad about our imperfect frames, but sometimes I could hear the silent comparisons with Morgan leak out from other people's minds.

My extended family, my parents' friends, even strangers like shop assistants or waiters — they were all charmed by Morgan. He was virtually perfect — friendly, funny, and nearly as good-looking as the guys you see in magazine ads for designer jeans. Whenever I was next to Morgan I noticed the way people beamed at him. They even beamed at me when I was beside him; I gained goodwill by association. You had to be a seriously hard case to steel yourself against Morgan. Confirmed homophobes even seemed to soften their anti-gay attitudes around him, usually unwilling to make an enemy of Morgan over something they'd label unnatural in someone else.

People loved Morgan no matter what he did, just *because* he was Morgan. Devin and I used to complain about it to each other, but Devin had his own exceptionalities going for him. Morgan was the popular one, but Devin was the one who'd qualified for Mensa at fourteen and had been doing my parents' taxes ever since. He was the one who'd won a full university scholarship and was always first in his class. Before last spring he'd never failed anything in his life.

That was *then*, before Devin turned every day into a twenty-four-hour exercise in tension when Dad dragged him home from university in March. He *wasn't well*, as my parents liked to call it. The results of Devin's *unwellness* were unpredictable, and whenever I was around the house I was too edgy to be hungry (you never knew what would happen next). You'd think getting rid of the source of that stress would help, but when Devin went AWOL in June my appetite curled up and died completely.

For months everyone in my family was too preoccupied to notice my dwindling waistline much, me included. No one except Izzy even mentioned it, and that was only once.

So I didn't really know I was thin until August 22. Devin was gone and the three of us still living at home weren't doing a fabulous job of dealing with his absence. Dad didn't talk about him or *it* if he could avoid the topic, but he didn't smile much anymore either. Mom was away from the museum with migraines so often — lying in the dark with her white noise machine amped up to maximum — that they'd hired her a full-time assistant.

That night in August Mom was supposed to take me back to school shopping because nothing fit anymore; all my clothes hung on me like an exaggerated "after" image in a weight loss commercial. The funny thing about shopping with my mom was how she'd turn into a teenage girl while doing it, laughing at stuff she wouldn't ordinarily find funny and asking me things about Izzy and Marguerite, as though the four of us were all friends. Then we'd stop for lattes and whisper silly things about passersby. Occasionally she'd try on things decades too young for her, just kidding around. It was embarrassing and comical at the same time. I'd be smiling while wishing for the power of invisibility.

This past August I didn't have to make that wish, and there were no lattes or laughing either. Mom complained that she had a crippling headache and handed me her ATM card. Dad was the one who taxied me over to the Glenashton mall, instructing me to call when I needed picking up.

But I never made that call. Instead I bumped into Jacob Westermark, who surprised me by flirting with me in the food court line, his dark blue eyes zooming in on my pupils like I was someone else. We sat and talked for a long time, him listening almost as much as he spoke. Then he drove me home and kissed me in his car. Jacob with his sexy basketball player arms and a T-shirt that fit so well it made me wonder if I was staring.

He was precisely the kind of guy Devin would've torn to pieces under his breath in a funny voice the minute Jacob walked away. Athletic. Popular. Cocky enough to believe his own hype. But he was also sweet that night, and when I finally stepped inside my front door various bits of me were purring shamelessly from the things we'd done in his front seat.

Jacob didn't pretend we'd never kissed. He didn't apologize for it either. We kissed a lot from then on. In Jacob's bedroom, the baseball diamond bleachers five minutes from my house, Chaz's basement, around the back of the school portables, at a booth in Pizza Hut where we both sat on the same side and the middle-aged waitress called us cute. For a while he made me believe I'd found the thing, the person, that would make me stand out from all the other average, nearly invisible kids I went to school with. No Mensa or MuchMusic for me. His name was Jacob Westermark.

CHAPTER THREE

❦

WHEN I WAKE UP, the back of my throat tastes like musty fall leaves and a thick strand of my hair is curled around my neck, a sweat mixture forming on my skin. I smell like last night's beer, which reminds me of Aya Yamamoto's hand on my knee and all the guys wanting to turn us into a live demonstration of *Girls Gone Wild*.

Jacob Westermark is a sleazy little asshole that I won't let myself miss. He should've stood up for me and told the rest of them to go fuck themselves. I'm embarrassed that I slunk off into the night like a woman shamed. I should've slapped Jacob across the face or dumped a drink over his head like a girl in a movie would. His friends would've laughed at him instead of howling at me. I'd feel so much better right now if I'd done that instead of running off.

I untangle myself from my death grip hair and drag myself into the bathroom. Surprisingly, I don't look as bad as I feel. I brush my teeth, gargle the stale grossness out of my throat with citrus mouthwash, and drag myself down to the kitchen for something to eat that won't make me feel like the icky insides of a recycle bin. The milk tastes sour, and the cola and orange juice burn on first contact. I settle for ice water and two pieces of plain toast, and my dad strides in searching for his keys while I'm chewing. "How was the party last night?" he asks absently.

I got over Jacob, high school parties, and the entire concept of sex in one night. That's how the party was. But I sigh and say, "Annoying. People drinking too much and acting like idiots."

Dad looks impressed with my maturity. "Well, it sounds like we don't have to worry about you too much, doesn't it?" He spots his keys on the counter next to a container of dried pasta and sweeps them into his hand.

No one would've thought to worry about Devin before either. Maybe you can never do enough worrying. "Where are you going?" I ask him.

"Home Hardware," Dad says. "I have some work to do in the upstairs bathroom and I can't find my caulking gun."

Some things went missing while Devin was home. Neither of us mentions this possibility in relation to the caulking gun. Dad goes off to Home Hardware and I shuffle upstairs and listen to my cellphone messages. The first thing I hear is Jacob shouting into my ear above the din of a Kanye West tune, demanding to know where I am. If he sounded worried maybe I'd soften, not enough to keep seeing him but enough to wonder if he cared a little.

Jacob doesn't sound worried. He sounds like the same pissed off, drunken dickhead he was last night. I'm glad that the next two messages are hang-ups, but when I press *end* my cell rings in my hand. I freeze at the sight of Jacob's phone number. What would a girl in a movie do? What would Morgan, who expects everyone to like and respect him, do?

"Hello," I say quietly.

"That's all you have to say?" Jacob says. "Hello?"

"Pretty much." I try to sound like I never cared about him in the first place. This is what you get for expecting another person to be your magical, special thing. Consider me educated.

"Shit, Serena." He grunts into the phone. "You take off in the middle of Wyatt's party and now you give me attitude. What's with you?"

"You really don't know?" How can that be possible? My heart jumps against my rib cage.

"How could I?" he asks. I wait for him to go on, but there isn't any more.

It's humiliating to have to say it. I can't believe I let myself get twisted up in this. What happened to the guy I sat with on the same side of a booth kissing? Is he still in there somewhere along with asshole Jacob?

I think back to how we were in the beginning. How tender Jacob's voice got whenever he thought I was feeling sad, the way he was always telling me how beautiful I was and how good I made him feel when we were touching each other.

"The way you see me ..." I pinch my lips together and pace my bedroom, my fingertips sliding across the contents of my dresser like they're Braille. "The way you see me isn't *right*. It's all about you. It's like I'm not even a ..." I stop moving and drop my voice. "It's just sex. That's the only thing that matters to you."

I loved making out with him, and when he'd tease my breasts and say how gorgeous they were. It's true, I was always ready to whip off my top for him and let him do it. But Jacob seemed to get bored of those things more easily than I did. He wanted more, so I tried.

The first time I put it in my mouth I almost gagged and had to pretend my jaw hurt instead. The main thing was, he liked it and told me I was good. Sometimes he'd say really dirty things while I was doing it. Some of them made me feel good because I knew he wanted me and some I didn't want to hear because they made me feel wrong and almost ... I don't know ... like ashamed or something. The thing was, back then it was never just the bad things on their own, there was always the nice things too — amazing kissing and Jacob's awe-inspiring basketball player arms, him nuzzling my breasts and talking to them like they each had beating hearts of their own.

"C'mon," Jacob says, like he can't believe what he's hearing through the phone. "We're not even *having* sex, Serena. There's never been any sex."

I'm quiet. He doesn't see that the balance between good and bad things has been weighing on the wrong side for too long already — him saying nasty things into my ear, always trying to convince me how much closer doing those things would make us. Or maybe he does see it, but it doesn't make any difference to him.

"We were just kidding around last night," he continues. "You know that. Why do you have to blow it all out of proportion? Nothing even happened, did it?"

Nothing happened because Aya upchucked and I pulled a disappearing act. Otherwise Jacob would've been quite happy to sit there next to me and watch Aya and I put on a show for all his friends, no matter how shitty I felt about it.

"I'm just sick of it, Jacob, okay?" My voice is whiny. I want to sound self-righteous, but I can't stop feeling sorry for myself. "I'm tired of things being wrong."

Jacob makes a frustrated noise into the phone. Then he says, "If it was just about sex I wouldn't be with you, would I? So, look, what do you want me to do?"

"Nothing, Jacob, okay?" For some reason I can't stop saying "okay." "This just isn't happening anymore. We're done. I'm tired of you pushing me, telling me what you want, making me feel like a slut — or *not enough* of a slut. I'm never just …" My tongue trips over my teeth. "… me." A single hot tear squeezes out of my right eye.

Jacob coughs out the same aggravated noise he made earlier. "You like when we're together too, Serena. You can't pretend you don't.

If *you* took things too seriously last night … hey, that's not how it was, so I'm sorry you got it wrong."

"I'm not looking for an apology," I tell him. "*Not that that actually was one.*" Yay for me, it turns out I can pop out some decent, movie girl lines after all.

"Hey," Jacob says, and now he actually sounds slightly worried, "I was loaded last night. I hardly knew what I was saying. If it was worse than I thought, I didn't mean it. I know you'd never do anything you didn't want to anyway. You're not like that."

Aren't I? I rub the tear off my face and act like it was never there in the first place.

"Do you want me to come over later?" he asks in a mushy tone. "We can watch that Emma Stone DVD you wanted to see. I can stop at the mall and pick up some of that almond popcorn you like first."

That sounds nice, but if I follow it through in my head I know it will always turn out the same way, maybe not tonight, if he's being good, but eventually. If I could cut out the things about Jacob that I like and keep them I wouldn't be left with anything close to a whole person. The whispering to my boobs, holding my hand when we walk, and telling me I'm beautiful just isn't enough.

"I can't, Jacob." My throat hurts but there are no more tears. "You should call someone else." I can't resist a final movie girl line. "And be nice to her, all right?"

I hang up before he has the chance to say something I don't want to hear. I switch my cell off, climb back into bed, and wait for high school to be over.

⊠

In some ways breaking it off with Jacob is like taking a step back in time. I'm still semi-popular at school (I'm still Morgan LeBlanc's sister and I'm still thin) but I'm not a hotshot point guard's girlfriend anymore. What's more, I don't want to be *anyone's* girlfriend (or anyone's FB either) and I let that be known, in subtle ways, to the guys who think I'm a fresh opportunity. Mostly I'm back to hanging out with Izzy and Marguerite, but it doesn't feel quite the same. I know they talk about things to each other that they don't discuss with me, and neither of them calls me at night unless it's about homework or TV.

Jacob gives me the evil eye in the school hallways but says nothing. Twice Wyatt calls me a bitch. One time Jacob's next to him and looks away. The other time Wyatt's with Chaz and Orlando, and Chaz tells me I'm damn cold. Nobody else seems mad at me, but I feel less important. Is it dumb to miss hearing someone tell you how pretty you are with a special kind of tremble in his voice when being pretty isn't supposed to matter anyway?

Dad seems to take my breakup with Jacob as inevitable. Mom asks if I'm okay and then zones out when I answer. Why do I bother when I know the only thing she wants to think about anymore — the one thing that seems to make her feel better — is shutting herself in the den to make eBay bids on retired Swarovski figurines to add to her collection? I always just end up feeling guilty for mentally interrupting her.

But if Devin (the old Devin, that is) were around he'd congratulate me on ditching Jacob's ass. He'd probably call me shallow for being tempted by basketball player arms in the first place but who is he to judge? And anyway, I'm not sure the old Devin even exists anyplace outside my head anymore.

Since he left I can't seem to get through two weeks without having a dream about him. I wouldn't mind except there are only two dreams that I have about Devin and both of them are bad. In dream number one he's on a shouting rampage. First he takes on my parents and then he turns on me. The dream Devin says scathing things I've heard him yell in real life, but he yells other awful things too. His mean streak is a mile wide and bone deep. It makes Jacob's selfishness seem like a walk in the park, like wildflowers and baby bunnies. When I wake up from that dream I feel like a hollowed-out egg, but the other dream is worse and that's the one I shake myself awake from tonight, a chill at the base of my spine.

The dream starts like a typical scary movie scene. It's night, and a young woman (me) is scurrying under a decrepit-looking city bridge. There aren't any stars or moon but somehow I can see my feet on the cement. It's not any particular temperature. I don't feel hot or cold and there's no wind and no traffic either. Quiet. Dark. Alone. My heart thumps frantically at the sound of footsteps behind me. Heavy. Slow. Like whoever or whatever it is knows it will get me in the end. I sprint for the other end of the bridge, where it should be lighter but isn't, and anyway my legs can't work up enough speed to escape. I run in slow motion, like I'm fighting air, until I'm sick to death of trying. I'm a goner and I know it.

I turn to see what's behind me, expecting my heart to stop in fear. I'm positive it will be a psycho killer with a knife or some ancient horned evil, but it's neither of those things. A version of Devin's standing there under the bridge with me. He's gotten so skinny that he looks like something from a medical journal. His head doesn't sit right on his shoulders and his anorexic arms are stiff like a zombie's. I know in an instant that he wasn't chasing me and doesn't mean to harm me. He doesn't even know I'm there.

He's gone. Lost.

I stare at the empty person in front of me and watch him walk. He thuds right by me, into the night, his eyes dull in their sockets and his face expressionless.

That's the moment I wake up, alone in the dark missing a brother. He could be anywhere. He could be dead. I shiver and sweat at the same time, thinking about that.

Back in mid-July a jogger in Newmarket stumbled across a body near a running path in the woods. The newspaper described it as a young white male, fully clothed. My mom's hands started shaking and my dad kept saying there was no reason for Devin to be in Newmarket, no reason. We live about an hour away from Newmarket, but I've never been there and I'd never heard Devin mention the place either. Like my father said, there was no reason for Devin to be in Newmarket.

Only maybe he hadn't started out in Newmarket. He could've been kidnapped or gotten himself in the middle of a drug deal gone bad. Maybe he was screwing some married woman and her husband found them together and got violent. My mind raced as my mom's hands continued to shake. *You never knew with Devin.* He'd become the kind of person anything could happen to.

By the time he left us, he'd already lost touch with lots of his old friends. The only people I saw him with were ones who either wouldn't look you in the eye or would stare for too long and make you want to take a step away from them. There were random girls too — one who wouldn't stop shouting while they were in his bedroom and who later stumbled out having forgotten to button up her jeans and another whom I caught a glimpse of him having sex with (her miniskirt hitched up and her thong around her ankles) through the wide open bathroom door before I realized what was happening and took off for Izzy's house.

"There's no reason at all for us to assume it could be Devin," my dad repeated, his face pale. "This article gives next to no details. The description probably fits a million people in this country."

My mother said we should call the Newmarket police department, and the suggestion made my dad raise his voice. "No one's calling the police department," he insisted. "Devin's not a missing person. He left of his own free will. We can't ring up police departments across the country every time we open the newspaper, for God's sake."

My mom scrunched up her eyebrows. "We're talking about our son," she said hoarsely. "If I have to call police departments across the country, I will."

Mom snatched up the cordless and dialled information to ask for the number. Dad listened to her without offering another word of protest. The two of us sat there trying to piece together details from the half of the conversation we could hear. Mom's fingers trembled worse than ever as she hung up. She said that the body had just been identified as a young man from Quebec but that the police wouldn't reveal any more as the family had yet to be notified. I silently cursed my brother for making us miserable, even as relief clawed at my throat.

My mind sifts through it all again as I roll over in bed — dream Devin, missing Devin, the Devin who would've applauded me for calling it quits with Jacob and the one who raged at my mother, accusing her of trying to make him fat when she was only trying to get him to eat some pot roast and peas.

It makes me so sad to think about that I can hardly stand it. Does anyone bother to coax Devin to eat dinner anymore?

CHAPTER FOUR

MS. YUEN PAIRS ME up with Aya Yamamoto for a conversation exercise in French last period. It's the first time we've spoken to each other since that night at Wyatt's but neither of us mentions it. Aya's French is almost as good as her English and that makes me angry with her. She's too smart to act like a skank for people like Wyatt and Orlando. What was she even doing at Wyatt's party? The people she usually hangs out with play the flute and top the honour roll.

I don't say goodbye to her when the bell rings. I'm not holding her fully responsible for that night but she's not innocent either. Now that I'm unattached I could easily spend too much time thinking about things that don't really matter, like why people do the things they do, but I've decided that I won't. What I need is to keep busy, and I've settled on the idea of a part-time job.

Last spring I started thinking that I'd like a baby blue scooter to cruise around town in. I could change my mind long before I have the money to buy one, but at least it's something to think about that doesn't involve high school guys or serious amounts of talent in an as yet undiscovered area.

If I had a scooter now I could hop on and be home in a couple of minutes rather than the fifteen it takes me to walk. Izzy's mom picks her and Marguerite up almost every day, but my house is in the opposite direction and since we've just started hanging out together again it doesn't seem like a good time to ask for a favour. Actually, even if I had a scooter I'd sooner ride in something with a roof this afternoon because it's starting to rain.

I pull my hoodie over my head as I step outside. Not only is it raining but it's cold. I bury my hands in my pockets and consider searching out Izzy after all. Her mom usually picks her up by the south doors near the office and I'm about to head that way when my eardrums pick up on Nicole Lapatas screeching at some lanky junior guy I don't know by name.

She's only six feet away and I can't avoid hearing her scream, "You're disgusting! You're going to be one of those guys whose best friend is his hand forever and who's still living in his parents' basement when he's forty because no girl will go near him!"

The lanky guy laughs, stares intently at his phone, and intones, "Ooh, you're sexy when you're mad, Nicki." I can't see the image on his cell from where I'm standing but the noise from it is clearly audible. Some guy's shouting encouragement to Nicole, telling her she's the hottest thing he's ever seen and *oh yeah, baby, YEAH, Nicki, baby, that's it …*

The guy looks up from his cell, a dirty grin stuck on his lips as he says, "You got some nice moves here. Why don't you want anyone to see them?"

Nicole grabs for his phone, but she's not fast enough. He yanks it into the sky above his head and laughs again as she jumps for it. "You *are* a frisky one, aren't you?" He whistles low but flicks his eyes away from mine when he sees me staring. His laughter turns embarrassed and then stops completely. "Okay, okay — there," he says, slipping the cell into his backpack. "Happy now?"

"Fuck you," Nicole declares, worry lines etching into her forehead. She reaches for his backpack this time, sliding the zip halfway down before he fights her off.

"Calm down," he tells her. "*Ree-lax*, Nicole. Just chill, would you?"

Nicole hasn't given up. Both her hands lunge for his backpack, all her weight and energy focused on it like she means business. The guy pulls back fast, spinning away from her and upsetting her balance. He doesn't glance back to see her crumple to the ground. He's halfway to the football field by the time I realize it's up to me to do something.

Nicole Lapatas is lying across the littered cement, one of her legs folded under the other and her skirt askew. I step towards her, realizing as I do that someone else is hurrying in her direction too. I bend down in front of Nicole and say, "Are you okay?"

Genevieve Richardson, last year's student council treasurer, crouches down next to me. She extends her hand to Nicole, who takes it and pulls herself up. "God, that looks sore," Genevieve declares, her eyes on Nicole's injured bare right leg, which is both scraped raw and covered in runny mud and itty bitty pebbles.

I groan inside as I stare at it. There's a cigarette butt on the ground between us which could easily have wound up fused to her skin too. "It's too bad you weren't wearing pants," I say sympathetically.

Nicole nods at me. Her eyes have filled with tears.

"Are you all right besides that, do you think?" Genevieve asks, her long red hair falling over her shoulders as she scrutinizes the wound. "Does it feel like anything's broken?"

Nicole places her weight solidly on her right leg and shakes her head. At that moment Jacob and Orlando strut right by us. Jacob eyes Nicole's leg and I'm sure he notices that she's crying too, but he doesn't say anything. Suddenly I want to run after him and thump him hard on the back. He'd either laugh at me or act like I was being hysterical and the thought eggs me on. I have the crazy feeling that I'd do it, if only Genevieve and Nicole weren't next to me.

"You'll have to clean that out really well," Genevieve continues. "You don't want it to get infected."

Nicole winces as she peers down at her leg. "I hope it doesn't scar."

"It doesn't look deep," Genevieve tells her. I nod in agreement, still visualizing smacking Jacob.

"Do you have a ride home?" Genevieve asks, throwing her hair back over her shoulders. "I can give you a lift."

Nicole sighs and stares off at a speck in the distance. "That would be great. Thanks."

I follow Nicole's eyes to the disappearing guy, who is now only a dot on the horizon. "Maybe you guys can run him over on your way home," I offer. On a normal day I'd pretend not to have noticed what happened between them, out of politeness, but it doesn't feel like an ordinary day anymore.

Nicole smiles thinly. "You promise?"

The fact that he seemed to be watching some sexy footage of her that she wasn't happy about is good enough for me. Like I needed another demonstration of how much high school guys suck. "If I can add someone to the list too," I quip.

Nicole smirks and wipes her damp cheek with the back of her hand. "Since Genevieve's driving I guess that's up to her."

The three of us are getting soaked standing there, but Genevieve, with her perfect features and A average, still looks like a cross between young Gwyneth Paltrow and teenaged Nicole Kidman. "Come on," Genevieve says impatiently, digging her hands into the pockets of her brown leather jacket. "I'm freezing." She cocks her head at me. "Do you need a ride too?"

"I'd love one." Genevieve has never bothered to suck up to me because of Morgan. I can't imagine her sucking up to anyone, and maybe it's dumb of me to feel mildly excited about catching a ride with her, but if I don't tell anyone it doesn't count.

I let Nicole take the front seat in Genevieve's not new but not ancient Honda Civic. Genevieve asks us where we live and begins driving in the direction of Nicole's house. It's quiet in the car and

Genevieve explains that her speakers are blown. "I meant to buy new ones," she says, "but I started to get used to the silence."

Then we're back to a semi-awkward quiet that lasts until we pull into Nicole's driveway. "Thanks for the ride," she tells Genevieve before turning to glance over her shoulder at me. "Thanks, Serena. I'll see you in English tomorrow."

"See you, Nicole," I say back. We just finished *Lord of the Flies* in English this morning and I'm never going to pick up the book again if I can help it. Who wants to read a novel about how we're all basically savages at the core? If that's true, I don't want to know it.

I hop in the front so Genevieve won't feel like my chauffeur, and as soon as I shut my door she says, "So have you seen the video? I didn't want to mention it to Nicole because she seemed pretty upset, but really, she should've known better. You can't let them film stuff like that." Genevieve clucks in disapproval. "But I feel sorry for her anyway. It's not like she can undo the damage, is it?"

"Actually, I didn't see the video. The guy Nicole was fighting with was watching it so I just heard a bit from his cell." I have that *Lord of the Flies* dread in my stomach and wonder if I really want to know more. "What is it? Like a sex tape?"

Genevieve shoots me a sideways look. "It was going around school today. I'm sure you'll see it soon enough. Basically she's doing a strip-tease for Liam Powers. Lots of shaking her naked booty and so on. You can imagine."

"That sucks." I frown and look out the window. Nicole and Liam Powers have been hooking up since last spring. He's a junior like Genevieve but not quite as popular. Whenever I saw Nicole and Liam together in the hall or cafeteria they were smiling. Now I'll probably never see them together again. It occurs to me that things could've been so much worse with Jacob. "I can't believe Liam would do that to her."

"Word is it wasn't him that spread the video — someone else stumbled across it on his cell and forwarded it around."

I groan. "Everyone's going to see it. That's so unfair." I have no idea what I'd do if it was me.

"Ridiculously unfair," Genevieve agrees. "Now Liam Powers is some kind of hero and she's a slut." She combs her fingers through her wet hair. "That's what people think."

I know it and I grumble, "I'm so off guys that it isn't funny." I don't know that I'd call them savages like in *Lord of the Flies* but they're not far off.

"Tell me about it." Genevieve tosses her head back. "None of them at Laurier are worth spending more than five minutes with, and with some of them five minutes is five minutes too long."

A grin curves onto my cheeks as I look at her. I had no idea Genevieve Richardson and I were part of the same bitter club. "That's way too true. I've actually sworn off high school guys entirely."

"You really think they'll be any better once they've graduated?" she asks with a dry smile. "Nope, I think we're out of luck until at they're at least thirty, Serena."

It's funny to hear Genevieve Richardson say my name. We've never spoken, but because of Morgan everyone knows who I am. At least seven different people have asked me whether my brother's having a secret fling with Ariel, Much's most popular vj, because they have such terrific on-air chemistry and the entire country's aware that he's bisexual.

"Why thirty?" I ask.

Genevieve shrugs. "I'm being generous, it could be forty or fifty before male adolescence ends. The jury's still out on that."

I laugh lightly as we hang a left onto my street. "You sound as jaded as I am. Maybe we can form a club and apply for school funding." It's nice to know that I'm not the only one who plans to avoid entanglements with guys for as long as I can. Izzy and Marguerite don't count because as much as they'd deny it, I know they'd secretly love for someone to flash them the hot girl look. Believe me, I know how that goes; I *was* an Izzy or Marguerite until August 22.

Genevieve smiles at my suggestion. The last I heard she was with Costas Gavril, who is a senior with a face like a WWE wrestler but a nice guy reputation. Since I don't want to sound like I've been following her life story I don't ask what Costas did to her. "It's the one with the green garage," I say, pointing to my house. "Right here."

Genevieve hugs the curb and shifts into park. "Trust me, no one's more jaded than me, dear." She arches an eyebrow and beams me a look streaked with weariness, boredom, and a side order of superiority. I have to admit she wears cynicism better than I do. Even the new, improved Serena can't compete with Genevieve Richardson, but inside I know I'm every bit as fed up with the male half of the Wilfrid Laurier student population.

"I wouldn't be so sure," I say as I open the door, "but thanks."

Genevieve nods, her eyes already back on the road. "Bye, Serena."

✄

By English class the next day I know what Nicole Lapatas's nipples look like. Technically no one's supposed to use their phones on school premises, but it's hard to enforce that rule in the cafeteria and the hallways. Not to mention the bathrooms, where a couple of guys in our class tell Nicole they've been jerking off to her image.

Nicole tries to ignore them, but she looks like she wants to neuter somebody. As we're leaving class I slow down to ask how her leg is. She's wearing pinstriped pants and we both gaze down at them as she says, "My mom cleaned it out for me last night. It hurt like a son of a bitch but Genevieve was right, it wasn't really that deep."

"That's good." I clear my throat.

One of the guys from our English class leers at Nicole as he ambles by.

"This is getting really, really old," she says in a sharp voice. "Don't you guys have anything better to do?"

If it were me I'd probably stay home and pretend to have bronchitis until someone else topped my drama. Nicole's holding up pretty well, all things considered. "None of them have anything better to do," I say, acidity swimming up my throat. "We go to Loserville High, Nicole."

Nicole plays with her hair and chews the inside of her lip. For a second I think I spot yesterday's ache in her eyes. "Listen, do you want to come over to my house after school?" I ask on impulse. "We can go over the English homework or whatever."

Nicole releases her hair. It flops against her shoulder. "I'm not in the mood for English homework."

"That's okay," I tell her. "We don't have to do English homework."

"Okay then." Nicole twirls a chunk of her hair around her finger again. "Where's your locker?"

I tell her, and we arrange to meet there after last class. It's funny how you quickly can click with someone you've never had a meaningful conversation with before. Once we start talking it's like we knew each other in another life, and we end up hanging out the next day and the day after that. I give her the behind-the-scenes tour of my relationship with Jacob, and she badmouths Liam Powers and everyone who's tried to mess with her over the video.

We get really good at tearing down certain people, especially when we're together. Not every guy has something nasty to say about her. Some of them are cool and act like the video doesn't make any difference, but we let ourselves get vicious with the rest of them, talking about how microscopic certain parts of their anatomy must be and how they probably couldn't last any longer than thirteen seconds. It feels good to be mean like that, way better than attacking a punching bag.

About a week after Genevieve drove us home I run into her leaving the library and she asks how Nicole's doing. "As bitter as us," I say with a half smile, "but she's cool."

"I told you — no one's as jaded as me." Genevieve gives a pointy grin. "I'm glad to hear she's okay though. At least she'll be wiser next time."

"I don't think there's going to be a next time any time soon." I explain that both of us have decided we don't want to waste our time. It's what I decided before Nicole's video anyway, but having two of us in it together seems less lonely.

"A one hundred per cent celibacy club?" Genevieve adjusts the paperback copy of *The Communist Manifesto* nestled under her arm. "You really think you two can stick with that?"

Excuse me? I know she's Genevieve Richardson, but it's not like I'm some tragically self-esteem-challenged girl who has to super-glue herself to a series of random guys to feel like life has meaning. I've only kissed three guys since high school started. I just got wrapped up in the newness of being skinny for a while. Maybe you can't imagine how that works when you've been as pretty as Genevieve Richardson all through high school.

"Just as well as you can," I snap.

Genevieve tilts her head to the right. "I didn't mean to sound harsh. Just — you know — we all have a way of being our own worst enemies at times." Her fingers stroke *The Communist Manifesto*. I bet Devin, with his near photographic memory, could sum it up for me in five minutes or less. "Listen, if either of you need a ride home you can meet me in the parking lot," she continues. "I pretty much always park in the same space. It's the silver Honda Civic."

I remember. "Cool. Thanks."

One minute I felt like there was no one at Laurier who could really understand me and the next there are three of us united in a common cause. Maybe I'm wrong about people always disappointing you. Maybe it's truer to say that *people will always surprise you.* When you think you can rely on them, they'll happily prove you wrong, and when you expect absolutely nothing from them, they become the people you can share your true thoughts with. All I know is that after that Genevieve, Nicole, and I tell each other everything.

CHAPTER FIVE

TOTAL DRUG MART HIRES me as a part-time cashier, which brings me one step closer to baby blue scooter ownership. I see a gorgeous, fully restored 1967 Vespa advertised online for $3499.99 and save the picture as inspiration. The Vespa looks like something you'd ride through the clouds on your way to heaven with classic R.E.M. songs playing as a soundtrack. If I had that scooter it would never rain again. It's like guaranteed sunshine and good luck.

Genevieve tells me that she rode on the back of one when she was in France last summer but that it was red and not nearly as cool as the one I want. "The back of one with *who*?" Nicole asks. "Some French guy? Was he hot?"

"It was a girl," Genevieve says. "And she was pretty hot, as a matter of fact."

"French girls are always hot," Nicole says knowingly. "They have flair or something."

"Confidence," Genevieve corrects. "It doesn't even matter if they have flair or not — just that they think they do."

"Uh-uh," I chime in. "That's like saying it doesn't matter if you're fat. Believe me, even if people don't think of themselves as fat, other people do. Not everything is totally subjective. Real life isn't like that *Hairspray* movie where the fat girl gets the cute guy just because she can dance. Guys don't want the fat girl or the girl who only *thinks* she has flair but doesn't."

"Some guys like fat girls," Nicole says, pulling her legs up on the couch with her. Her right leg has healed perfectly, with no scars to give the incident away. "You know, they get off on it."

Genevieve reaches over and flicks me in the knee. "You know you were never fat though, right?"

My face smarts. I didn't mean to sound like I was talking about me, but that's Genevieve, she always picks up on things. "I just mean in general, but I was chubby enough that no one really gave me a second look before last August. That still counts."

Genevieve wags her finger at me. "I guarantee there were guys ogling you before last August. It's easy not to notice when you're not interested in them."

"Great, so none of the cute guys are interested in you when you're fat," I amend. "Does that sound more accurate?"

"Probably." Nicole reaches for the gold nail polish on the coffee table next to her and gives it a shake. "But what can you expect? Hot guys like hot girls and vice versa. People pair up with people who are roughly at the same level of hotness as themselves."

"But you were never fat," Genevieve insists, her eyes on mine. "So, no, that doesn't count."

Nicole unscrews the top from her nail polish and slips a coat of gold on her big toe. "She's right, you know. You were never fat. You were barely bigger than average."

I was definitely bigger than average. And I've put a few pounds back on over the past few weeks. It's hard not to eat when you're hungry, and lately my appetite has come back some. There's a bag of open pretzels lying between Nicole and me and I slide my hand into it as Morgan's image flashes onto the TV in front of us.

"I really like this next one," Morgan enthuses. "You know we've talked about this before, and I think she's really developed a style of her own with this new —"

"I know," Ariel interrupts with her perky smile. "You *luuuuv* this video. You can't stop raving about it. I hear she's going to be in the studio with you this weekend. Maybe you can get her to do a little unplugged for us here." Ariel knocks her shoulder against Morgan's. They're like two peas in a pod, as my grandmother would say.

"You have to know I'll try." Morgan beams us a vision of his orthodontically repaired pearly whites. He had a slight overbite at one time, supposedly, but Devin says that he never remembers Morgan's teeth being anything less than perfect.

I crunch on pretzels and listen to Genevieve say, "Attraction isn't just based on physical attractiveness. You see a lot of people together where one person is clearly better-looking than the other."

Genevieve isn't the only one who picks up on things; what she just said was really about Costas. Before we became friends with Genevieve, Nicole and I both guessed that Costas Gavril had wanted an all-access pass to her body or treated her badly in some equally cliché way. But that wasn't the case; back in October, Costas confessed to Genevieve that he was obsessed with someone else. Nicole and I are supposed to keep it a secret, even though Genevieve hates his guts and could make his life hell, but the girl — woman, actually — is Ms. Halliwell, his economics teacher. Costas told Genevieve that he's not going to act on it but that he can't stop thinking about her and didn't think it was fair to keep his feelings a secret.

Genevieve isn't in his econ class but shares a biology class with him and says she gets a stomach ache before class every day. Ms. Halliwell isn't sexy like a teacher in movie. She has a good body but her hair is always a mess, like she doesn't care how it looks. She's not a flirty teacher either, so Costas having those feelings for her is one of those weird accidental things. I guess I should just accept the fact that I don't understand guys.

Genevieve, Nicole, and I have lots of conversations like this, but we talk about deeper things like communism and poverty too. Nicole's usually the one who burns out on those discussions first and makes us dance or go cruising. A couple of times Izzy and Marguerite or some of Genevieve's and Nicole's other friends join us, but the various groups don't naturally gel. It's so much easier when it's just the three of us, so we root our New Year's Eve plans in that. Nicole's dad won't care if we drink ourselves into a stupor at their place, but the plan is just watching movies, playing video games, and making fondue (which Genevieve has been wanting to do since she read about it in some 70s book about a couple that keeps screwing and then breaking up).

I'm going to bring finger food like samosas and sausage rolls, and every time I think about it I smile. Making fondue will be exponentially more fun than wondering why no one worthwhile wants to kiss me at midnight.

Unfortunately, I have the Christmas holidays to get through first. With no word from Devin, my parents avoid the season until the last minute. One night when Dad picks me up from Total Drug Mart I notice that they've put up the tree while I was work. Devin's allergic to real trees so we have one of those fold-out fakes you buy at Walmart. It looks pretty good for an artificial tree, but I can't imagine doing the holidays without Devin.

"Are the lights going up outside too, then?" I ask my father.

After a three-second delay he replies, "I suppose so. I'll have to bring them up from the basement."

"You don't have to," I tell him as I stare at the Christmas tree. "You'll only have to take them down again in ten days."

My father steps towards the tree, plucks a silver snowflake decoration from one of the middle branches, and repositions it on a barer lower branch. "Morgan's coming for Christmas dinner."

So that's why everything has to look passably festive. Morgan. "I thought he wanted everyone to go to that hotel in Toronto," I say. Morgan told me his idea over the phone a few days ago. He did Sunday brunch at the King Edward Hotel a couple of months ago and thought it would be the perfect place to take our parents (plus me and his boyfriend, Jimmy) for Christmas dinner — high ceilings, a seven-course meal, and old-style opulence.

"Your mother wants to stay in," Dad tells me. "You know she likes to do her turkey and stuffing. It's tradition."

I suspect the point of Morgan's idea was to distract us from LeBlanc traditions — and Devin — but he should've known Mom wouldn't want to get dressed up and go out somewhere for Christmas. The only places she goes these days are work or the supermarket. If we were rich she'd probably never feel the need to leave the house.

At Total Drug Mart I'm constantly surrounded by customers lining up for glossy wrapping paper, expensive skin cream gift sets, and boxes of Belgian chocolates. All the Christmas merchandise feels like theatre props and now it looks like I'll have to put up with them at home too. There's no escape.

In fact, the next day my dad asks me to help him hang the outside lights, and on Christmas Eve my mother emerges from the den and insists I chop celery and onions for her stuffing recipe. It shouldn't look like Christmas at our house and it definitely shouldn't smell like it, but it does. After the stuffing's done and sitting in a sealed container in the fridge I wash the homey smell out of my hair and go to bed before my parents can force any other fake seasonal activities on me.

Why couldn't we have skipped Christmas altogether just this once? It'd be more honest than the four of us (plus Jimmy) pretending that we feel happy together and aren't wondering where Devin is and whether he's still *not well*. I should've volunteered to take the Christmas evening shift at Total Drug Mart and then lied to Morgan and my mother that I never really had a choice in the matter, being a new employee.

Because it's too late for that I stay in bed for as long as I can on Christmas morning. When I get downstairs Mom and Dad have already opened the presents I left for them. I can't afford the good stuff my mom goes crazy for, but the keepsake box I got her has tiny aurora borealis crystals on it, and when you hold it on a slant it shines like a rainbow. The engraving on it reads: *For Mom at Christmas. Love Always, Serena.*

Mom smiles stiffly at me as I shuffle into the living room. My eyes land on the keepsake box, unwrapped under the tree next to the business card case I bought for my father. "Good morning, hon," my mother says. "Thank you, that's a beautiful gift."

It doesn't really matter what I got her or what she got me. We both know that. "You're welcome," I tell her.

Dad squeezes my shoulder. "Most of them left here are for you. I'm going to make some coffee. Can I get you a hot chocolate?"

If this year were like the ones before it, Devin would already have brewed coffee. He always got up early on Christmas Day, and the first thing Devin used to do on a daily basis was either make coffee or head out to pick some up. The smell of strong java would be permeating the room now.

I nod at my father and set to work opening my presents. If I were with Genevieve and Nicole everything wouldn't feel like it was about Devin, but when I'm with my parents none of us can forget. Sitting under the tree with masses of stuff I don't care about makes me feel raw like I did last summer. If someone turns on the radio to Christmas tunes my eyes will begin to sting.

I rip through the gifts as fast as I can so that the three of us can put some distance between us and the tree. Then Mom disappears into the den while Dad and I dispose of all the torn wrapping paper. We'd normally head over to St. Stephen's on Christmas morning, but I'm relieved that no one says anything about church.

Later in the day Mom ropes me into assisting in the kitchen.

She asks how it's going at work and I tell her about one of my lazy co-workers who keeps coming in fifteen minutes late and how a couple of days ago I saw a teenage guy drop out of my line and join one with an older cashier because he was buying a package of mint tingle condoms.

My mom smiles when I mention that. Not with the forced smile she had on her lips when I came downstairs but a real one. We talk more than we've talked in a long time. It feels nice, but I know better than to think it will last or to let myself miss it when it stops again. Not that I used to pour my heart out to my mother every day, but mostly now it feels like she's rationing her words, saving energy for eBay bids and potential future Devin emergencies.

While we're cooking together it doesn't feel like Christmas, exactly, it's just boiling, baking, and basting. Busywork. When it's time to set the table with poinsettia napkins, though, we both clam up. Next to opening presents, Christmas dinner feels like the hardest part of the day. Last Christmas I gave Devin a goofy-looking Einstein tie and $E=mc^2$ tie pin that I ordered off the Internet, and when everyone else was either cleaning up or entertaining my grandparents he asked me about Clara, the ghost I used to see upstairs in our old house. I was really little at the time and my parents thought she was an imaginary friend, but I insisted she was real. It's so long ago now that I honestly don't know whether I made her up from bits of a dream I'd had or if there was something more to her. The image in my mind's blurry, but Clara has a fancy black and white striped dress on, like something women would've worn a hundred years ago.

Being older, Devin could remember more of the things that I'd told him about her than I could remember myself. "You said she had a nice person face," he told me. "And that she smelled like flowers."

I hate that just setting the table on Christmas can make me remember good things about Devin. My parents tried to help him and he repaid them by throwing it back in their faces. Then he disappeared and made us wonder if he was still breathing. It's not fair. I shouldn't miss him. He doesn't deserve it.

"Serena, can you pour some filtered water into the pitcher and slice in some lemon?" Mom calls from the kitchen. Her voice is tired and I know that she's dealing with her own Christmas memories.

I do what she asks, my mind reaching for another memory to snap into place and stop the Devin ones. Like the first time Jacob took off my top, and then my bra. I loved watching him undo the little green buttons. He was so careful about it, and the size of his fingers made the buttons look even tinier. After we were finished rolling around together I wanted to ask him to button them up again for me, but it seemed silly. I should've asked him, though. It's a nice thought, someone doing up your buttons, taking care of you. It wouldn't have made him the person I wanted him to be but it might have made me regret him less.

God, what's wrong with me today? Just because it's Christmas doesn't mean I have to go soft inside like a rotten banana. There are people who would love to have my cushy life.

Sometimes I can pep talk myself out of sadness and sometimes I can't. This feels like one of the *can't* times and I'm starting to surrender to gloom when Morgan and Jimmy arrive. The doorbell even sounds like Morgan somehow. Jaunty. Like it should make me feel better.

My dad answers the door and soon Morgan and Jimmy are carrying plates into the dining room for Mom. Jimmy's the only male redhead I've ever seen that I would describe as good-looking. He has freckles, like most redheads, but the minute Jimmy starts talking to you they disappear. He and Morgan look impossibly glamorous standing in our kitchen in form-fitting shirts and black pants and a familiar jealousy slides under my skin. My brother shouldn't be prettier than me.

"This looks fabulous," Morgan says, stopping to give Mom a peck on the cheek. "My mouth's been watering since we walked through the door."

Mom looks pleased. "I have containers for leftovers. You can take some too if you like, Jimmy."

"I most definitely will," Jimmy tells her. "Thank you, Tessa!" Jimmy speaks in exclamation marks a lot but it's always positive things. He turns to me and says, "Cute highlights, Serena. You look like summer!"

"Thanks, Jimmy."

My father has never quite figured out how to talk to Morgan's boyfriends and usually ends up doing lots of polite smiling. Christmas dinner isn't any different. Dad smiles and nods as the three of us listen to Morgan and Jimmy chat their way through dinner. Listening to them is easier than forming our own conversation, but eventually Morgan gets impatient. "You should've let me take you all to the King Edward," he says, facing my mother. "It would've been so much less work for you."

"I like to do it," Mom says, although her face seems to project the opposite.

Morgan's chin dips towards his collar. He looks like he wants to say something but Jimmy aims a cautionary glance his way. Morgan's chin pops up again. His eyes settle on me across the table. "Do the Sandhars have their Christmas lights extravaganza up again this year? I thought I'd walk over there with Jimmy later and have a look."

"They have an ocean theme this year," I tell him as I cut into a piece of white meat. "All the lights are green and blue. Santa has a boat instead of a sleigh and three dolphins are pulling it."

Jimmy laughs. "You're kidding! I have to see this."

"They do something different every year," Morgan explains. "One time they did Noah's ark with tons of animal statues covering the yard and roof —"

"They even had monkeys in the trees," I cut in.

"They did." Morgan smiles as he nods. "And they were holding fluorescent bananas."

"Poseidon's there this year," I add. "He's holding a … what do you call it … a pitchfork thing. He looks fierce."

"A trident!" Jimmy suggests in an exuberant tone. "Poseidon in a Christmas display, I love it!" An impish grin tugs at his lips. "I just hope he doesn't smite Santa. Disaster! Who would deliver the toys?"

"Maybe Neptune himself." Morgan's left hand brushes Jimmy's right. For a second it makes me miss having someone to hold hands with. "We'll check it out after. You can take some snaps."

According to Morgan, Jimmy shoots photos of everything, for reference. When you're an artist like Jimmy is you have to take notice of things.

"They hire the same team of people to put the display together every year," Dad says with one of his polite smiles. "They must spend a fortune on it."

The Sandhars' spectacular Christmas lights give us all something to say, except Mom. I see that she's barely touched her turkey and that there's a mound of stuffing and garlic mashed potatoes left on her plate too. The vegetable medley is the only item she's made any headway on, and when I notice that I lower my own fork and wonder if Devin even knows about the Sandhars putting up a Christmas Poseidon. It was in the Glenashton newspaper a couple of weeks ago but Devin probably wouldn't see the Glenashton paper where he is.

Vancouver. New York. Mexico. Newmarket. It's Christmas everywhere on the planet today, and wherever he is, I hope Devin hasn't given up on getting well because I can't give up on him, no matter how much I wish otherwise. I can help my mom make stuffing, ring up thousands of dollars' worth of seasonal sales, and smile with Morgan and Jimmy about a Christmas Poseidon, but inside my heart's pounding with a single half-broken wish: Devin, come home.

CHAPTER SIX

AFTER CHRISTMAS I BEGIN to perk up. Why should I worry about Devin when he's probably not giving any of the other LeBlancs a second thought? Most likely he's busy being a paranoid asshole, smoking up, staying awake for days, and stealing from his friends (if he still has any).

Genevieve, Nicole, and I have the best New Year's Eve ever. Actually there are seven of us altogether (including Izzy — Marguerite came down with bronchitis and has to stay in bed). First we kill things mercilessly onscreen. Then we dance, eat huge amounts of tiny edibles, and toast each other with champagne at midnight. Genevieve brought over an old movie with George Clooney and Jennifer Lopez and it makes us all so hot that we're practically climbing the walls.

"Thanks, Genevieve," Nicole says with a pronounced pout. "How are we supposed to stay off guys when you force us to watch movies like that?"

"C'mon, you ever see a guy that smooth around here?" I ask. "There's no comparison with the Laurier guys. Zilch. George Clooney's like the perfect man in that movie, except for being a bank robber." There's always *something*, isn't there? Because if a guy's too perfect he's either boring, like in chick lit flicks where guys seem like they've had every bit of personality drained out of them along with any potential savageness, or unbelievable: the guy who acts like a bad boy with everyone but the female lead.

We drink a little more champagne and make Swiss cheese and mushroom fondue from Genevieve's recipe. Nicole's dad comes down for a beer and samples some of the fondue. I can tell he likes being surrounded by all us girls. Not that he flirts or anything, but his eyes sparkle. I wonder what it would be like to go out with an older guy, like George Clooney in the movie or Mr. Lapatas, if he wasn't Nicole's dad. Would someone older be better about things like doing up your buttons?

Okay. Obviously I've drunk too much champagne. And that sexy paperback Genevieve lent me hasn't helped. I have to quit reading the sex scenes over and over.

It's time to stop snacking so much too. Otherwise all the clothes I bought at the end of August won't fit anymore. Even if I'm not going to be with anyone I don't want to go back to being a girl that a cute guy would only make out with if he's drunk.

"There's lots left," Genevieve says, stirring the pot. "Does anyone want more?" I'm the first person she looks at, and I'm sure she doesn't mean anything by it, but it makes me silently repeat my vow.

"We can save the leftovers," Nicole says. "I looked it up online." With all of us full to the brim with cheese and champagne, Nicole insists that it's time to dance again. If aliens landed on earth and made the human race their slaves Nicole would still find the energy to dance.

Her dad tells us good night and, "Have fun, girls." Once he's gone the seven of us break into wild and hilarious movements, dancing however the hell we want because there's no one there to watch us, no one to impress. I fold the bottom of my top into my bra and wriggle around like a belly dancer to "Girls Chase Boys." Then Pharrell comes on and we all sing and do chorus line kicks. Izzy tries to belly dance too and then I know I'm not the only one who's had too much champagne because normally Izzy doesn't do anything silly.

I wish every day could feel like this. I don't want the night to end, but even when it's time to go, hopefulness clings. With friends like this, the new year won't be like the last. Nicole and Genevieve don't care who my brother is or whether I go back to being chubby. When I'm around them I don't even care how popular or unpopular I am. We're all in this together.

There are seven Total Drug Marts in Glenashton, and the one I work at is in a plaza with a flower store, toy shop, Quiznos, Starbucks, TD Bank, The UPS Store, The Nutty Chocolatier, a nail salon, and a dentist's office. As you can see from the list, there aren't many places to buy food. Total Drug Mart carries some frozen dinners and essentials like canned vegetables, cereals, and milk but there are times when I really don't want to eat something out of a package for dinner and then I usually opt for a small honey bourbon chicken or turkey ranch sub from Quiznos. They're the two subs that have the fewest calories.

Today I go in to Quiznos at about ten after seven and get served right away because the only two other people inside are already sitting down at a table, munching on salad and sammies. I watch the woman behind the counter set my honey bourbon chicken sub on the grill conveyor belt. I'm so hungry right now that I could eat something crazy like a prime rib cheesesteak sub with oatmeal raisin cookies for dessert, but the chicken will be fine. Everything's fine until Jacob and Wyatt barrel through the door bringing the cold air with them. We see each other at school all the time but at school I'm never trapped with them; I'm not near them long enough to feel the full weight of their hostility.

Jacob looks at me for a split second. His eyes say: you bitch.

I have to move away from the counter so they can order. Wyatt keeps his face pointed at the menu like he's determined not to see me. Then he turns to Jacob and says, "I can't believe you were almost hitting that. You got out just in time, dude. She's packing on the pounds again."

Jacob smirks and glances my way to make sure I've heard. I'm still waiting for my stupid chicken sub to come out of the other end of the grill. My palms begin to sweat as I turn my head slowly away from Jacob, like him and his asshole friend don't matter.

If we'd been at school or if Wyatt had said some other nasty thing, I would've told him to go fuck himself, but the comment about my weight caught me off guard. The words hurt. I angle myself towards the window and watch a dirty red minivan pull into a parking spot. It's snowing lightly but not enough to stay on the ground. I don't want my stupid low-cal sub anymore. I won't be able to swallow a bite while I feel like this.

"Would you like a drink with that?" the Quiznos woman asks as she runs around the other side of the grill to pluck my honey bourbon chicken from the conveyor belt and wrap it in paper I'd normally tear off only seconds later.

I shake my head, my cheeks probably turning pink as I wrestle a ten-dollar bill out of my pocket. She plops my dinner into a bag and hands me my change.

I trudge to the door, hoping Jacob and Wyatt won't say anything else to my back. They don't, not anything I can hear anyway. The two people already seated and eating are talking about transmission problems and I walk past them, out into the snow. If my cheeks are red the way I think they are everyone at Total will think it's because of the cold.

Across the parking lot, the Total Drug Mart door automatically opens for me. I head for the staff room at the back of the store, which is empty except for me, and snap my hand out over the garbage to drop my Quiznos bag inside. It's a dumb thing to do and I regret it forty-five minutes later when my stomach starts to growl.

I hate that I don't make sense. Jacob and Wyatt are trash. Why should I care whether I look hot to trash? My Total Drug Mart uniform isn't exactly clingy like lingerie and I wore my winter coat over to Quiznos so how could they even know if I'd gained weight?

My stomach sinks as I scan in a box of tissues for the chunky woman in front of me. Why is it that the first thing I've noticed about her is that she's overweight? Maybe she's an amazing humanitarian or the best brain surgeon in the country.

For the record I've gained eight pounds back in the last six weeks. If I don't stop I could *be* that woman and the first thing that cashiers will notice about me is my weight.

I act extra nice with the woman to make up for all mean things I'm thinking about us both. I need to get back to that headspace I was in on New Year's; I can't let a single comment from a loser like Wyatt bring me down.

The next guy in line takes all the items out of his basket for me and then hands over the basket itself. "Thanks," I tell him. I scan his shower gel, shaving cream, copy of *Sports Illustrated*, and a package of ladybug hairclips, all the while thinking he probably jerks off to the swimsuit issue of *Sports Illustrated*, fantasizing about orgies. If he already knew me he'd smile at me to my face but secretly think that my chub was returning.

"Shit," he says under his breath. His hands disappear swiftly into his pockets. "I don't think I have my ATM card."

"We take cash," I tell him, sounding vaguely bored. He's too good-looking for me to want to smile at, but of course I can't be rude.

"Yeah, I know." He smiles at me. His almost shoulder-length hair is half a shade too dark to qualify as dirty blond, and he has grey eyes and a couple of freckles on his nose but not anywhere else. The grin makes him look like a nice guy, but do you think I believe that?

"Do you want me to cancel the transaction while you go look in your car?" I suggest.

"No, that's okay." He pulls out a wad of bills from his back pocket. "I have cash too."

Congratulations, I say silently. *You're quite the superhero.*

The guy presses a couple of bills into my hands and waits for me to punch in the numbers on the register. *Hang on, what's this?* I separate the bills he's given me and stare at the glittering pink heart sticker in my hand. I flip it over automatically, like when you're checking both sides of a twenty-dollar bill to make sure it's genuine. There's a wobbly "A" printed on the back of the sticker in orange crayon.

Does he think he's being cute or was it an honest mistake? "Here," I tell him as I hand the sticker over, "have your heart back." I say it with a hint of accusation (because guys suck and good-looking guys suck the worst) but like I'm really kidding around underneath it all.

He makes a kind of *ah-ha* noise, like the thing must've gotten mixed in with his bills by accident, and slips it into his wallet. "Have a good night," I say and present him with his Total Drug Mart bag.

"You too." He pats his wallet in his front pocket. "Thanks for noticing that."

How could I not notice? It was glittering and pink.

I nod and turn to the next person in line, my stomach gurgling at the sight of a box of Oreos in front of me on the counter. I don't need them, I tell myself, and I don't need to be hot either. I don't need to be any one thing in particular to be happy. It sounds so true that I wish I could one hundred per cent believe it.

CHAPTER SEVEN

MY SECOND SEMESTER CLASSES are science, intro to business, civics, and history. Mr. Cushman, my science teacher, is recently separated (or so the rumour goes) and is mostly in a dire mood, but aside from that I don't have much to complain about. It's okay being back at school where everyone asks each other how their holidays were and what they did on New Year's, like they're really glad to see each other.

Not long after I'm back Morgan calls while Genevieve's driving me and Nicole home from school. I could let the call go to message, but if I don't answer a corner of my mind will wonder if it's some kind of emergency I shouldn't ignore. "Hey, Morgan," I say from the back seat.

Morgan says hello in his giddy voice and quickly explains that Muzzy Ryan, this New Zealand band I used to like (but that he obviously doesn't realize I've stopped listening to), are coming into the Much studio in two days. "They had a shake-up in their schedule," he continues, "and it's a last-minute thing but I know how much you like them. If you can skip your last class and make it down here I'll be able to introduce you and give you a couple of minutes with them."

Because I don't want to rain on his parade I don't mention that Muzzy Ryan's last album sounded like paint drying but without the drama. "That would be cool but I have to work, Morgan."

"Maybe you can get someone to switch with you," he goes on. "Jimmy might be able to pick you up at school. I can check with him."

Truthfully, I do have to work and don't want to waste a sick call on something I don't have enthusiasm for. I thank Morgan and say that I really don't want the whole ditching class thing to blow up in my face. Morgan says he understands but sounds disappointed and after that's over with we run out of conversation pretty fast. "So did they take Poseidon down?" he asks. "I'm surprised nobody stole that trident of his."

"They took him down," I confirm. "Back to business as usual until next year." If I were talking to Devin there'd be more to say. I'd tell him how fantastic New Year's was and explain what a genius appliance a fondue maker is. I could say that to Morgan too, but he goes to so many glamorous parties and happenings that if he told me it sounded cool I'd think he was humouring me. Poor Morgan, he can't win.

Devin used to refer to our big brother as the golden boy. One time he said, "There can only be one golden boy in the family but at least you have a chance of being wonder girl."

I laughed because I had no chance of outshining Morgan. He'd probably even look better than me on a baby blue scooter.

"Well, keep in touch," Morgan tells me. "You know you can sleep over here whenever you want, if you need a change of scenery. There's a lot to do in the city."

My little finger slides along the edge of my cell. "There's stuff to do here."

"Oh, I know," Morgan says genially. "But we have the subway here and the city never sleeps. It has a different energy to it. Clubs, theatre, festivals, there's more than one person could ever keep up with. There's nothing wrong with Glenashton. It's just got those family burb vibes."

He's right — if anyone wants to do anything really cool they have to head for Toronto — but I don't want to admit it. His life is cool enough without me telling him how cool it is so instead I say to have fun with the band and get an autograph for me.

"Sure thing, Serena. Talk to you later."

When I get off the phone we're pulling into Nicole's driveway. She snaps off her seat belt and says, "I can't believe you won't cut class and work to meet Terry Preece. He's so sexy. Those cheekbones make me want to cry."

Terry Preece is the lead singer of Muzzy Ryan. When I used to listen to them I kind of preferred their guitarist, who looks like the kind of guy who could keep a secret, if you can ever really sense something like that just by looking at someone.

Genevieve reaches over and pokes Nicole's thigh. "Whatever happened to swearing off guys? God, you're such a lightweight, Nic."

"What's the difference between drooling over George Clooney in a movie or drooling over Terry Preece at MuchMusic?" Nicole asks sharply. "Neither of them are real people to us."

"Yeah, guys like that don't count," I say, siding with Nicole. "Only guys you're actually in danger of making out with." Which means Nicole's dad doesn't count either, not that I've been thinking about him, I swear.

"Rock and roll, babyyy!" Genevieve sings. "I bet Terry Preece would make out with anyone over fourteen and under forty."

I bet he would too. Terry Preece is a total slut.

But it really is impossible to stop thinking about guys entirely. I'm not tempted to think about Laurier guys because even the ones who seem okay usually have a couple of friends who aren't, and anyway, probably every last one of them has seen Nicole's striptease, which should've just been between her and Liam Powers until the end of time. But sometimes I think about guys on TV or strangers I pass in the mall.

Every now and then an especially cute one, like that guy with the glitter heart sticker, wanders into Total Drug Mart too. I don't flirt with them because I don't want them to know I think they're cute but I still think it to myself.

Actually, the first time I saw the sticker guy it didn't occur to me that I might see him again, but he must live nearby because he comes in to Total just a few days later and buys a bag of milk and a box of Cheerios. I wonder if his mom asked him to buy cereal and milk for her or if he lives alone and will be the only one eating the Cheerios. I can't really look at him hard enough to figure out how old he is and which scenario is more likely, because if I do that he'll think I'm checking him out.

My voice rasps as I'm telling him the total for the Cheerios and milk. I really don't feel that sick but I've been losing my voice on and off all day and there's a tickle in my throat that makes me want to clear it every twenty minutes or so. I grab my half-full water bottle from beside the register and swallow some down before repeating myself.

"Should you be here?" the guy asks with a sympathetic look. "You sound terrible."

"It sounds worse than it is."

"It sounds bad," he tells me, his grey eyes hanging on mine. "It sounds like a good excuse to go home early."

"Ah, but if I leave early I won't get a full night's pay." My voice wobbles on the word *early* and the sound makes the guy wince a little. "It doesn't hurt," I insist. "It's just annoying."

"Okay." He points at me the way Genevieve does when she's being bossy. "Drink some more water at least."

I uncap my bottle again and go for it because it happens to be what I want to do anyway. The guy swipes his ATM card and punches in his PIN as I'm gulping. It gives me an opportunity to look at him some more while he's too busy to notice. Then I hand him his bags and he groans and says, "I suck. I keep forgetting to bring my cloth bags with me."

"Next time." I offer him my customer service smile, thinking that he probably won't be in again for months and that even then we won't notice each other because I'm hardly Total Drug Mart's only cashier.

Wrong. He gets in my line again three days later with batteries, a four-pack of fruit cups, and a Dora and Diego book that he must be buying for a young sibling or cousin. This time he has cloth bags with him and a beat-up-looking DVD in his left hand. I squint at the cover, which seems to say *Haunted Hunting*. He notices me checking out the DVD and says, "I borrowed it from a friend," as though I'm about to accuse him of shoplifting.

I'm reading upside down but I think I see the words *Canadian Edition* underneath the title. I swipe his batteries and then the rest of his things. "You like that paranormal investigation type stuff?"

He answers my question with a question: "You're not into the supernatural?" His hand rushes through his hair. Now that I think about it his shaggy hair reminds me of Muzzy Ryan's guitarist. Maybe the guy standing in front of me plays in a local band that practises around the corner and lives on Cheerios.

He's not a real person to me, like Nicole pointed out about Terry Preece, so I can make up a backstory for him and think whatever I like. It won't mean anything in the real world.

"I believe in it," I say honestly, "which makes it too creepy to watch stuff like that. If there are any spirits around my house I just want them to keep quiet so I don't have to know about it."

His head dips as he smiles. "I know what you mean. It's a freaky thing, people hanging around after they're gone, but then there's the flip side."

"Flip side?" I motion for him to swipe his card.

He follows through with the transaction and then stands in front of the counter with his hands on it like we're not done yet. "If there really are ghosts that must mean there's some kind of afterlife," he says.

I nod, thinking of Clara. I always took it on faith that there was an afterlife, but even if I needed proof, I don't think I'd want it to come in the form of shadowy figures and flying objects. According to Devin, I didn't feel like that about Clara, though. She seemed almost like a friend.

I hand the guy his cloth bags and don't say any of the things that are charging through my head.

"Thanks," he says. I think I catch him checking out my name tag for a split second but I can't be sure. "You sound better today."

I am. I stayed home from school for a day so I could avoid talking, and the day after my mom gave me a note to show all my teachers, explaining why I'd be staying silent in class. Today I didn't need the note but if I have to shout I bet my voice will let me down.

"And you remembered your bags," I say cheerfully.

He smiles and holds them up triumphantly before turning to disappear out the sliding doors and towards band practice or whatever it is he does in real life. A tall woman in a fur coat thunks a value pack of tampons down in front of me so I don't have time to add any details to his fictional backstory. It turns into a busy night, as though every family in Glenashton ran out of at least one essential item at the same time and Total Drug Mart was the only store open for miles. For a while I don't have time to think of anything beyond Total, not even with the portion of my brain which is usually reserved for remembering that Devin is missing. I'm just a cashier girl, scanning makeup remover, cough syrup, and cottage cheese like a robot with a human face.

The big news at school the next day wouldn't come as a shock to anyone who was at Wyatt's birthday party. Everyone's forwarding a video of Aya Yamamoto making out with a drunken blond girl I don't recognize. Their lipstick is smeared across each other's faces and there's plenty of tongue involved. Now Aya's officially the slut of the day and Nicole says she feels sorry for her.

Maybe I should feel bad for Aya the same way I felt bad for Nicole, but I can't. It was different with Nicole, she thought she was just doing a striptease for Liam, but Aya's acting like a trained seal for the crowd. If she hadn't gone and tried to pull me into things that time in November, I might be more understanding now. As it stands, I look past her when I see her in the hall.

In the cafeteria later Nicole nudges me and points to the spot where Aya and her friends normally hang out. Most of Aya's friends are sitting there, talking with their heads close together, but not Aya. "I wonder where she is," Nicole says. "I bet she's afraid to come in here in case people start acting up."

"Maybe." I shrug. "She should've thought of that before."

Nicole frowns at me. Her fingers tighten around her plastic fork.

"I told you what happened at Wyatt's," I go on. "Obviously she's just like this all the time. Maybe she *wants* all the guys talking about her."

"In communications this morning she hardly raised her head," Nicole says, still frowning. "Does that sound like somebody who wants all the guys talking about her?"

I glance over at Aya's friends across the cafeteria. They're like an Asian version of Devin's high school friends — studious, quiet, and well-behaved. What do they think of Aya now? I squash the sympathy pang that's beginning to twist in my chest. *Remember Aya's butterfly lashes blinking slowly at me, her hand on my knee?*

"We should talk to her," Nicole continues. "Stand by her."

I nod reluctantly, not wanting to say no to Nicole but wondering why it should be up to us to perform some kind of intervention.

Nicole clicks into her let's support Aya/common sisterhood spiel again for Genevieve when she's driving us home later, and Genevieve says, "I saw her crying in the hall today, stupid girl. It's like she learned nothing from that time with Serena."

Because Genevieve's driving she doesn't see Nicole fold her arms, her chin drooping into her puffy white and blue coat. "So is that what you guys think of me too?" Nicole blurts out. "That I'm skanky and starved for attention?"

"Nic! Of course not!" Genevieve shakes her head, her red hair shining in the sun. "All of us here have made mistakes, but Aya's starting to make hers seem like a habit."

"Twice is a habit?" Nicole pouts in the back seat. "I can't believe how judgmental you two are being."

"How are we being judgmental?" I ask. "We haven't even said anything to her." Jacob has probably watched Aya's video multiple times by now, impressed by how hot her and this blond chick are together. It pisses me off to think about.

Nicole goes quiet. When it's time for her to get out of the car she zips up her jacket and says, "Well, I'm going to try to talk to her anyway. You two can do what you want."

Obviously, and I don't intend to do or say another thing about Aya. She doesn't show up for school the next day and then I know she's probably pretending she's sick, just like I would've under similar circumstances. Maybe she is feeling shitty about things, like Nicole said, because she's not around the following day either.

When she does show it seems like she didn't stay away long enough because plenty of guys are still talking up the video. On my way out to the portables for civics I pass Aya's locker where a stocky blond freshman and two of his scrawny friends are hovering around her with X-rated thoughts pulsing in their beady eyes as they ask what she's doing this weekend.

Aya keeps her eyes on her locker, shoving the textbooks from her arms into the locker and gathering up new ones as swiftly as she can. "What — you don't like freshmen?" the stocky guy says, jutting out his jaw. "Aren't you at least going to say hello?"

"Maybe she only likes girls," a second guy says with a toothy smile.

"I like girls who like girls," the third guy declares enthusiastically. "What school does that other chick go to anyway?" He stares down at Aya as he leans against the locker next to hers. "How old is she — that chick you made out with?"

I stop walking about ten feet down the hall and glance back at the four of them, feeling guilty for not taking Aya's side sooner. No one could mistake the look on her face for someone who's enjoying herself and I'm thinking that I'll have to do something about it after all — thinking that I've been just as bad as everyone else, although I should've known better — when Joyeux Maduka veers over to Aya's locker. Joyeux gives the freshmen trio the evil eye and says something that makes them shake their heads and look panicked.

Joyeux is six and a half feet tall and the captain of the senior basketball team. He has a reputation for swooping in when he sees someone being bullied so no one ever does anything mean while Joyeux's around to see it. Apparently he's real religious too and helps coach at-risk kids in a bunch of different sports. But I can tell you, it'd be easy to forget his soft side if Joyeux was shooting you the evil eye because he looks terrifying when he's mad. If those freshmen were scurrying away any faster they'd have dust kicking up behind them.

I can't hear Joyeux and Aya from where I'm standing. I imagine she's saying thanks and he's saying, "No problem, Aya."

I don't know Joyeux personally but I've heard enough to know that he wouldn't hold some stupid make-out video against her. He's probably the biggest (literally) gentleman at Laurier.

Aya shuts her locker and cradles her textbooks in her arms. She and Joyeux notice me staring at them at the exact same moment. Aya's eyes are tired and she instantly looks away but Joyeux holds his gaze a couple of seconds longer. I don't want them to get the wrong idea about my staring so I amble in their direction, even though I haven't figured out how to handle this yet.

Joyeux bobs his head at me. He's so tall that I feel like a child next to him.

"Hi, Serena," Aya says quietly. "What's up?"

"Not much." Anything I can think to say leads back to the video and I don't want to bring that up in front of Joyeux. "We don't have class together anymore so I thought I'd say hi."

Aya's eyebrows knit together in suspicion. We weren't buddies in French class so why would I want to speak to her now?

I shift my weight to my left foot and add, "And … you know … Nicole was saying we should all hang out sometime."

"Nicole?" Aya repeats, puzzled. "Nicole Lapatas?"

"Yeah. I guess she hasn't talked to you today?"

Joyeux takes a step back and says, "I'll catch you two later, all right?" With his long legs he's halfway down the hall in no time. Meanwhile Aya and I are about to be late for class.

I don't have time to explain but I say, "She will. She told me she was going to talk to you. We have this, like, buddy system going to deal with douchebags. It might help you."

Aya blinks at me, but her blink doesn't look at all like it did that night at Wyatt's. She's smart, school-edition Aya but with a tarnished reputation and her eyes are drilling into mine like she's trying to find some sense in what I'm saying.

She pinches her left earlobe, her lips open a sliver. "So I'll talk to Nicole when I see her," she says finally. Then she turns and strides away from me before I can say goodbye.

CHAPTER EIGHT

✦

IT'S NOT LIKE WE adopt Aya and become a gang of four. She still hangs out with her other friends most of the time, but she's definitely into the idea of swearing off guys. Once I get to know her better my hard feelings about how she acted with me at the party fade. I know what it's like to want people (especially cute guys) to like you. And Aya's so uptight at school that I understand why she'd want to have a bunch of drinks at a party. Getting hammered can easily seem like a better option than acting like a loser if you're not good at talking to people.

The thing that Aya's most worried about isn't assholes bugging her in the school hall (although that makes her crazy too); it's that her parents would kill her if they ever saw the video. Whenever she mentions the possibility her eyes bug out like she's about to have a seizure.

"They're never going to see it," we assure her. "Don't worry. You know how much worse stuff is out there? This is nothing. People will all but forget about it soon." They'd probably forget about it quicker if Aya wasn't such a good girl type but this is the way these stupid things work. It's a lose-lose situation. If you're too much of a good girl people get on your case about it, but if you show the slightest bit of skank they jump down your throat for that too.

It's different at work. The only things that matter at Total are scanning barcodes, making change, being polite to customers, and balancing your cash at the end of the night. Nobody cares what you act like when you're away from work because while you're there you're interchangeable with any other cashier. Well, mostly interchangeable. There is one cashier girl who goes out with one of the stocking guys, but Mauricio and Ki never get too cozy at work. I've never even seen them hold hands.

Today it's really icy and most people have stayed home rather than cruising over to Total to fill prescriptions or buy toothpaste. When Mom got home she grumbled about sliding all the way home in the car and grumbled again when she found out she'd have to drive me to work because Dad wasn't home yet.

I know precisely what Mom did after dropping me off, even though I wasn't there to see it. There's always something that needs adding to her Swarovski collection and nothing has come in the mail for her for at least a month. That last package had a kangaroo figurine with a baby in its pouch inside. You'd hardly notice the kangaroo mother in Mom's den display case now. There's so much crystal in there that it's almost as blinding as a solar eclipse. In the summer I spotted a receipt for a pair of mandarin ducks on her desk and they cost $164 plus $14.50 in shipping. They were tiny ducks, so I can't imagine how much an entire display case full of crystal would be worth.

My shift is over and I have a headache (just a regular one, not a superturbo) so I'm waiting outside in the cold air, eyeing every black sedan that gets near the Total end of the plaza parking lot, hoping it's my dad. If he's not here in another three minutes I'll call home and see what the holdup is. Probably just the bad weather.

Here we go. Black four-door. But not my father's. A guy in jeans and running shoes opens the driver's side door and gets out. The second I see his hair I realize it's the guy with the imaginary band who wants to believe in ghosts and may or may not eat Cheerios and may or may not live at home. He's wearing a light leather coat that obviously isn't meant for winter and he grins when he sees me. "Cold enough for you?" he asks.

Well, if you're going to wear a jacket like that naturally it would be. "January," I say, pricking up my shoulders. "It's supposed to be cold, right? What can you do?"

He nods as he passes me. "Not a lot." When he exits the store two minutes later Angela, a woman who just started in the cosmetics department last week, is with him. Like everyone else who works in the cosmetics department, Angela is wearing perfectly applied foundation, eyeshadow, lipstick, and blush. She's probably almost as old as my mother but looks like a Hollywood actress ready for a photo shoot.

I'm still hanging out in front of the store with my back against the wall, scanning for my dad's Audi, and I overhear Angela say, "I still can't believe it. I feel like I should've suspected something. Now and then I'd see him walking his dog around the block but he was never around much."

"I had no idea either," the guy says. "I guess you never know about people."

"No, you don't," Angela declares. "You certainly don't." The two of them have stopped walking and Angela pulls her coat collar tight around her neck. "You say hello to your mother for me, Gage. Tell her I'll be booking an appointment soon." Angela glances over in my direction and waves. "Good night, Serena."

I say good night back and then listen to her and this Gage guy say bye to each other. It sounds as though the Cheerios and milk were for his mom after all and I catch myself smiling at the thought.

Angela continues teetering to her car but Gage stops, turns, and cocks his head at me. "Are you waiting on someone?"

"My ride should be here any minute," I tell him. "He probably got held up with the ice."

Gage arches his eyebrows and folds his arms in front of his chest like the cold is getting to him in his flimsy jacket. "Maybe you should call him," he suggests, hunching over a little. I see his hot breath on the winter air and it makes me feel the cold in a way I didn't before. "Make sure he didn't forget."

"If he's not here soon I will." I cross one leg over the other and bury my hands in my coat pockets. "Don't worry, I'm fine."

"Are you sure I can't drop you off somewhere?" he asks. I guess it hasn't occurred to him that his offer could appear creepy rather than concerned. Maybe guys don't think about that unless they're somebody's father or brother. I'm not at all scared of him, but Devin would probably say that I should put my psycho girl act on, or at least have it ready.

"No, thanks. Honestly, I'm sure he'll be here any minute." Could it be that he's trying to get me into his car so he can be alone with me? I shouldn't feel flattered just because he's good-looking. I thought I was over that. I *am* over that. It's just because I haven't been thinking of him as a real person and suddenly he is. George Clooney doesn't pull up at Total Drug Mart and offer you a ride.

"Okay," he says, his hair blowing in the wind as he turns his back on me. "G'night."

His hand's reaching for the car door handle when I call, "Hang on." I whip out my cell, my pulse sprinting like I'm on the verge of drama.

"Hmm?" He looks over at me fast.

How dumb that I feel sorry for him in his spring jacket. He probably just gets warm in his winter one when he's in the car, like Devin did. That's no reason to feel sorry for someone.

"Can you just wait while I call to see if he's coming?" I ask. Dumber still, I don't want him to know that I'm talking about my dad rather than a boyfriend.

I've already hit speed dial when he says, "Sure." He smiles again, and I don't think he can actually be any older than twenty. His dimples look boyish. Sweet.

I hope he's not about to spoil things by giving me some line about how if we were together he'd never keep me waiting.

Dad answers on the third ring. "Serena, oops! I'm supposed to be out in front of the drugstore now, aren't I?"

"Yup." I push my hair back behind my ears. "But —"

"I'm grabbing my coat as we speak," he interrupts. "I'll be there in five minutes."

"It's okay. Don't worry. Someone here is going to drop me off. I'll be home in a few minutes. Bye, Dad."

Crap. *Bye, Dad.* I'm such an idiot. So much for my ride actually being some cool boyfriend.

"So where do you live?" Gage asks as I approach his car. I start to give directions, but he cuts in before I can finish. "Sorry, I'm Gage. I guess I shouldn't have offered you a ride without introducing myself first. I just didn't like to see you standing out here in the cold, waiting."

At least he didn't tag on the rest of the cliché about the benefits of being his girlfriend. "I'm Serena," I say. I finish giving my address and walk around to the passenger door. Once I'm inside the first thing I notice is that there's a child seat strapped into the back seat. Then I think about how I'm in a strange guy's car and how potentially that's a seriously bad idea. Okay, he's not a complete stranger because he knows Angela, but what does that prove? I hardly know Angela myself.

Gage sees me looking at the child seat but doesn't mention it. "Angela lives in my neighbourhood," he explains. "There was a grow-op just three houses down from hers. They had homemade booby traps on all the windows and doors set up to give anyone trying to get in an electric shock." He shakes his head. "Crazy. The guy had a pug he'd walk around the neighbourhood. It looked like a puppy. I talked to him a couple of times. He seemed like a regular guy."

"I heard about that on the news," I tell him. "We had a robbery in our neighbourhood two years ago. They took all the electronics and stuff while the family was asleep upstairs. At first they thought the cat was stolen too but it'd just gotten out when the robbers broke in. She came home the next day."

Gage scratches the side of his nose. He's driving nearly as slowly as my dad does when the roads are icy. Jacob liked to speed all the time, not that I'm comparing them. I know that we'll end up at my house safe and sound and that I don't need Devin's advice, but I promise myself I'll never get in a car with anyone I don't know again. Hopefully that promise will stop fate from throwing some other bad thing my way. Most of the time I don't think I believe in fate but when I find myself thinking things like that, I have to wonder. Maybe I'm hedging my bets.

"I guess everyone needs alarms now," he says. "It's too bad."

Sometimes my mom brings up how she used to walk to school with her sister every day when she was six and her sister was eight. She says it like it's a highly disturbing fact; she would never have let Morgan, Devin, or me walk to school when we were that young.

But who wants to go on and on about how bad and dangerous things are now? Not me. "Did you watch that ghost DVD your friend gave you?" I ask. "Was it any good?"

Gage smiles. "You probably wouldn't have liked it. One family wouldn't believe their son about the bizarre things he was seeing in the basement. He really started losing it. In the end they had to have him hospitalized."

"You see," I tell him. "Ghosts suck. They don't care if they're tormenting you. It's all about them."

"Self-centred." Gage laughs. "The bastards." I've never met anyone with the name *Gage* before. I still don't like that he's good-looking, but aside from that he seems okay. Someone who makes all those trips to Total for his mom can't be too much of an asshole.

"So what happened to the son? Was he okay in the end?" I wish Gage would tell me something about his real life. If Jacob had never happened I'd probably do something stupid like lean in close to him once we're in my driveway. He might kiss me, like those other guys did, and then act like it was nothing the next time he walked into the store.

I'm better off without that kind of stuff happening in my life. Completely. This is just a hormonal challenge. I can absolutely get through this. I have to. I'm not going to spend my life stuck in a vicious cycle.

Gage tells me he doesn't know what happened to the kid after that. We're almost at my house and I know I can trust myself not to do something stupid but I wish I didn't have the stupid ideas in my head in the first place. My cheeks are hot. I imagine what Gage would look like undoing my buttons. No, I'm not wearing any buttons. He could unzip my coat then. What does he look like under his jacket? I've never seen him without a jacket. Does he have basketball player arms?

George Clooney, Mr. Lapatas, and now Gage the drugstore customer with no last name. Thank God no one can read my mind.

CHAPTER NINE

MR. CUSHMAN IS IN a worse mood than usual. He lectures our class about how disappointed he is in our performance so far. The year has barely started and he's already disappointed. Uh-oh. "I know not all of you will end up pursuing a science-related career but there's a distinct lack of enthusiasm for the subject as a whole here that I simply can't tolerate," he complains, hurling one hand into the air. "And I've had more than enough of your incessant chatter while you're supposed to be reading or listening to me." His pointer finger shoots out like a semi-automatic weapon. "Is that clear, *ladies* and *gentlemen?*" He pronounces ladies and gentlemen with a sneer, and I have to agree with him about the gentlemen anyway. At least sixty per cent of the guys in my science class are more savage than civilized.

But still, our class shouldn't have to suffer on account of Mr. Cushman's separation. He should take his problems out on a licensed therapist.

"And if some of you feel you're not getting anything from this class, perhaps you should question your presence here," he continues with steely eyes.

"We need two science credits to graduate," Jon Wheatley quips from the back of the class. "That's what we're doing here."

Sometimes Jon gets away with his smart remarks because he's not the delinquent type and tends to give the right answers in class, but this time Mr. Cushman glares at him like he's waiting for Jon's head to explode. Then Mr. Cushman pinches the top of his nose between his thumb and forefinger. He looks so tired of Jon and all of us, down to the bone exhausted with the way his life has turned out so far, that I get a lump in my throat. I know just how he's feeling. That's how my parents and I felt when Devin left in June.

Suddenly I want to get an A in science, just to show Mr. Cushman that he's not wasting his time with us. The thought stays with me through second period but starts to ease off a little during third. I guess Mr. Cushman is right. I don't really care about science class as much as I could. I don't know what I want to do with my life (it's hard enough for me to imagine next summer, let alone graduation) but I don't think it will require an extensive background in science.

The good news lately is that most people are over Aya's video. Between the four of us we've perfected our drop dead stares, and it's gotten so that most of the guys who would've been inclined to aggravate us with their comments don't bother anymore because they don't want to listen to us get mean. They leave us alone and we leave them alone.

I know I'm not really a mean person at heart, though. I just don't want to listen to people say nasty things about me or my friends. Mom let Devin say a lot of bad things to her last year, and I let Jacob say things I didn't want to hear too, but I've learned my lesson. What bothers me about my mom is that it seems like she hasn't learned anything; she's just faded away. She pretends eBay and her Swarovski display are hobbies, but hobbies are what you do with your spare time.

She's already getting professional help but I think she needs a new therapist. After Devin left Mom, Dad, and I went to see Doctor Berkovich together and for most of the appointment the doctor didn't even say anything, just listened to my mother explain about Devin not being well. My ears kept zooming in on the tick-tock of the clock, like it was going to hypnotize me, and then Doctor Berkovich looked into my eyes and asked whether I wanted Devin to come back. I stared at him like he had three heads as I told him yes.

"There were lots of problems when Devin was around," Doctor Berkovich declared. As if I didn't realize. I didn't want to go back to the therapist after that and neither did my dad. Mom still goes once a week but I can't see that it's helping her any; she's the worst off of all of us.

When I get home from school there's a package with a return address in Delaware sitting in the mailbox for her. I think about getting rid of the evidence and pretending it never showed up. What would she do? What if I intercepted every package addressed to Tessa LeBlanc from now on? Would it bring my mother back from her hiding spot of choice or would it send her into a full-out breakdown?

I set the package down on the kitchen table and blend myself a fruit smoothie. I'm still trying to be disciplined, so the yogurt is the low-fat kind. The good thing about feeling like crap was that I never had to be careful; now I crave things that I shouldn't eat all the time. I don't skip meals but it's a struggle to keep them medium-small and to avoid snacking too much in between. A struggle that I've been winning. I've already lost three of the eight pounds I'd put back on. That only leaves another five to go.

The smoothie helps tide me over to dinner, but I'm hungry again by the time I hear the front door swing open at five-thirty. "Hey, Mom," I call, bounding into the front hall with her. She's unzipping one of her leather boots and says hi back. Gloom bunches around her mouth like it hung around Mr. Cushman's earlier, making me feel fresh guilt for both lacking science class drive and imagining snipping my mother's lifeline.

"Something came for you!" I add, turning to snatch the delivery from the kitchen. I rush over to my mother, feeling childish even as I do it — as though I'm looking for approval in the most obvious places — while she's hanging her coat in the closet.

Our hall closet still has Morgan's and Devin's old winter coats in it; making space for your own jacket is always a battle, and it takes Mom a minute to cram her coat in with the rest. Finally free, Mom holds out one hand to take the package and I think she's got it in her grasp when I let go. Truly, I do. This isn't a continuation of the withholding the package from her idea. I sincerely thought she had it and that I was free to let go. I thought I was doing a good thing.

Wrong.

The package thuds to the floor. I don't hear anything shatter — there's just the subtle thump of cardboard hitting tile floor — but Mom yelps.

"Sorry," I squeak. "I'm sure it's in tons of bubble wrap anyway." Someone wouldn't send it all the way from Delaware without adequately packing it, would they? I bet I'd have to stomp on the thing to break it, and I bend to pick up the box and prove it to her.

"Stop!" Mom shouts. "I'll get it, Serena." Her cheekbones sharpen as she plucks her precious package from the hall floor.

"I can pick up a box, Mom. *God.*" I shouldn't let her get to me; I should just walk away and let her obsess over her package to her heart's content, but now I feel like a kid with chocolate milk spilt down the front of her best dress. Do you know what it's like to feel invisible to your mother, except when she's forced to deal with you? "Anybody can drop something once in a while. *You* were the one who didn't take it in time."

"You know how I treasure my things, young lady." Mom begins walking away in her stocking feet. Her pantyhose have a run in them at the little toe. "Don't be difficult."

"Difficult?" I croak. "You're calling *me* difficult?"

"Not now, Serena," Mom barks, heading for the kitchen. "I want to make sure it's not damaged." I stalk into the kitchen behind her, my stomach growling in recognition of its regular feeding place.

Difficult? *Really?* Did I get myself hooked on drugs and sell off a couple of figurines I didn't think she'd notice missing? Do I hide out in my room 24/7 trawling shopping sites rather than finishing homework and interacting with the outside world? *No and no. She must be mistaking me for someone else.*

I lean in the doorway with my arms knotted in front of me. Mom pulls a utility knife from the bottom drawer and slices carefully into the package. My nostrils flare as I watch her.

Whatever's inside the box is swaddled in masses of bubble wrap, just like I said it would be, and Mom rips through it swiftly with her fingernails. Then she cradles the glittering naked figurine in her palm and holds it up to the light. A small clear crystal bear offers a golden sunflower to the track lighting above us. He's cute, but his dazzling perfection annoys me at the same time.

"I told you it wouldn't be broken," I say. "And anyway, it's not like you don't have a thousand of these things gathering dust in the den."

"Serena." Mom's voice has wholly iced over. "Just because you don't realize the value of my things doesn't mean they don't have any."

"But it didn't break." I point to her palm. "You freaked out over nothing."

Mom folds the bear back into the safety of his bubble wrap box. "I'm going to change out of my work clothes. Would you mind sticking some of the chicken breasts from the freezer in the oven? The temperature's on the box."

"I don't know," I say. "I might *break* them or something." I want to stomp my feet and scream so she'll really look at me. Devin isn't dead — he's just gone — and I'm still here. She could notice me for a change.

Mom yanks up the box from the kitchen table and shoves it

towards me, the cardboard scraping against my arm. "Take the damn box, Serena. Balance it on your head, if that's what you want to do."

That's not what I want to do. I really don't want to make her mad either. A lump squeezes down my throat for the second time today. I don't want to sit at the kitchen table for dinner if she's going to be mad at me.

"Calm down," I tell her, projecting equal parts attitude and regret. "I don't want the box."

Mom's eyes are lined with a tender-looking pink. She holds the box against her stomach and says, "These are my special things. I just want people to show a little care. Is that too much to ask?"

It's not about me dropping the box anymore; it's about me not being wonder girl. Devin was wrong about not being a golden boy. He must've been. Because now that he's gone it seems obvious that the world revolved around him. My parents and I are just hanging around like movie extras, waiting for the main action to crash back onto the set.

✄

I'm glad to be out of the house during dinner the next day. I smile extra hard at everyone, even the grumpy guy with wispy bits of grey hair growing out of his ears who complains that the copy of *The Notebook* that he bought for his wife keeps freezing in their DVD player. "If you bring it in with your receipt we'll exchange it for you," I tell him in the sincerest tone I can muster. Irritable customers are easier to deal with if you make their problems sound important, and let's face it, *The Notebook* should not skip. I'm sure his wife doesn't want to miss any quality Ryan Gosling moments.

And, you know, Ryan Gosling — not a real live person, so I can stream *The Notebook* from Netflix again after work if I want to. I can cry and lust at the same time; one doesn't preclude the other.

Michael Bublé's voice is bouncing through the air around me as the grumpy guy pops the upset stomach pills he just bought into a Whole Foods bag and mumbles that he supposes he'll have to rummage around and find the receipt. "Have a good day," I tell him.

I think I know all of Michael Bublé's lyrics off by heart now. He seems to be Total Drug Mart's favourite person. I wonder who's made more girls cry — Michael Bublé singing "Lost" or Ryan Gosling in *The Notebook*?

The next girl in line has really cool purple hair and tons of piercings. She sets a package of Monistat and a bottle of conditioner in front of me, opera music leaking out of her earbuds. As I'm scanning her Monistat my eyes zing in on a male form sauntering over with a big bag of Doritos. *He's back.* And this time he's wearing a black wool coat, unbuttoned and hanging open. He smiles when he sees me notice him. Why am I always noticing him? It's good that he has a winter coat on, though, and he did give me a ride the other night so I should definitely thank him. It's only polite.

I throw the purple-haired girl's things into a plastic bag as Gage gets into line behind her. Thinking his name makes me tingle. *Gage, Gage, Gage.* It doesn't sound like a name I'd like — it's too short, weirdly functional — but I like it on him. What would he do if he knew I was standing here thinking his name over and over? Would he be all over me in no time? Would I even mind?

"Hey," Gage says as the Monistat girl moves away from the counter. "How're you doing?" He points at my name tag. "I feel like I'm cheating but I honestly did remember your name was Serena."

"Liar," I tease. Yes, I'm flirting, but that doesn't mean anything. It only counts if our lips touch.

"I'm serious," he says, the strength of his grin making it impossible for me to avoid grinning back. "Why would I lie? I actually ..." He drops his voice, his expression turning slightly sheepish. "I noticed before you told me."

"Uh-huh, you committed it to memory the minute you saw me, huh?" I'm kidding, but I'm also glad that my skin doesn't happen to be breaking out and my hair hasn't decided to do anything weird today.

Gage tilts his head, his grey eyes shining like high gloss marble. "I'm not really good at this, but when are you getting off?"

Not good at this? *Yeah, right.* When you look like Gage you're automatically good at macking on girls. Everybody knows that.

"Do you want to pay for that?" I ask, motioning to his Doritos. A second ago he had me believing his shy-boy expression but he ruined it with that last line, overplayed his hand. I shouldn't be surprised that he's another Jacob; it was obvious from the first time I saw him.

Gage hands over his Doritos without a word. I scan them in and recite the after tax total. "So ..." He presses a five-dollar bill into my hand, looking as though he's holding his breath. "Is your dad picking you up tonight?"

"Uh-huh." I look him in the eye, all business. "So I don't need a ride if that's what you were going to say." I know that's not exactly what he was going to say, but this is my way of telling him to stop, that I'm not going to be an easy target for him.

Okay, I know twenty seconds ago I was having fun, but if he thinks he can drive me home later and get lucky it's better to let him know he's wrong straight away. I was on the verge of repeating a mistake and caught myself just in time.

I haven't given Gage a bag or anything. He's stuffed his receipt into his pocket and is holding the Doritos in his right hand. An old woman in a brown knit hat's standing behind him, her basketful of items on the floor in front of her. Gage leans over the counter, blinks, and bites down on air. He's probably wondering why I went cold on him all of a sudden, and if I was judging solely by his expression I'd feel a little sorry about it all, but then again, I made a promise to myself that I'd be different.

"Okay," Gage says at last. "Then … do you think I could get your number?"

The old woman behind Gage smiles at me like we're sharing a private joke: aren't men funny, the poor dears, putting their delicate egos on the line for the sake of a telephone number? I glance back at her, smiling automatically because it's what I've been doing all day. Your total is whatever, whatever. *Smile.* The item you're looking for is near the back of aisle four. *Smile.* Have a good day. *Smile.*

But underneath my autopilot smile, I feel a mix of sympathy and satisfaction. Gage is standing in front of the two of us asking me this thing and I could easily say no. I could say it nicely or I could be cruel about it and make him feel stupid and insignificant. This isn't the kind of power you should enjoy, probably, but I am.

"Are you really sure you want it?" I ask, my voice dancing and my lips grin-shaped. Heat floods my face and my heart speeds up. I can make him ask me again. This doesn't need to be easy, it could be difficult for him and he might still want it.

"Only if you want to give it to me," he says, not quite smiling back. "I don't want to tread on any toes or …"

There aren't any other toes involved, but I nod and go back to being normal Serena. It's not like me to make guys jump through hoops. I'm not exactly used to guys wanting my number. It's a confusing thing. Good and bad. I can't get a handle on it at all.

"Let me just …" I grab our weekly flyer from behind me and tear off a corner. Then I print my number on it without my name, which Gage should remember if he really wants to call me.

"Thanks, Serena." He sounds so grateful that I feel a bit sick. He folds the small bit of paper into his wallet next to the glittering pink heart with the "A" on the back. "I'll call you." He lopes off with his Doritos still in his hand and leaves me staring at the old woman in the brown knit hat.

"You made his day," the woman tells me.

My polite smile sticks to my teeth. "He probably has a hundred numbers. I bet I'll never even hear from him."

She winks at me from across the counter, curly silver hair spilling out from under the edges of her hat. "Oh, I bet you do." It's exactly what I wanted her to say, and my real smiles bursts out from behind the forced one and lights up the entire store. Who needs *The Notebook* when you have real life?

CHAPTER TEN

EVERY TIME I HAVE the dream feels like the first. I think I'll die or that someone or something will hurt me. Normal life has disappeared, taking with it all the grass, flowers, birds, and sunshine. All that's left is darkness, dread, and the thing that's chasing me. Whatever it is, it's gaining, and I know I'll never be able to run fast enough to escape it.

So I stop.

Not because I'm brave but because it's inevitable.

I turn to see Devin's almost skeletal body lurch along in front of me like it doesn't know there's a head attached to it. It's the worst sight you can imagine. So much worse than the dread itself. My brother but not my brother. No one. Nothing.

Normally I stare at this ugly, lifeless echo of Devin for what feels like a long time, until I can't stand it another second and begin fighting my way back to consciousness. This time the staring's cut short, and I'm glad, but then the ache sets in. Where are you, Devin? Is this how things will always end? With the real you disappearing?

My cell's ringing on the nightstand. I changed the ringtone to Ellie Goulding on New Year's Eve so at first I don't recognize the *and we gonna let it burn, burn, burn, burn* as the sound of my phone. The second I realize I throw my hand out and snatch it up so that

I won't have to lie there alone with my soul-sucking Devin sadness.

"Hello," I mumble. Anyone who knows me would be able to hear that I've just woken up.

"Serena?" a male voice asks.

"You got me." I sit up in bed, pressing my shoulders back against the wall. Sweat fuses my T-shirt to my spine. "Who is this?"

"It's Gage," he says. "From yesterday at the store. Did I just get you up?"

"It's okay." I clear my throat. "You did me a favour. I was in the middle of a dream I wanted to get out of." The Devin sadness clings to me like it always does. I need Gage to stay with me there on the phone until it fades.

"What were you dreaming?" He sounds nice about it, and I want to be nice back, maybe say something flirty, but the heaviness in my lungs won't let me.

"It doesn't matter," I say finally.

"Serena?" Gage's voice has changed too. "I wasn't sure if you really wanted to give me your number or not — if you felt like you had to because of the situation."

If that's some line he uses he's really got it down. I can hear uncertainty but at the same time he's not overdoing it. He's too good-looking for my own good, and I'm not supposed to be noticing guys in the first place, but all of that seems dumb while I'm listening to him feel out our situation, like he's at least halfway sensitive.

"I didn't feel like I had to," I admit. "It's okay that you're calling." More than okay. I'm glad that the old lady was right, even if I shouldn't be.

"Good," Gage says more confidently. "I was hoping you'd say that." He pauses for the briefest second. "Do you want to do something on Tuesday? A movie maybe ... dinner and a movie?"

Dinner and a movie sounds like a real date. Like something that happens in a George Clooney movie before he seduces a woman, and it dawns on me that Genevieve and Nicole wouldn't approve of this conversation. Especially Genevieve. She's so definite about things. I'm sure if I was Genevieve I'd tell Gage, in a casual but polite way (because Genevieve isn't indiscriminately mean) that I'm not in any frame of mind to date. I might even thank him as I was turning him down.

But I'm not Genevieve and I'm tempted. Is it really possible to get close to a guy without having him turn it against you? I feel my insides warm up as I cradle the phone.

Damn. I promised myself I wouldn't do this.

"Or maybe some other time if Tuesday's not good," he adds, a touch of insecurity slipping back into his voice.

Tuesday isn't good. Tuesday is the day of Jimmy's art show opening in Toronto. Morgan's going to pick me up at school and the two of us will have dinner before catching up with Jimmy at the gallery. According to Morgan, Jimmy's always too nervous before an opening to eat a bite.

"How about Wednesday?" I ask. Genevieve's right; I can't stick with the one hundred per cent guy-free program. I want Gage to have whatever feeling he's having about me for a while longer. We only have to see each other a few times, maybe only once. How wrong could once be?

Gage makes a half-groan, half-sigh noise into the phone. Before he can explain why he can't make it I remember that I'm scheduled to work on Wednesday anyway, and tell him that. "Maybe it's just not meant to be," I joke, but I'm only saying it to make him try harder.

"The best thing that never happened," Gage kids back. "Or we could always try for Thursday ..."

"Thursday," I agree. I'm nervous as I say it.

"Okay." Gage sounds like he's smiling. "I'll pick you up around seven."

I picture his cute self on my doorstep next Thursday, ringing the bell, and smile too. I know that could make me seem as hopeless as Genevieve originally predicted, like some clingy girl who needs a guy in the picture to make her feel worthwhile. Then again, doesn't everyone want the people they like to like them back? That can't always be pathetic.

"Seven's good," I tell him. "See you then."

I hang up, stumble to my feet, and yank my T-shirt off. I stand in front of my mirror, inspecting my all but naked self. There are parts I'm happy with, but mostly I'm just not sure. I wish I could see myself the way someone else would see me, not with my usual eyes. I don't weigh that much more than when I started going out with Jacob but I feel different.

It occurs to me that examining myself this way directly after talking to Gage might be another sign I should've turned him down. *Might be.* I can't ignore that he took my mind off Devin and gave me something else to think about. Maybe nothing's all good or all bad, or maybe I just can't easily recognize the difference, like a form of colour blindness.

If there was someone I could talk things over with I might be able to get a clearer idea about it all, but anyone I can think to ask is the wrong person, for one reason or another. And anyway, that's a hell of a lot of "mights" and "maybes" for someone who's already agreed to seven o'clock on Thursday.

Morgan invited my parents to Jimmy's opening too, no doubt knowing that they wouldn't come. Like I said before, Mom doesn't like to go out much these days and as soon as Morgan asked her she suggested that it sounded like "something fun for you and Serena to do together."

Jimmy's parents won't be there either because they live in Regina, but Ariel from MuchMusic has promised she'll drop by with her live-in bass player boyfriend. I've never met her before and the thought of having a conversation with her makes me a little anxious, like she's destined to find me ordinary in comparison to my brother. This is the way I usually feel about Morgan's friends, but never with Jimmy, who's good-looking and cool but in the most humble, generous way: the kind of person who won't let you suffer an awkward moment if he can help it.

So I'm happy to tag along to Jimmy's opening, even though Morgan and I have to catch dinner by ourselves first. He picks me up in his Mini Cooper at four-thirty after school on Tuesday and we go straight to a Mediterranean restaurant where the entrees start at $21.95. It seems like a nice place but I can't imagine swallowing squid or octopus so I end up with steak and hand-cut frites (which are too gourmet to just be called "fries").

"How's life treating you these days?" Morgan asks while tackling his warm goat cheese salad appetizer.

I should have just ordered a salad myself. Now I could be heavier by Thursday. I resolve to leave at least two-thirds of my frites on my plate, no matter how gourmet they are.

"Everything's pretty good," I tell him.

Morgan's lettuce dangles from his fork. "Yeah? The parents aren't driving you too crazy? I feel bad for you at the house alone with them sometimes. I wish you'd come downtown more often. They never ..." He flicks his free hand through his hair and puts his fork down. "I mean, we all miss Devin, don't we? But we have to keep on keeping on."

This is the kind of thing Morgan can say without sounding ridiculous. *Keep on keeping on.*

"I know." It's on the tip on my tongue to ask him the question I've posed a dozen times before. *Where do you think he is?* I swallow my impulse and stay quiet. No one knows the answer to that.

Devin's been swallowed up by elements we don't want to think about.

"You okay?" Morgan asks, squinting at me.

"I just … worry." I sip at my water and scope out the room for something other than Morgan's inquisitive eyes to look at. A teenage girl just a year or two younger than me averts her gaze when my stare veers in her direction. She's seated between a man and woman who I assume are her parents and she's wearing dark pink makeup around her eyes, which makes them look sore, like an infected raccoon. The girl raises her chin and tosses her long blond hair back with attitude, like she's decided not to be embarrassed that I've caught her staring.

People always stare when I'm with Morgan. Sometimes they march over and say hi in a way that makes it clear that they feel as though they already know him.

"Me too," Morgan says. "But we can't let it grind our lives to a halt." I look back over at him as he chews his salad. "That won't help him and it won't help any of us."

I don't know how he can be so rational about it. I swallow more water and watch the pink-eyed girl to see if she's staring again. Some people can't seem to help themselves.

"You have a fan in the house," I say, steering us away from a topic I don't really want to talk about. I incline my head in her direction.

Morgan looks for only a split second.

"So Jimmy didn't want to come?" I say, stating the obvious. "How come you didn't stay with him, keep him calm?"

Morgan's eyes open wider like this is an interesting question. "Jimmy has his own way of keeping calm. He likes space when he's anxious. If I'm there for him to bounce anxious energy off it only amplifies."

Imagine having someone understand those kinds of things about you. Now imagine that very same person's in love with you and you're in love with them. Sometimes I feel jealous of Morgan and Jimmy.

"I get nervous for him when I see him nervous." Morgan tilts his head and smiles. "And that gets him going even worse. Would you mind if I called him, actually? I'll just see if there's anything I can bring him at the gallery."

"Go ahead." I wave my hand at him and listen to Morgan's voice tense up when he gets Jimmy on the line. His left hand plays with his hair while his right clutches the phone. He laughs, making the fangirl shoot her gaze over to him again. I dig my own cell out of my pocket and check text messages. There's one from Nicole telling me to have fun tonight and that I can flirt with all the guys if I want because they'll probably all be gay anyway. I don't think being gay's a requirement for visiting Jimmy's show but I text back and forth with her until Morgan's finished with his call.

When Morgan and I get to the gallery on Queen Street West Jimmy's shimmering with what I take to be a mix of fear and excitement. He's wearing grey pants and a form-fitting violet sweater over an eggplant-coloured shirt, and he flings his arms around me and says, "Hello, gorgeous! Thanks for getting Morgan out of my way for a couple of hours. You know I love the boy but these shows make me bananas. I hardly know what to do with *myself!*"

I make way for Morgan, who looks more casual but just as fashionable in jeans and a grey vest over a white and blue striped shirt. Having never been to an opening before I didn't know what to wear and thought I might be overdoing it in buying an almost knee-length silk floral-print wrap dress but Genevieve's eyes popped open when I tried it on at Banana Republic on Sunday.

"That is *the* dress," Genevieve said. "You're a vision. You should wear it every day for the rest of your life until it disintegrates."

So for once I don't feel that Morgan's five times prettier than me. The dress gives me confidence the same way a good hair day or Gage's invitation does. As soon as Morgan and Jimmy are done with their hello kiss Jimmy reaches for my hand and twirls me around in admiration. "Look at you!" he declares.

Honestly, I'd love to be able to hear the same thing from someone else's lips on Thursday but wearing the dress then would seem like trying too hard. After all, I can't imagine Gage will be taking me to someplace where the dinner entrees start at $21.95.

Once the gallery starts letting the public in they swarm around Jimmy, fawning over him as they grasp their wineglasses. Morgan's engulfed in the appreciative crowd too. He introduces me to a couple of people, but mostly I just wander around on my own, checking out Jimmy's paintings and eavesdropping on clusters of men and women declaring them to be about artifice, the end of innocence, and cultural appropriation. I don't know about any of that but I do like them. Each painting includes at least one vintage Fisher-Price Little People figure. The toys are from long before my time; I only know that's what they are because Morgan mentioned it at dinner. He had one in his pocket and set it on the table when he was having his dessert coffee: a two-inch tall figure of a man with several strands of hair drawn on his otherwise bald head.

So far my favourite painting is one where a little girl with a smudgy face clutches a Little Person with a red baseball cap. You can only see the girl from the chin up, one of her hands reaching up over her head. She's standing in a motel room window, behind gauzy cheap-looking curtains, illuminated by what must be headlights from a car parked outside. Looking at her you can't help but wish the little girl was someplace better and wonder if she's been left alone by whoever's in that car.

Another one of the pictures I especially like is of a thirty-some-thing-year-old man posed outside his gorgeous suburban house next to a life-sized Fisher-Price woman with yellow plastic hair and a blue plastic body, curves marking the presence of her bust and hips. The man's hand is lying flat on top of her head, the same way you'd pet a dog or maybe a child's head. I stand in front of the painting, taking a second look as I try to figure out what I think it's about on my own, without the words I've already heard other people apply to Jimmy's work.

"Hey, Serena," Morgan says, his hand falling lightly on my back as he guides me across the room. "I want you to meet Ariel and her boyfriend, Grover."

Ariel's every bit as gorgeous in person as she is on TV, even though she has a big nose and her eyes are too far apart. "It's nice to be able to put a face to the name," she says, her teeth blinding me as she smiles and reaches out to squeeze my arm. "Morgan talks about you *a lot.*"

I smile back at Ariel and her boyfriend, whose band's newest video is on heavy rotation on Much at the moment. He looks neater and less edgy in person, like someone who would sit behind you in science class and actually take notes.

Grover happens to be standing quite near the door, and as I fumble for something to say I spot a flash of something behind him the way you do in a scary movie, something you're supposed to notice but not quite make out. My heart jumps. I squeeze by Ariel and Grover and rush for the door. My hand swings it open. Outside it's the kind of cold you block from your mind as soon as June arrives, and I'm instantly freezing in my silk dress, but that's not important.

I spin around, my eyes desperately scanning for the hint of dark green I saw pass by the door. Across the street, in front of a trendy clothing store with bare-chested mannequins, my stare catches and holds. He's striding away in a green shell coat and I can only see his back now, but it was the side of his face, a glance of cheek and chin, that I caught sight of a few seconds ago. I haven't laid eyes on him in seven long months, but I'd swear on the Holy Bible that my brother Devin's darting along Queen Street in a dark green coat.

I run into the street, sprinting as fast as my high heel shoes will let me.

CHAPTER ELEVEN

CROSSING THE STREET AGAINST the light, in my thin dress and delicate, winter-unfriendly four-inch heels, a taxi honks at me. My heart's thudding erratically, like it's forgotten how to keep time. I stop and look at the angry driver, and that's all the time it takes for a streetcar to swoop Devin up. By the time I reach the other side of the road the streetcar doors are closing.

The patch of sidewalk Devin just walked down seems too ordinary to be the place where this just happened. I fold my arms across my chest and ogle it, stunned.

I'd probably stare for even longer only it's so cold that my teeth are already chattering. As I turn and wait for the traffic light to change, I see Morgan, minus his coat same as me, standing directly across the road, glaring at me like I've lost my mind. Once the walk sign flashes, I hurry towards him, rubbing my arms.

"I think I saw Devin," I say quickly. "He just crossed the street and hopped on a streetcar. We *missed* him. He was right here and we missed him." My lips quiver as I go on. "Maybe he even lives around here. Do you realize he could live in your neighbourhood?" Maybe he's been here all along, just blocks away from where Morgan works. The thought comes as a second shock. All this time and he's been right here. How could we not have known?"

Morgan's jaw has fallen. His head slants down towards mine. "Are you sure it was him? You were inside the gallery. How much could you actually see?"

"I saw the side of his face as he passed by. He walked right in front of the gallery." I'm speaking faster than I mean to. I can't seem to slow down. "I only saw him for a second but it looked exactly like Devin. He looked like *thin* Devin, you know, how he looked near the end." Now I've made it sound like my brother's dead. "How he looked when he left, I mean."

Morgan's eyes cloud over. "Serena, you know that could've been anyone."

"It could've been, but maybe it was him." I pout as Morgan touches my arm. "Don't you want it to have been him? Why don't you believe me?"

Morgan sighs and pulls his head back. "It's not that I don't believe you or don't want it to have been him. I just don't think you should get your hopes up too high when the odds are it was some guy with a passing resemblance."

"You'd have thought it was him too, if you'd seen him," I insist. My heart sinks as I process Morgan's doubt. Now he's making me doubt it too, even as I tell him otherwise.

"Maybe I would." Morgan nods diplomatically. "But it's freezing out here and whoever it was is gone. Let's get back inside. They'll think there's some kind of emergency."

I've managed to step in some gum and I feel it sticky underfoot as I head for the gallery with Morgan. Inside Ariel gazes at us with concern. "She's fine," Morgan says with a hint of *please don't ask* in his voice. Grover returns to Ariel's side with two glasses of red wine in his hands. Ariel thanks him as she takes one.

After a couple of seconds, during which Grover silently absorbs the undercurrent between the three of us, he turns to Morgan and says, "Your boyfriend's paintings are really interesting. I feel … unsettled but intrigued at the same time."

I'm glad he didn't use any of the more intellectual words I've heard tonight. I guess I've missed my chance to impress Ariel, and I don't know why I should want to measure up to Morgan anyway; none of that matters. I'm not sure whether the person I saw on Queen Street was really Devin or not, but the more I think about it, the more I realize whoever it was gave me hope. Devin's not dead and he's not a zombie. He's out there walking around like the man in the green jacket, waiting for me to spot him.

"Morgan." I involve my oldest brother in my giddy, distracted state by steadying myself against him and plucking gum from the bottom of my right shoe.

"People are disgusting, dropping their trash like that everywhere!" Jimmy says from behind us. He hands me a linen napkin to deposit the icky green-grey gum in. "Sometimes I wish I lived in the country."

"Who're you kidding?" Morgan quips. "You know how much dirt there is in the country? And remember how bored you were when we were at Orla's for the weekend?"

Jimmy and Morgan squabble playfully over the merits and disadvantages of rural living, but my heart's still galloping, thinking about the guy on the streetcar who may or may not have been Devin. Anyone's findable. No one can hide forever, especially someone like Devin who didn't have much money when he left and probably doesn't have much now. I want to talk to Morgan about it, ask him where the streetcar ends up and why we can't follow it, but I guess we're too late, and anyway, my oldest brother has obviously already pushed the matter out of his head.

By the time Morgan drives me home hours later I'm angry. Jimmy, exhausted from the success of his opening, has gone home to bed and I tell Morgan that we should've jumped in his car and tailed the streetcar along Queen Street until the guy in the green shell coat hopped off.

Morgan screws up his eyebrows and says, "You're telling me I should've run off in the middle of Jimmy's show to chase down a streetcar, which would be gone by the time I reached the parking lot by the way, just *in case* the guy you *think* you saw was someone who doesn't want our help in the first place?" Morgan sighs like he's exhaling cigarette smoke and eyes me warily. "Is that what you're saying?"

I shake my head in frustration and slide down in the passenger seat.

"Devin knows where to find us," Morgan continues. "It's not like any of us have disappeared. If he wants to get in touch, he can do it at any time."

"He needs help," I snap. "Do you think it's so easy to ask for help after everything that happened?"

Morgan rubs the side of his face and keeps his gaze on the road. "He doesn't want our help. That's why he's not calling."

"*Wait.* Do you know something I don't?" Is that why Morgan's in such a hurry to throw me off the scent? Does he think he's protecting me somehow? "Have you seen Devin in Toronto before? Have you talked to him?"

"*No.*" There's a prickle in my brother's tone, and an expression to match it. "*Of course not.* I haven't seen or heard from him since he left home. Do you really think I'd keep something like that from you?"

"If you thought it was for the —" I begin, before Morgan cuts me off.

For the best.

"But I haven't," he counters. "That's not what this is about."

"Promise me," I insist.

My brother's voice softens despite the impatience in his face. "I promise, Serena. I haven't seen or heard a word. I'm only saying, you remember how it was before Devin took off. All the shouting, the stealing, and the lying. Even if that was him outside the gallery, do you think he's any different now? You know you can't help someone if they don't want it, and when you insist on trying they drag you down with them."

Morgan's pupils plead with me. "I really hope you won't say anything to Mom and Dad. You can do what you want, obviously, but just think about it. They've been through enough."

I think about that but don't make any promises. Odds are that Morgan's right and Devin's still hooked and wants nothing to do with the rest of the LeBlancs, but the next day at school I can't stop going over the moment on Queen Street in my mind. If it were me in Devin's place, what would he have done?

I think about how when I was young Devin seemed to be the first person to notice whenever I was upset, like the time when I was ten and went trick-or-treating with some friends on Halloween. At one of the houses a woman with no hair and a baby on her hip answered the door. Her face wasn't wrinkly but the baldness made her look older than she probably was. She was really skinny too, the way Devin is in my dreams now, and my friends and I stared at her and forgot to speak.

"All I have left now is bubble gum," she said apologetically, reaching towards our bags to deposit the tiny packages. The baby on her hip seemed too chubby and healthy to belong to her, and the woman didn't seem to care that we were seeing her without her hair. We went to a lot of houses that night — I ended up with two jumbo bags full of chocolate bars, potato chips, gummies, and concentrated sugar products — but the bald, fragile-looking woman stayed in my head.

When I got home I was quiet and Devin asked if I'd gotten into a fight with my friends or something. I told him about the woman

and the baby and he said she was probably going through chemo-
therapy for some kind of cancer.

"Cancer?" I repeated. So maybe she'd die and the baby wouldn't
have a mother?

"Yeah, but she's lucky she's getting the chemo," Devin continued.
"In the old days mostly people just died when they got cancer. Now
she's got a fighting chance." He bit his lip like he realized he wasn't
calming me down any. "But you know, it could always just be something like alopecia, that can make people — women too — lose
their hair when there's nothing else wrong with them. I bet that's what
she has."

"Really?" I asked suspiciously. "You're not making that up?"

"What? Like I'm going to make up a word like *alopecia*?" Devin
shook his head at me. He would've been sixteen at the time and a
master at rolling his eyes, but he usually saved that for Mom and
Morgan or people he didn't like. "You can look it up on the Internet
and read all about it if you don't believe me."

I can't remember whether I looked it up or not but what I do
remember was that neither of my brothers ever tormented me the
way other people complain that their older siblings often do. There's
only a year between my brothers, so you'd think they'd have been
close to each other growing up, but it was always Devin and I who
were close. Morgan just never seemed to take that much notice of
either of us.

A few months after that Halloween incident, and not long after
a record-breaking snowstorm and cold spell left Glenashton covered
in white, two boys who took the same school bus home as me pelted
me with snowballs three days in a row. Some of the snow was closer
to being ice and on that third day I slipped and fell while trying
to avoid the pain of being hit. I got the wind knocked out of me,
and when I told Devin my face was still red from trying to catch
my breath. He was waiting for me when I hopped off the bus on

the fourth day and he fixed a death glare at the boys. Their heads dropped down towards their chins as they turned slowly away, like any sudden movement might provoke him.

If my mom knew about the snowballs she probably would've said one of the boys liked me (as though no one ever has a *mean* motive for singling someone out) but Devin advised that I should give "idiots like that" withering looks and build up a force field of anger around myself that wouldn't let them get near me. I guess that's what Aya, Genevieve, Nicole, and I have done lately. Sixteen-year-old Devin would've approved but he'd also count Gage out on looks alone. Does that make him wrong, or am I the one who's wrong now?

After school Genevieve drops me off at Total Drug Mart for my shift. Ki can't stop throwing up in the bathroom, so we're down a cashier. I barely have time for a break, but that's good because it stops me thinking about Devin on Queen Street — or Devin, wherever he may be. Ki's mom picks her up and says her brother's already home with the stomach flu and now she'll have two patients on her hands. I don't want to pick up the stomach flu before my date with Gage; I buy chewable Vitamin C and coat my hands with liquid sanitizer every chance I get.

As I count the contents of my register at the end of the night my mind flips back and forth between tomorrow's date and what my parents would say if I ignored Morgan's wishes and told them that I thought I saw Devin downtown. My best guess is that Dad would agree with Morgan that I was imagining things and Mom would go into hysterics and get straight on the highway. She's taken Devin's disappearance worse than anyone; I don't want to be responsible for getting her hopes up again only to have them shredded worse than ever. There's not enough left of my mother to handle that right now.

Drug addict Devin would break her heart. Who else could we hope to find but him, and why then do I insist on thinking there's some hope left?

CHAPTER TWELVE

IN CIVICS CLASS THE next day Nicole wants to know if we're hanging out after school. She keeps talking about ordering pizza at her place later and pondering various topping configurations, never mind that we just had lunch last period. Almost all of Nicole's pizza ideas include pepperoni, but my favourite pizza of all time is Pizza Pizza's Bacon Chicken Mushroom Melt with Italian sausage added on (my mouth tingles with desire at the thought of the Italian seasoning and mesquite chicken).

"I can come over but I can't stay for pizza," I tell her. I have an alibi at the ready and I act extra casual so she won't suspect I'm lying about tonight. "My parents have a new bed on order. The delivery guys are coming anytime between five and nine and guess who's stuck waiting for it?" I grimace like this is highly vexing. "I'd ask you to come over instead but my mom's been in a really bad mood lately — like even more so than usual — and doesn't want anyone around."

"She doesn't want anyone around even when she's not there?" Nicole says, wriggling her eyebrows.

"We had a fight the other night and I'm not sure what time she'll be home from her work thing tonight. It could be, like, seven or it could be nine-thirty." Nicole's mouth sags in sympathy for me. "But I can hang out at your place for an hour or so," I add brightly. "Is Genevieve coming?"

Sure enough the three of us lounge around Nicole's living room after school. Hiding my plans from the two of them gives me a tickly sensation at the back of my throat, like maybe I'll cough up a furball. I still haven't mentioned my Queen Street drama either, and it's not that I don't want to confide in them — because I do, I want to relive the entire incident and get their opinions on it so badly that I feel like a fake talking about anything else — but it's easier to keep the news from my mother when no one on the planet aside from Morgan has a clue what I suspect.

We officially agreed over the phone last night, Morgan and I. It's better not to upset my parents unless we have "further evidence."

"Did you tell Jimmy?" I asked him.

"Of course," Morgan replied as though I should've taken that as a given. "But he'll keep it quiet too."

So there are multiple things I'm keeping quiet lately — one of them Morgan knows, another would make my friends scowl, and the third is my obsession with weight, which is something I don't like to talk about, although I never stop thinking about it. Maybe it wouldn't sound like a big deal to naturally thin people, but I wish that I hadn't finished off half my gourmet fries at the restaurant the other night because I have yet to drop the extra pound I picked up there. A pound is nothing, I know. But I swear I feel heavier, which is the last thing I want to feel when I'm about to go on a date. And why did Nicole have to go and mention pizza?

I need to fill up on water more from now on. That's what I'll do tonight; chomp on iceberg lettuce and guzzle calorie-free fluids. Being thin is almost as bad as being fat if you have to spend all your time *thinking* about food rather than eating it. And not only thinking about food but pretending to yourself that you're *not* thinking about food. It's so exhausting that it makes me want to break down and order Bacon Chicken Mushroom Melt pizza with Italian sausage.

I remind myself that I'm stronger than that and think about how much better I look in my jeans when I'm not filling up on things like pizza and fries. After about an hour at Nicole's place, she and Genevieve drop me off at home, completely buying into my alibi. "You know you should've gotten your folks to buy you a new bed too," Nicole says as we pull into my empty driveway. "You're too old for a twin."

"I have a twin," Genevieve reminds her with a pointed expression. "If there's no one sleeping next to you there's plenty of room."

I laugh in agreement to cover my guilt at lying to them. "So exactly what are you getting up to in your double that we don't know about, Nicole?"

"I don't have any secrets," Nicole reminds me, smiling ironically. "Whatever I've gotten up to in the past, everyone knows about. I'm like a teenage cautionary tale."

Genevieve flicks her hair back over her shoulder with a toss of her head. "If you were a cautionary tale you'd be pregnant or have gonorrhea — we're not cautionary tales, any of us; we're just new and improved versions of ourselves. We got smart, unlike a lot of people we go to school with."

Nicole and I nod at this. I desperately want to be a new, improved version of myself but the new me and the old me are trapped inside the same body. Genevieve honks as she and Nicole pull away from my house in her Honda. Thankfully today's not one of Mom's "sick" days so I don't have to explain what she's doing home when she's supposed to be conducting unspecified late business, serving as my cover story.

Inside my bedroom, I slide open the closet and stare longingly at my silk floral-print wrap dress but reach for a dark denim skirt instead. I pull grey ribbed tights on under it and tug my arms into a matching tight grey sweater. Jacob always said I had great breasts. Well, most of the time he used other words instead but that wasn't one of the things I minded about him.

Stop thinking about Jacob, I lecture. I don't want my mind hanging on him as some kind of bad example to avoid. Better to start fresh, with the sky as the limit.

Dad has a container of deli-bought ravioli with him when he arrives home but Mom has already started on a homemade rice and vegetable medley. "I'll grab dinner while I'm out," I tell them. "I'm going to a movie with a friend."

Dad's head swivels on his shoulders. "A friend?" he repeats. "Do you already have Jacob's replacement lined up?"

I pin a smile onto my face, the mention of Jacob turning my stomach sour. "I'm not looking for any replacements. This is just a friend, a work friend."

"A friend with a male name," Mom surmises, dragging a wooden spoon through her rice and veggies.

A friend with a male name and male appendages, but I know Mom will only be interested in this revelation for a few more minutes. If I spilled the news about my possible Devin sighting any questions about what I'm doing tonight would instantly evaporate. I'd go back to being supporting cast for Devin, even in his absence.

"His name's Gage," I confirm, still smiling. "You've heard that men and women can be friends, right? I think that was legally decided in the 70s."

My parents would probably let me leave with Gage even if I admitted that he doesn't work at Total and that we're about to go on an actual date together but I don't want to watch my mother and father cobble together some manufactured additional concern when I know that their true priority is their missing second son.

As it is, my parents take my word for it and don't insist on coming to the door when Gage rings the bell at a quarter after seven. He stands on my doorstep in black cargo pants and the same light leather coat he was wearing the day he drove me home from work. "Sorry I'm late," he says, his face creasing apologetically. "There was something I had to take care of at home."

"Fifteen minutes isn't really late," I tell him, wondering why I'm already making excuses for him.

Gage eyes my body up quickly, like he doesn't want to be caught doing it. "I'm usually on time," he continues, his almost dirty blond hair fluttering in the wind.

"You'll catch cold in that jacket," I lecture to make up for letting him off the hook about the fifteen minutes. "You're going to get hypothermia, which will be a much bigger deal than being fifteen minutes late."

I wait for him to make some joke about sharing my body heat, like Jacob would've done. Instead Gage nods like I could be right and that he's not surprised to have his mistakes pointed out to him. "It's all bad, isn't it? Should I drive home and get another coat?"

"Then you'd be later still," I point out. I love watching Gage's eyes take me in. They look warm, even as the rest of him is probably about to freeze to death on my doorstep. I smile at him, glad we're doing this even though I had to lie to my friends about it. Watching him watch me, I feel like someone just lit me up from the inside.

Gage tosses his head back and bites his lip, a grin stealing onto his face. "So it looks like I'm screwed."

"You really are." I pause for a few seconds, as though I'm thinking it all over. "Let me get my coat, at least then it will be only one of us with hypothermia." I beckon him inside and pull my wool coat out of the closet.

Seconds later we sit inside Gage's car where he says, "I was think-ing we could go to Kelsey's, but whatever you're in the mood for is fine with me." He smiles again and reaches quickly into the back seat to pick up a scrap of newspaper. "I ripped out the movie listings.

There are a couple of things that might be worth watching. See what you think." He hands me the paper, shaking his head as I take it. "I don't know why I'm giving you this now. You can wait and read it at the restaurant. Or maybe you already know what you want to watch." He winds his left hand around the side of his neck, his smile slipping from his face. "Sorry, I'm not great at this."

"This?" I repeat.

"First dates." Gage's hand massages his neck. "All the getting to know you and *what should we do* small talk."

If his show of nerves is an act it's a good one. I'm starting to believe him. "We can pretend we're just hanging out," I tell him. "That we've known each other for years."

Gage tilts his head as he stares at me. "If we've known each other for years I already know that your last name is ..." He stretches out the last word and prompts me with his eyes.

"LeBlanc," I tell him. I hope he's telling the truth about not being great at first dates. I don't want to find out at the end of this that I've been played.

"LeBlanc," he repeats slowly. "And that you're ..."

I'm not sure what he's looking for here. I stare quizzically back.

"Okay." Gage laughs. "It's going to be really hard for me to pretend we've hung out before when I don't know a thing about you besides your name and that you work at Total Drug Mart and believe in ghosts."

"That's true. But you've got one up on me. I still don't know your last name."

"It's Cochrane." He turns his key and starts the engine. "Why don't you tell me where you want to go before we fill each other in on the rest? Otherwise we might never get out of your driveway."

"Kelsey's is perfect." I glance at the torn newspaper page in the dark. "We can look at the movie listings together later."

Gage waits until I've put my seat belt on to back out of the driveway. "There's really not all that much to know about me," he continues. "Right now I'm working at a warehouse, getting some money together. I guess you could say I'm at a point where I'm try-ing to figure out what to do with myself. I didn't know what to do when I graduated so …" He shrugs. "I'm hoping it'll fall into place, but I'm not in a hurry."

"I don't know what to do with my life either," I confess.

"You'll work it out," Gage says confidently as he glances at me. "You've got time."

"A few years, I guess."

Gage's eyes hang on me longer this time. "How old are you anyway?"

Seeing as I just found out that he's already graduated, "fifteen" doesn't seem like it would be a popular answer. Why make things trickier than they have to be? I twirl my hair around my finger and quote him a number that will be true in three months.

"Sixteen?" he repeats, surprise leaking into his voice. "I would've guessed seventeen or eighteen. You're just a baby. You have all the time in the world. What are you, like, in eleventh grade?"

"Eleventh grade," I echo, fudging the truth imperceptibly. "Yep. How old are you?"

"Nineteen. Eleventh grade seems like …" He exhales loudly. An expression I can't decipher sweeps across his face. "Like a lifetime ago."

"Well, it would," I tease. "You're ancient. I mean, *nineteen*. Wow. I don't see how you could even be interested in me with the big gap in our maturity levels and all."

"You're a mid-life crisis date," Gage jokes, his eyes crinkling up, and God, he looks so gorgeous when he smiles that I want to spend the rest of the night saying things that will make him break out in grins.

Over dinner I do my best to make that happen repeatedly. The entrees don't start at $21.95 but the restaurant's nice just the same and we have a good time. I order salad and water, like I promised myself, and Gage cuts off a piece of his steak for me and drinks one beer and then 7-Up. He says he only ever has one beer if he's driving. I also find out that he lives with his mom near the big rec centre on Laird.

"I had swimming lessons there when I was younger," I tell him. My mom used to love to swim. There was a time, when I was seven or eight, that we'd go to the public swim here together pretty regularly. The pride in her eyes when I showed off my newly learned diving skills courses through my memory, leaving muddy waves in its wake. I must've made her watch me three or four times in a row. She beamed at me every single time.

"Me too," Gage says. "Used to have hockey practice there too. They have everything at that place. There's even a really good library just next door."

I've never heard any guy my age comment on the quality of a library before. Gage adds that he's bigger into soccer than hockey these days and that the team he plays for will start up again in the spring. He's a big Toronto FC supporter, even though "their midfield sucks." I pretend to be interested and ask him follow-up questions about the team. He's so enthusiastic that after a while it actually becomes a bit contagious, although I've never once watched a professional soccer match. "I can pick up a couple of tickets for us when the season starts," he offers. "I mean, you know, if you like the idea and if we're still hanging out."

For some reason the idea that we could still be hanging out in the spring makes my face tingle. We spend a long time talking about ghost-hunting and I tell him a bit about Clara. That gets Gage even more excited than the soccer and he asks me a ton of questions. I wish I could remember more for him. He says young kids seem to be more "sensitive" when it comes to ghost sightings.

"I think maybe Clara even used to talk to me," I say. The memories are so faded that I feel like I'm making them up but once upon a time I remember *remembering* the sound of her voice, hushed and lyrical, an accent probably.

We're still on the subject of the supernatural when we get to the movie theatre. Afterwards, walking to the car, we pick apart some of the stupider points of the thriller we've just seen. Then, out of the blue, as Gage is starting the car, he says, "I thought I saw my dad once. In the backyard of our old house about thirteen years ago." Gage stares out the front window, blinking as he continues in a steady but quiet voice. "The sun was coming up. He smiled at me through the sliding door in the living room."

At first I don't know what Gage is talking about. Then, in a lightning bolt moment, I get it and feel like an idiot. Gage is talking about seeing his father's ghost. Gage's dad is *deceased*. This is something I should've clued in to earlier in the evening. All along he just mentioned his mother and I never even thought to ask about his dad; I assumed his parents had split up and that his father wasn't in the picture.

"My mother said it was one of those things you imagine when you're still half-asleep," Gage continues. "And maybe it was." He shrugs lightly. "Who knows?"

The car's moving now, and as we navigate our way out of the parking lot I feel a rush of sympathy for him. "Maybe it really was him," I say. "Maybe he was checking in on you." I swallow the dryness at the back of my throat. "How long has he been gone?"

"Since I was two," Gage says. "Leukemia."

"I'm sorry." My cheeks are heavy. I stare down at my lap.

"It's okay. It was a long time ago. I mean, obviously I would've liked for him to be around, but I can't really remember him. That time in the backyard — I only recognized him because of the photo and, well ..." Gage nods a little. "It *felt* like him. I can't really explain it."

I nod too. Then I notice we're driving back exactly the way we came. Another few minutes and we'll be on my street. "Are you taking me home?"

Gage swings a look my way. "It's late. Your parents will probably be waiting up."

Maybe. "I thought we could talk for a couple more minutes." I don't want to end the night on a sad note. Besides, Gage could be right about my folks and the possibility alone means we'll barely be able to share a kiss in my driveway. Even if my parents aren't waiting up they might hear us pull up to the house and feel some kind of legal guardian compulsion to peek out the window.

We definitely need more time alone. Gage can't just drop me off, leaving us both with this unfinished feeling. I gaze hopefully at him, trying to convey all that without seeming skanky.

Gage blinks slowly back, the air in the car feeling spiky with expectation. "My place isn't good," he admits. I can see my disappointment reflected in his eyes. "We can get coffee somewhere," he adds. "Or maybe ..." Gage's cheekbones tighten. He presses his lips together and stares at my legs. They'd be more tempting if they weren't covered by thick grey tights but it's nice to see him checking them out anyway.

"Or maybe what?" My heart's speeding. It feels good to be wanted again.

"I know someplace close that we can talk for a while." Gage looks me in the eye, a more intense look than I've seen on his face so far. "Somewhere no one will bother us. It's deserted at night."

"Okay," I tell him. My lungs feel like they're expanding, like whatever oxygen I can take in won't be enough for them. "That sounds good."

"You might not think so when you see it." Gage laughs lightly. "Promise me you won't be insulted. We don't have to stay if you don't want to."

I take the fact that he's offering me an out as a good sign. He doesn't just want me with him; he wants me to want it too. He hasn't touched me all night, unless you count our hands brushing against each other in the popcorn tub. The anticipation is starting to make me a little crazy. I want to sink my teeth into his neck like a vampire. He has beautiful lips. I can't wait to find out how he kisses.

Gage cruises into an industrial area, weaving his way casually through dimly lit streets like we're stuck in a maze he'd know blindfolded. Finally we pull into the parking lot of what's clearly an abandoned structure. A sign proclaims the narrow two-storey building "J.N. Malzar." There's a letter missing between the "l" and "z," which I guess makes the defunct company something like Maltzar or Malezar. Crooked shutters are still hanging inside some of the windows, making the red brick building look even more dilapidated.

"You're creeped out," Gage notes. "I knew we should've gone for coffee." He taps the fingers of his right hand against the steering wheel. "Sorry, we'll go somewhere we can get a decent cappuccino."

"No." I reach out and touch his arm. "This place is pretty creepy, but you don't have to be sorry. Just come here." I unbuckle my seat belt and lean brazenly across the divide between our bucket seats, before either of us can lose our nerve.

Unfortunately, Gage has no idea I'm planning on lunging for him and our teeth collide. The noise sounds like something you hear in a dental office. I've never knocked teeth with anyone before and it makes me feel like a complete amateur; I want to shrink into the space between our seats and disappear. Gage laughs at me. I recoil and frown into the fake fur of my coat, embarrassed.

"Hey," Gage says. He unbuckles his seat belt, his hand landing on my thigh and squeezing. "Hey, come back. Do I only get one shot?"

"You're laughing at me," I point out. I feel like sulking, and it makes me wonder if I'm ready for any of this. Maybe I need longer to deprogram myself from Jacob and my fat-girl thought patterns.

"I'm laughing because I'm an idiot," Gage explains, his thumb stroking my thigh as his four fingers remain motionless. "I'm laughing because I've got a beautiful girl sitting in my car, in front of this sleazy-looking dump of all places." He motions over his shoulder at the remains of J.N. Malzar. "And she *still* wants to kiss me, but I can't even do that right.

"What else can I do but laugh at the idiocy of that, Serena?" He takes his hand off my leg and touches my hair where it spills over the shoulder of my jacket. "C'mon, I swear I won't laugh this time, no matter what happens." He leans closer towards me, his face so close that I imagine I can feel his breath. I let him press his lips softly against mine, softer than anyone has ever kissed me, the way you kiss someone in their sleep if you don't want to wake them. He lets the kiss rest on my mouth for three long seconds before repeating it, his bottom lip dropping open a little. Our lips rub and catch, catch and rub, our tongues sliding cautiously out to explore. We're teasing each other, giving just enough to make the other demand more.

"Hold still," I demand finally, impatience getting the better of me. I grab the back of his head and hold him there in front of me. His tongue slips into my mouth and he kisses me deep and long, exactly like I want. One of his hands rests on my neck. He strokes my hair, pulls it just enough to make me feel good but not enough to hurt.

"Do you want to get in the back seat?" he whispers, his face still close to mine. "We'd have more room."

"Okay," I whisper back. It doesn't occur to me to step outside and open the back door; I climb over my chair and into the back seat. Gage gets out and slips into the back with me. The cold air from outside gusts in with him and makes me shiver.

"I can leave the car running," he says, about to swing his door open again.

"No. Stay." I grab the end of his jacket, helping him out of it. Then I press my hands against his shirt, feeling his heart beat under my palm. It's running as fast as mine. I tell him that and lay his hand over my own heart to prove it. "See?"

Gage nods and slowly shifts his hand, his eyes on mine as if to ask whether I'm okay with this. I'm perfectly okay. Better than okay. Gage scoops his hand around my breast, one of his fingers circling my nipple. We kiss hard, making ourselves comfortable in the back seat, his hands boomeranging back to my breasts every chance they get. My sweater's only in the way and I yank it over my head, my cheeks stretching into a smile as Gage stares at my bra. "Does this open at the front?" he asks, his finger resting on the centre clasp.

"Yeah," I murmur, waiting for him to do it. What's the holdup? I know he wants to. The feeling's taking over his whole face.

"Serena," he says. His tone is almost stern, and I watch his jaw turn rigid and feel the dynamic between us start to shift. Maybe he doesn't want this as much as I do after all and he's already figured out that the next time he sees me he'll want to pretend none of this happened.

"What?" I ask. But if it's something bad like that, I don't really want to know. Everything's gone pretty well so far tonight and I mean to keep it that way. I go for Gage's pants before he can answer me. The zip slides down easy. The boxers are easy too. I find my way inside with no problem. I bend over him, my hair falling down around my face.

"Serena," Gage whispers. One of his hands lightly cups my head. I hear a shivery awe in his voice that I used to hear in Jacob's. He tastes different and sounds different, but that tone, it's almost identical.

"Serena," Gage repeats. "Serena." The urgency makes me think we're almost finished.

"Hey," he says, removing his hand from my head. "Stop, Serena. Stop."

I'm so into what I'm doing that there's a second delay as my brain translates the syllables. Stop? Why?

"Stop," he commands. "Stop!"

I raise my head slowly, averting my eyes as he pushes his hard-on back into his boxers and zips up his jeans. Gage gets out of the back seat, slamming the door behind him like I've done something wrong. Then he stands outside with his shoulders hunched as though he's waiting for me to follow his lead. I have no idea what I've done, but I pull my sweater on and open the back door, my throat scratchy with regret.

Why did I think this time things would turn out right?

CHAPTER THIRTEEN

"I'M SORRY," GAGE SAYS once we're both sitting in the front seat again. "This was a bad idea. I'm just going to take you home, okay?" He glances warily at me from the corner of his eye. I guess the prospect of facing me is too horrible to contemplate.

"Whatever," I tell him. I lost my cool there for a little but I'm not going to dissolve in front of his eyes. He doesn't have to know how he's rattled me.

"Sorry," Gage repeats. I wish he'd quit apologizing every two seconds. It obviously doesn't mean anything.

He called himself an idiot earlier, but I'm the real idiot, the grandmaster idiot. Thank God Genevieve and Nicole don't have to know about this. No one at school does. It'll be like tonight never happened.

Gage's car is quieter than any library. I reach out and turn on his stereo. Considering what I did earlier, I'm not worried that touching his car stereo could qualify as overstepping boundaries. On the radio Natasha Bedingfield's grooving about her "Pocketful of Sunshine." Meanwhile my throat's on fire. Inside I'm waging an epic battle to convince myself that I'm not really upset and that Gage is the one with the problem here, not me. Never mind that he seemed nice earlier, guys under thirty are a lost cause, just like Genevieve said.

I home in on the radio because it's obvious that Gage and I don't have anything left to say to each other. He hasn't even bothered to explain himself beyond his minimalist *sorry*. I don't have a "Pocketful of Sunshine" like Natasha does, but as I listen to the lyrics I find that they fit my situation after all. It's one of those *I'm gonna be all right no matter what anyone tries to do to me* songs. Go, Natasha! Go, me! Goodbye, Gage.

But what did I do wrong?

Nothing, I remind myself. It's not you, stupid. It's him.

We veer into my driveway, a thumping hip hop tune replacing Natasha's triumph. Gage turns the volume down and glances at me, his hand back on his neck, kneading away in full stress mode. "Thanks for coming out tonight," he says. Maybe he's in a band after all and expects me to applaud.

I nod silently. If I open my mouth he'll know how upset I am within two seconds.

"I'm sorry, you know …" He drops his gaze for a second before pointing it back at me. "I should've taken you somewhere else."

"Maybe," I mumble, unbuckling my seat belt. I open the door, slip out, and slam it shut behind me without another word.

Gage stares out at me from the car. He rolls down the window and leans over the passenger seat. "Are you okay?" He sounds concerned, but I'm not going to poke my head into the window and explain what he should already know. He didn't have to yell at me and practically shove me off him, making me feel like a leper.

"Fine." I wave him away, forcing myself to deliver an almost casual-sounding, "See you."

I step away from his car, the thought that Devin would've written Gage off from the start jumping up and down inside my head, making it ache worse than my throat.

Devin's not here but he's still right. I *am* here and I'm dead wrong.

Time to evolve into that new, improved version of myself Genevieve was talking about. I'm a little screwed up, I know, but I have no intention of being anybody's cautionary tale.

※

I score fifteen out of fifteen on a science quiz the next day, which is funny because I feel unfocused and tired. Jon Wheatley bumps into me on the way out of class and catches a dazed expression on my face when he glances over to apologize. "Hey, your heart still pumping oxygen to your brain there, LeBlanc?" he asks as we head into the hallway. "You look like you're about to go zombie."

So maybe that's what's wrong with me: I'm about to go zombie. Who knew that people were so fuzzy-brained just before they turned? The state's eerily similar to what it feels like to be shunned by the good-looking guy from the drugstore while your missing brother shambles along Queen Street, probably looking for drugs and/or the money to buy them.

"Check your pulse," I tell Jon. "You're the one who walked into me, Wheatley." I smile like I'm just kidding, but by the time the lunch bell rings I'm heavy with a sadness that I can't hide. I stride up to Nicole in the cafeteria and command her, "Walk with me."

Nicole's eyes darken.

"Walk with me," I repeat, my face falling. "C'mon, Nic." My voice cracks, and Nicole's up in a shot, her shoulder pressed against mine as we stomp across the cafeteria together and into the hall.

"What happened?" she asks on the other side of the door. "Is it Jacob?"

I shake my head and rub my eyes, catching any tears before they can wet my skin.

"His turd friends?" she continues worriedly. "What? Tell me what's going on, Serena."

"Maybe nothing." I squash another tear under my finger and begin to describe Tuesday's crucial events. They're not the only reason I feel like someone ran over me with a semi, but talking about seeing Devin is easier than confessing what happened last night.

Nicole and I hang out between the inner and outer doors to the north parking lot and she listens to me, curving a hand around my shoulder. "Do you think he saw you?" she asks when I pause. "Maybe that's why he jumped on the streetcar."

"I don't think so. He never even looked in my direction. I had my eyes on him the entire time."

"Like a private detective," Nicole comments. "Maybe you should hire one. Have him tracked down."

"That would cost a fortune. They're something like forty bucks an hour." I looked it up on the Internet when Devin walked off last June. Part of me was sick to death of all the drama and almost relieved that he'd written himself out of the family picture but there was still a huge chunk that needed to know I could find him if I had to — or at least that my parents could. I never asked them if they thought about hiring someone, though. I held the idea in reserve. A last chance.

The funny thing about the Devin drama is it didn't end when he walked out; it just mutated into the way my parents and I live now, like we're forever waiting. I'm not even sure whether it's something good or something bad we're waiting for. Both probably. Hope for the best. Expect the worst. *Waiting, waiting, waiting.*

Nicole nods thoughtfully. She folds her arms in front of her and leans against the wall.

"You can't say anything," I warn. "I told Morgan I wouldn't let our parents find out." Nicole's head slants up, and I begin to explain our reasons for the secrecy, knowing that's the question on her lips. I've never gone into any depth about Devin with her or Genevieve before. Unloading some of the details makes me feel at least two pounds lighter. "And maybe it wasn't him anyway," I add. "He could've lost more weight by now. I haven't seen him in seven months. I might not even recognize him anymore."

I know this is a logical thing to say, but in my heart I still believe there's a good chance it was Devin I saw swallowed up by a Toronto streetcar. I wonder if that's how Gage felt about seeing his father's ghost. He admitted he could've imagined it but somehow I think he believes what his heart told him, just like I do. My lungs twinge at the thought.

"So …" Nicole says slowly. "Do you think maybe you can just think of it that way — decide for yourself that it wasn't him and move on — or do you feel like you actually have to know?"

I freeze in place, my eyes dry. That's the million-dollar question, isn't it? "I don't know." My mascara has clumped. I stroke my sticky lashes. "I think maybe I should at least go back to Toronto, walk around. *See.*" I know that the odds I'll find Devin waiting for a streetcar in exactly the same spot as last time are a thousand to one, but I can't shake the feeling that I need to retrace his steps along Queen Street. If he passes by there a lot, someone might recognize him.

"We can comb the area," Nicole suggests excitedly. "Bring a picture of him. Do you have one from before he left?"

I'm touched that she wants to help, and I realize I might have better luck if she, Genevieve, and maybe even Aya make finding Devin a group effort, but I don't think I can do it that way. Even with what I've told her, Nicole doesn't have any real idea of what it was like to live with Devin those last few months. Only my parents and maybe Morgan know what it was like to watch him be possessed before our eyes. Somehow involving anyone else would make the effort feel small, like a summer project to build a deck. I know Nicole has only the best intentions and I feel bad for not being able to work my way around the feeling that Devin is our problem — Morgan's, my parents', and mine — but I just can't.

"I'm going now, Nicole," I say. "I'm going to ditch my afternoon classes, and you have that presentation in English later."

"We can go tomorrow," she tells me. "It's Saturday, we'll have all day."

"I can't stop thinking about him." I glance down at my shoes. "Being here feels like a waste of time. I'll call you later, okay? Let you know if I find anything."

Nicole frowns. "How're you even going to get there?"

"I'll take the bus." There's one at the Glenashton mall that hooks up with a commuter train travelling west to Toronto. My dad used to take it to work before he opened up his own audiologist practice in Glenashton. It'll take me close to an hour and a half to make it to Queen Street, but it's doable.

"You sure?" Nicole's hair obscures one of her eyes as she tilts her head. "What if you need backup? What if he gets weird or ..." She shrugs. "You sure?" she asks again.

I am. I let Nicole write a note excusing me from class for a dental appointment. "What's your mom's name?" she asks.

"Tessa. But she usually signs her name T. LeBlanc."

Nicole signs my mother's name as I described. It looks nothing like my mother's real signature but at least Nicole will feel like she's done something to help.

I hand in the note at the attendance office and then bus it over to the train station. In total my journey is a bus ride, one commuter train, and a subway ride long. An hour and forty-five minutes later I'm roaming along Queen Street, past clothing stores and coffee shops. It's not as cold as it was on Tuesday but I can still see my breath in the air. Here and there, sitting outside convenience stores or in doorways that are the closest thing to warm you'll find outside, homeless people sit begging. Some of them have signs explaining why they've fallen on hard times or what they'll do with any money you hand over. I feel guilty strolling past them. Devin could be feeding himself this way, for all I know.

An old guy with a scraggly white beard and a spotted dog sitting next to him looks up at me as I approach. "Have any change for me, darlin'?" he asks. His cheeks are lined with broken blood vessels.

The dog looks up at me too. He has sadder eyes than the man.

"My best friend in this life," the old guy tells me. "Everyone should have one." I glance down at the tin can in front of the man and his dog on the sidewalk. I wonder how much money he's gotten so far today. His cardboard sign doesn't explain his life story; it simply reads: "Donation$ appreciated." I notice his navy jacket is thick and has a good hood on it. I hope it keeps him warm.

"What's his name?" I ask, pointing to the dog. "Or is it a her?"

"He's a he." The guy's gloved hand lands affectionately on his spotted dog's head. "Call him Bucky. Another old friend gave him to me. Got sick. Couldn't take care of him no more." I nod and listen to the man continue. "Not sure that I can do such a good job myself but at least we keep each other company."

The beginnings of a sob are forming in my chest. I nod again to keep it trapped under my ribs. I don't have much cash on me, and now that we've been having a conversation it feels like an insult to give the man money, but at the same time I know he could use it. I wriggle a five-dollar bill out of my pocket and press it into the man's glove.

"You're very kind," he tells me, his lips jerking up. One of his bottom teeth is missing but he still has a nice smile.

I pull my cellphone out of my knapsack before I lose my nerve. "Do you think you could have a look at a photo for me and tell me if you've seen the person in it?" The man stares up at me, bewildered. I guess I don't look much like a cop. "He's my brother," I explain. "He's been missing since summer. I thought I saw him around here a couple of days ago."

"Well, then." He scrutinizes the image on my cell. It was taken about a week after Dad first brought Devin home from Queen's University last March. He'd already lost about twenty-five pounds, and by the time he left in June at least another fifteen had vanished. Mom cooked up his favourite foods nearly every night (and even some mornings): steak smothered in mushrooms, chicken and ribs, fettuccine alfredo, fajitas, potato pancakes, deep dish peach pie.

I ballooned up worse than ever for a while, before the stress level surrounding Devin crushed my appetite. Sitting next to him at the table became the worst moments of each day, a test he almost always failed. He'd manage only a couple of bites before either making some lame excuse for why he didn't have an appetite or just pushing the food restlessly around his plate until it got cold. Later he started getting angry with Mom, accusing her of wanting to keep him fat and saying things like, "The kind of things you're putting in front of me, no one should be swallowing that garbage. What're you trying to do — give me a heart attack before I'm thirty?"

"You're wasting away, Devin," Mom would lecture in a weepy voice. "Do you think we don't know why you're never hungry? You have to eat something. Your body can't just run on …"

Mom couldn't bring herself to use the word *meth* or even *drugs*.

"Here we go," Devin would say, his mouth and eyes full of disdain. "Cry," he instructed. "*Cry.* You never stop, do you? You can't leave me alone for two seconds?" He'd push his chair away from the table and storm off, his food barely touched on the plate.

The Devin on my screen doesn't look sick, but that's a lie. He's sitting in the kitchen in a khaki striped hoodie and smiling an overly bright smile, annoyed that I'm taking his picture. I didn't think it'd be the last photo I ever took of him. I was just testing out my new phone at the time. Snapping everything in sight.

The old man in front of me is sitting on a flattened cardboard box. He takes his time staring at Devin's image, like he really wants to be sure. Finally he looks up at me and hands back my phone. "Sorry, darlin'," he says regretfully. "Can't say the fella looks familiar to me. You say you saw him around here?"

Bucky's glossy brown eyes are suddenly alert. The dog sniffs the air as an Asian woman strides by with a pizza box in her hands. I can smell the cheese and pepperoni too, and agree with Bucky that it's unjustly tempting.

"I thought so," I tell him. "But I'm not positive. It could've been someone with a resemblance." I tuck my phone away again. "Thanks anyway."

"Ask around." The man stretches his arms out to indicate the scores of people passing. "Don't take my word for it. Someone else might have seen him."

I thank the man and continue slowly along Queen Street, searching out friendly faces, my hand clinging to my phone in my coat pocket, ready to pull it out. Some people don't even wait for me to finish asking the question before shaking their heads at me and striding off. I give five dollars each to the two other homeless people I ask, feeling guilty for requiring something of them when they have so little. An Arab guy in a convenience store studies the picture on my cell before advising me that I shouldn't approach people I don't know because someone's liable to steal it on me or worse.

"I'll be careful," I assure him.

Inside a coffee shop I question a cute barista guy with spiky blond hair and a barbell through his eyebrow. In Club Monaco two employees with sleek dark hair glare disapprovingly at my cell like it's covered in Ebola germs. Restaurant hostesses, shoe store employees, and people behind deli counters, nobody has seen Devin.

I'm disappointed, but I don't take it as proof one way or the other. I could come back down here a dozen times and never find a trace of him, even if he's living around the corner.

Morgan wouldn't be happy with my undercover work. I fully expect to run into my golden boy oldest brother at any moment. He lives just blocks away himself, and the MuchMusic studio is only about a hundred feet away from where I'm standing right now, my face getting prickly as the wind picks up. Above me, a mass of grey is gathering. Soon there'll be snow. Do Bucky and his master have someplace to go when it snows heavy?

The cry I resisted earlier rumbles around in my lungs. I think of that morning in early June when Devin left us. He'd taken my mom's car the night before. He wasn't allowed to drive it anymore but that didn't stop him. I had a geography exam at one o'clock and didn't have to be up for hours but my parents' frustrated voices woke me. Mom was due to leave for work and Dad was pacing the kitchen, his eyes bursting with tension. By then several of Mom's crystal figurines had already gone missing, including one of her favourites, four lovebirds perched on a branch. Money slipped periodically out from my father's wallet and mother's purse. Morgan's old flat screen TV, which he'd left on top of the walnut bureau in his former bedroom, disappeared into the night along with a ten-speed he'd stored in the garage.

"Nobody even cares about that old thing," Devin said when Dad raised the subject of the disappearing TV. "It'd just been abandoned there. I didn't think it mattered. If it's so important I can see if I can get it back for him."

But Devin didn't return things. They slipped through his fingers never to be seen again. Like the night he knocked at my door at 1:47 a.m. and said a friend of his was in trouble and did I have any money he could borrow?

I stared warily at him in the dark. "*Devin.*"

My brother's jaw tightened. He shoved both hands into his sweat-shirt pocket. "Serena, you know I'm getting help. You know that. That's what I'm doing back here. Mom and Dad, they don't trust me anymore and, okay, I can see why. But I'm trying to change." His running shoe tapped up and down on my floor, the motion silenced by my bedroom carpet. "This isn't about any of that. I have a friend with a big problem and she needs my help. You know how hard it is for me to ask you this? I'm like ..." He turned and faced the wall. "Jesus, Serena. You know I'd always help you."

"Help me get high?" I asked in a low voice. Inside I felt sick, incredulous that I could speak to him that way.

A bitter chuckle dropped out of Devin's mouth. "Right," he said flatly. "Because that's all I do and all I am. Nothing's ever about anything else and anyone I'd know isn't worth helping anyway." He pulled his hands out of his pocket and crossed them against his stomach. "*Thanks, Serena.* I don't have to guess where I stand with you."

"How can I give you money when I don't know what you'll do with it?" I said pleadingly.

He shook his head like he was disappointed in me. "I'm in *treatment* now, Serena." Day treatment, but my parents and his counsellor didn't believe it was enough so he was on a waiting list for an in-patient facility in Quebec — a place where they keep you for months. "The way you're all acting, it's like no one will ever trust me again anyway, so what's the point in staying clean?"

I wanted so much to believe him, to see him as the person he used to be. If he'd shouted at me the way he yelled at Mom it would've been easy to turn him down.

The money I gave him didn't make its way back to me, just like Morgan's old TV didn't make it back to his room. My mom's car, on the other hand, arrived back in our driveway at just after nine in the morning. Honestly, I was starting to wonder if we'd ever see it again, but when Devin strolled into the kitchen he acted like it was no big thing.

"Your mother's late for work!" my father yelled, blood rushing to his face. "*I'm* late for work! You know you're not supposed to take the car. I've reached my limit, Devin." Dad's head bobbed aggressively on his shoulders. "This is it. One more incident and I'm locking you out, understand?"

Devin shut his eyes tight and exhaled noisily. "You have the car back," he said, eyelids flying open again. "How is that even an incident?" He motioned with outstretched palms. "You're blowing this way out of proportion. When Morgan had the car back late he'd get a slap on the wrist. When I do it it's the end of the world." He shook his head and rolled his eyes. "Do you have any idea how crazy you sound? You're all so pathologically paranoid — it's like living inside a loony bin."

Mom's hands twitched. She opened and closed her mouth, no sound escaping.

I was standing against the counter, about to load my breakfast dishes into the dishwasher. Devin's dilated pupils homed in on me. "What are you looking at?" he asked me. "Why don't you just go on and open the cupboard there and stuff your face with some cookies — that's what you're good at."

My cheeks twitched like Mom's hands. I turned my head, my whole face stinging.

"Where are they?" Dad said, barrelling towards him. "Where are the drugs, Devin?" He reached around Devin's back and grabbed at his jean pockets.

"Get your hands off me!" Devin shouted, pushing him backwards.

Dad stumbled backwards towards me, his gaze never leaving my brother. "You put them up here now." Dad's hand thumped the counter behind him. "I won't have any more drugs in my house and I won't have you taking things that don't belong to you. *This is the end of the line, Devin.* Everyone here wants you to get the help you need, but none of us can do a thing for you if you don't help yourself."

Devin's laugh sounded like a coiled sneer collapsing in on itself. "It's that easy, is it?" He cocked his head and dragged his top teeth across his bottom lip, smiling crookedly. "I just have to want it."

"We know it's not easy," Mom murmured, her eyes darting between Devin and my father. "We can't keep going on like this if you don't try."

"Oh, I don't know about that, Mom," Devin said snidely. "You seem to try enough for all of us."

Dad took three heavy steps back towards Devin and stood in front of him as if to block his way. "Empty your pockets, son," my father instructed. "Then you can go up to your room."

"This is bullshit," Devin snapped, jostling by him.

Dad's arm flew out and gripped Devin's shoulder. They pushed back and forth against each other, knocking the nearest chair to the ground. Mom jumped. I scuttled towards the stove, as far away from them as I could get. Then Devin drew his right arm back, his fingers forming a fist. He swung at my father's jawline and sent him reeling. Dad collapsed onto the upended chair, one of its legs breaking off under his weight.

Mom rushed to Dad's side, kneeling beside him while Devin watched. "He wouldn't let go of me," Devin said flatly. "You both saw. He should've let go."

I stared at my brother with my mouth gaping and my face still in flames.

"Fuck this," Devin said to himself, both hands scratching through his hair. He turned and lurched out of the kitchen, back the way he'd come. The front door slammed as Mom and I crowded around Dad and the broken chair.

I'm numb when I think of that morning now. For a long time the image of Dad on the tile floor beside the remains of a wooden chair shocked me. It's weird how something can shock you time and time again, even though it's already happened. I couldn't believe that Devin would talk to me like a dumb fat girl either. Nobody cares what you think, his spiteful tone said. *No one will ever really like you.* We'd been imperfect together for all of my life. I didn't fully realize the togetherness was over with until that moment. It was almost as much of a shock as Dad broken on the ground.

Why am I even looking for Devin?, I ask myself again. Why do I care? I shuffle along the street and into Second Cup, where I sit over a steaming hot chocolate, fighting back angry tears.

That's what you're good at.

Jacob told me I was good at other things, but apparently Gage Cochrane doesn't agree, and I can see with absolute clarity how the tangled mess of my former blubber, personal insecurities, and stupid need for some kind of male approval have shaped me into a person I don't want to be.

My coat's behind me, draped on the chair, and I wrestle my cell out of my pocket, determined to right one of my own wrongs.

"Hello?" Gage says into my ear.

"It's Serena," I say in a steely voice. "Would you mind telling me what I did last night that was so horrible that we had to evacuate the area?"

At first there's no answer; I've stunned him silent. "I'm at work," he tells me after a long pause. "I can't talk right now. Can I call you back later?"

If he ever planned to get in touch with me again, my call will have changed Gage's mind in a hurry. "Right, like that'll happen," I mutter bitterly. I hang up on him and drop my cell down next to my hot chocolate. Thank God I didn't wear my magic dress to dinner last night. It would've been wasted on him.

And we gonna let it burn, burn, burn, burn. Ellie Goulding's voice has such ache and strength that every time my cell rings I forget everything else for a millisecond. Inhaling the sweet smell of my hot chocolate, I pause before sweeping up my ringing phone.

"You don't know me well enough to hang up on me," Gage says, annoyed. "What makes you think I even need to explain?"

I rub my temples with my other hand, frustration whipping through my veins. "You jumped out of the car, sped back to my place, and barely said a word. Is that the way you normally act on a date?"

"I can't talk now," Gage repeats in a barbed tone. "But if you rewind the whole night and play it back in your head maybe you'll be able to figure out what went wrong for yourself." The annoyance he heaps on that last sentence makes me want to empty my hot chocolate onto someone's head.

"I think I actually figured it out just now," I snap. I'm about to tell him that he's a first-rate asshole when a woman in tall brown boots and a red coat bends to address me. I've had a couple of training shifts at Total's makeup counter and I'm pretty sure the whiff of perfume I catch is by Stella McCartney.

"Is that seat taken?" the woman whispers, motioning to the empty chair across from me.

"You can have it," I assure her, not bothering to cover the phone. She thanks me and drags the chair towards a friend at a nearby table.

"If I thought you were the kind of person who'd freak out like this over nothing I wouldn't have asked you out in the first place," Gage tells me.

I thought I wanted to argue with him, but as I sit in Second Cup watching wispy bits of white dance in the wind outside I suddenly feel drained and empty. This hasn't been a good day, and fighting with some random guy I barely know over the phone won't make me feel any better.

"Serena?" Gage prompts.

"What?"

"I gotta go."

"I know. You said that before. So *go*." My voice cracks on the word *go*. It's not even him or what we're talking about in particular. Everything has just backed up on me. It's probably a good thing I haven't been able to find Devin. If he said something cruel to me, like that day in June, I would either dissolve into tears or scream at him until both our ears bled.

"*Listen*." Gage's anger has eased up, making it obvious he heard my voice break. "If you still want me to call later … Sorry I got so —"

He's doing that thing where he can't stop apologizing again, but I don't want to listen. "Look, I'm having a really shitty day here," I say, talking over him, "so whatever you …"

Behind me somebody hiccups out a laugh. I noticed a guy with a laptop and a latte sitting at one of the tables behind me when I first grabbed my seat. Whatever he's looking at must be hilarious because now he's laughing so hard that it's a wonder there's enough oxygen getting to his brain. Someone will probably have to call an ambulance for him any second now.

"Where are you?" Gage asks, so I guess he can hear hyena guy too.

I sneak a look behind me. The guy's bent over in his chair, his shoulders shaking. I wish he'd shut up already. His manic laugh, the smiling homeless guy on the street with his dog, Bucky, and me, out on the pavement looking for someone who doesn't exist anymore — it's all exhausting and wrong.

"Toronto," I mumble, my voice still unsteady. "I was looking for someone, but it hasn't worked out."

"I really have to go," Gage says. "But if you …" He doesn't sound sure of his words. "Do you … have a ride home?"

Together, last night and my follow-up phone call have warped whatever potential Gage and I had before. I don't know that I want to sit in his car knowing that he just feels sorry for me, the girl who never seems to have a ride.

"I'm off in thirty minutes," he continues. "If you don't have another way home I can come get you."

"Why would you want to do that?" I ask, and then I'm crying.

CHAPTER FOURTEEN

AN HOUR AND A half later Gage calls my cell and tells me he's outside. He looks nervously over at me when I open the passenger door and sit down next to him. I guess he's worried I might freak out on him about last night again. Instead I thank him for picking me up and lean my head against the window.

Gage has a news radio station on low and we listen to it as he heads for the highway. A report about a mid-air small plane crash that killed three people concludes that there's too much congestion around the Toronto airport. Meanwhile, some ex-NHL player has just signed a deal to star in his first movie about a time-travelling bounty hunter, and in real life a twenty-two-year-old man was stabbed at King and Jarvis this afternoon and is in stable condition at St. Michael's Hospital.

"That's not too far from where I picked you up," Gage says, mostly to himself. Then there's more news (mostly bad) and about ten minutes later he clears his throat and goes, "Last night — it's not that you did anything wrong — it was just really fast. It's not ..." He glances out the driver's side window before fixing his eyes back on the road ahead. "It's not what I'm looking for."

I keep my head snuggled against the window and slouch down in my seat, wishing we could drive and drive and never really get anywhere.

There's something comforting about being on the road. You're fixed in place while still in motion.

I stare into space, processing what Gage has just told me. "I thought you wanted to go to that place after the movie," I say evenly. Less than two hours ago I wanted to pour my hot chocolate over his head and now it feels like we're well past yesterday's drama, like it happened a long time ago and can be discussed rationally.

"I did. It just got out of hand."

The thought that I was the one who made things get out of hand comes as a surprise. There was a moment in the parking lot when I thought he was losing interest, but it never occurred to me that it had anything to do with me overstepping boundaries. Maybe he only really lost interest when he started seeing me as slutty. Gage could be the religious type that wants any girl he's with to be one hundred per cent pure. It's not like I'd normally go down on a guy during a first date, but if I explain that to him it will only sound like I feel bad about having done it in the first place.

"I wish you'd said something instead of jumping out of the car," I tell him. I actually do feel bad about it now, but mostly because it turns out I was almost forcing myself on him. It's not that I think a blow job is a dirty thing by definition, but the truth is that I'm not really happy that I did it just to get his attention either.

"Yeah." Gage's grey eyes gaze at me as he nods. "I can see how that would've been a good idea now. You made me nervous. I don't know …" He shrugs, his light leather jacket hanging open so that I can see the striped zip top he has on under it.

It's hard for me to believe that I could make anyone as gorgeous as Gage nervous, and I feel a measure of annoyance creep in under my calm. Why do I insist on judging people based on their looks?

"I didn't realize I was doing that," I admit. "I know you said you were nervous that night, but I just thought you didn't like first dates. I didn't realize it was *me* putting you on edge."

"It was both, I guess." He frowns. "This might sound weird to you, but I just want to stay away from sex stuff for a while."

I laugh into my coat collar. He's got me so wrong.

Gage shoots me an uneasy look, frown cementing on his face. "I'm not laughing at you," I say. "It's just, you make me sound like some kind of sex addict and I've never actually done it. I've barely even ... I mean, there's only been one other guy that I've done *that* with." I fight a blush.

The surprise shows in Gage's eyes. "I didn't mean to make you sound like a sex addict." He smiles ruefully. "I guess we didn't get a clear picture of each other last night."

"I guess not." I shift my head away from the window and sit up in my seat.

"I told you I wasn't great at first dates," he says.

"I didn't believe you." I'm kind of teasing and kind of not.

"I'm not sure whether that's a good thing or what," Gage says, but he smiles wider so I guess he's flattered.

I hope having this conversation will make things less weird the next time he comes in to Total. Jacob's still giving off hostile vibes every time he sees me; I don't need any more guy tension in my life. "At least we've had a chance to clear things up," I say and thank him again for picking me up. Most guys wouldn't do that if you'd gone off on them over the phone after only having been out with them once to begin with.

"No problem," he tells me. "You seemed pretty upset so —"

"Yeah," I cut in. I don't want him to think the crying was because of him; I'm not that pathetic. "Going downtown today was a waste — I went looking for my brother. No one has seen him in months." I briefly explain about Tuesday night and Devin's drug problem. Not the details of what happened the morning he left, just the bare facts of him walking out on us.

"Devin LeBlanc?" Gage's expression turns curious. "*That's* your brother?"

"You know him?"

Gage scratches his chin. "Not personally, but we went to school together. I was a freshman when he was a senior. I remember him getting some math award near the end of second semester. Wasn't he practically a genius?"

"He was. I don't know how many brain cells he's got left." I feel guilty as soon as I say it, like being negative will invite more bad things into Devin's life. "I didn't know you went to Laurier."

"It feels like ancient history," Gage declares, and I remember him saying something similar last night. "I don't know if this is a good time to ask this, but depending on your answer, there could be something I should tell you." He goes quiet and points his sombre grey eyes at me.

I stare back, suspense rising until I have to ask, "What's your question?"

Gage blinks, shifting his weight a little in his seat. "Do you think we'll be hanging out in the future at all?"

"I don't know." I'm definitely not mad at him anymore but after this bizarre beginning I can't picture how things would go with us. "Do you still want to?"

Gage tries to smile, but he looks like he's about to break out in a sweat. "That's what I'm asking *you*. Okay, look, I'm just going to come out with it anyway." He motions over his shoulder. "You see the car seat?"

I peer into the back seat at the blue child's car seat. It wasn't there when we went out last night and when I climbed into the car a few minutes ago I was too upset to notice it.

"It's not for a little brother or sister," he continues, his cheekbones flaring and his eyes focused doggedly on the highway. "It's my daughter's."

CHAPTER FIFTEEN

❧

I'M CONSCIOUS OF TAKING too long to answer him, but in my mind I'm doing math — that's not a baby's car seat, just how old is his daughter, and how old would that have made Gage when she was born? My brain splutters with questions about his daughter's mother — is she still in the picture and if so what does he think he's doing asking me to hang out — as Gage glances at me from the corner of his eye with a resigned expression.

"Her mother and I aren't together," he says, like he can read my mind.

The honesty in his face and tone makes me nod that I believe him. Someone who wants to have a fling with me behind his girlfriend's back would hardly tell me he wanted to stay away from sex. But the truth is a shock.

"You took the seat out of the car before we went out last night?" I ask finally. It was there the first night he drove me home from Total Drug Mart. I remember that now. On some level I must've assumed the most obvious explanation about a little brother or sister was the truth. The miniature chair hadn't even formed a concrete question in my mind.

Gage slowly bobs his head. "It's a lot to bring up on a first date.

Not everybody can handle it, and I didn't know if we were really going to click."

I guess I wouldn't want to drag out all my personal issues in front of someone I'd just met either, not that I'm calling his daughter an *issue*. I'm still just struggling to catch up with him.

"So how old is she?" I ask.

"Four." Gage's eyes mirror my surprise. "*I know.* I was really, really young. Thought my life was over and all that." He taps the steering wheel. "But she's great, so I can't regret it."

I think of the ladybug hairclips he bought at Total and the glittering pink heart sticker with a wobbly "A" printed on the other side and try to let the reality of what he's saying sink in. "What's her name?"

"Akayla." He digs into his back pocket and hands me his wallet. "I have a couple of pictures of her in there."

I flip it open, ignoring his driver's licence and collection of bank cards, etc.

"In the side compartment," he tells me, and the first thing I see is a photo of a sleeping baby with long eyelashes and dark curly hair. Her complexion's pretty dark too, much darker than Gage's, so her mother must be black. In the second picture a child-sized Akayla's sitting on a couch with her legs crossed, her arms planted on her knees, and her fists tucked under her chin. Her hair is tied back, and she's beaming into the camera like she loves getting her photo taken — either that or she loves the person taking it, which could very well be Gage, the nineteen-year-old guy next to me.

"She's gorgeous," I say honestly.

"Thanks." He smiles proudly. By this time we're almost at my turnoff and I have yet to answer his question about whether we'll be seeing each other again in the future. Something tells me that he's not going to ask again, that he's just going to pull into my driveway and let me off the hook.

I slip the photos back into his wallet and set it down in the compartment behind the gearshift. Since he's been so truthful with me the least I can do is not leave him hanging. "Um ... I'm not really looking for anything seriously long-term myself at the moment so ..."

"Why would you be?" Gage says, like he agrees with me that casual is the way to go. "I'm not either. I just don't think it's fair to hide such a major thing from someone if we're going to be hanging out. It's the same as lying.

"But anyway," he continues, "it's cool if you're not into the idea anymore. No harm done. I just thought I'd ask."

"Hey," I say it loudly, the same way I did last night when I told him to hold still so we could get down to some heavy kissing. "That wasn't a no. With all the miscommunications we've had so far I just didn't want to be unclear and lead you to believe that I'm ready to get ultra-attached." I'm making it sound like he asked me to marry him and become his daughter's stepmom. I bite my tongue and cut to the chase. "But it's cool with me if you want to call sometime." I think I still want him to. I haven't been able to calculate all the ways that Gage having a four-year-old could change things, but why get ahead of myself when he's only saying he wants to hang out? "We can arrange a do-over."

Gage gives me a grateful look. "I'll wear a warmer coat," he says, grin inching onto his lips. "I think maybe that's where things went wrong. You did try to warn me."

"I did." I feel a smile burst onto my face too. This has been one weird day. My brain is still sorting through the backlog of emotions — disappointment (at not being able to find any trace of Devin downtown), last night's anger with Gage (which no longer seems to make any sense), and Akayla's existence. On top of that Gage is looking better than ever as he watches me beam at him, like my smile is making him grin even harder.

We flirt a bit, recovering some of the vibe we lost in a deserted industrial parking spot last night, and when he pulls up to my house

I'm sorry that it's time to get out of the car. "I'd ask you in," I tell him, "but I don't think you really want to sit down to dinner with my parents."

"That could be weird," he agrees. "I'd invite you over to my place, but that could be pretty weird too, and anyway, I'm low on food. I think all I have right now is a box of mac and cheese and frozen peas."

"We're not very gourmet at home these days either." When Devin was home Mom made meals from scratch, but now most of our dinners come from the freezer or the deli next to my dad's work.

"'Scuse me?" Gage says, pretending to be insulted. "Macaroni and cheese out of a box is better than gourmet if you know what you're doing."

"If you know what you're doing?" I echo. "You mean, like, if you can *read* the instructions on the back of the box?"

Gage explains that there's much more to it than that and says he's ready to prove it if I want. I hesitate, wondering if we'd be eating with his daughter and whether that's such a good idea. He reads my mind and adds, "Akayla won't be around if that's what you're worried about. I have her a couple of nights a week but I'm on my own tonight."

So we drive back to his place just around the corner from the rec centre on Laird. There's a black Toyota Camry already in the driveway, which must belong to his mother. But since Gage has his own private entrance around the side of the house it turns out we don't even have to see her. He leads me down to the basement and through a cozy-looking family room with matching floor lamps on either side of the chocolate brown couch. I understand right away why he told me we couldn't come back here last night. Evidence of his daughter is everywhere. A folding pink castle, with three wooden royalty figures propped up against the interior walls, is spread out on the beige carpet. Two horse figures have been deserted on the couch next to a shimmering purple baseball hat with butterflies, flowers, and a mermaid pasted on its front. An empty plastic glass sits on the coffee table, which has some kind of stamping kit half-pushed under it. Gage reaches down to scoop up the glass as we head for the kitchen.

I'm impressed that everything's as clean as it is. Sure there's stuff left out in the family room but the carpet's been vacuumed recently and the kitchen's tile floor is spotless. "This is really nice," I tell him.

Gage has a list of emergency numbers stuck to his fridge along with a wipe-off calendar that has Akayla's visiting days clearly marked. I see another picture of her there too — a large fridge magnet with a photo of her in a crushed red velvet dress, sitting primly on an uncomfortable-looking wrought iron chair. She's holding a plush lamb doll and smiling with her mouth closed. I stare at the image, trying to spot a resemblance to Gage but not finding one. Maybe she looks more like her mother.

"Thanks." He motions to my coat. "Hey, you want me to hang that up? We missed the closet on the way in."

"Oh, okay. Sure." I wriggle out of my coat and hand it over. He said he wanted to stay away from sex and I know his daughter isn't around so why am I so nervous? Messing things up more than we did last night doesn't seem possible.

"So let me see this mac and cheese magic," I say when he steps back into the room minus our coats. Suddenly my mouth is so dry that I'm afraid my smile will dissolve into dust on my lips.

"Maybe I should blindfold you first so you won't give away my secrets," Gage says. My cheeks burn at the mention of the word *blindfold* as though I really am a sex addict liable to pounce on him at any moment.

"I kinda don't believe you have any secrets," I joke, pushing my nerves down under my rib cage so he won't be able to hear them in my voice.

"I think I've actually told you one of them already," he says with a half grin. "Sit down." He cocks his head at the fifties-style Formica table in the middle of the room. "You can watch me do my chef thing."

I slip into the nearest chair and watch him pull the macaroni and cheese box from one of the higher cupboards. Then he checks the freezer and reports, "I have broccoli and peas. You want both of them, or are you the kind of person who's not really into vegetables?"

"I like everything," I tell him, my entire face on fire because of the multiple ways that sentence can be misconstrued. "Let me do something to help."

If I could kiss him I wouldn't have to think so much but there's no way in hell I'll be the one to make the first move — or even the second — after the way things went down last night outside J.N. Maltzar/Malezar.

"Okay." He closes the freezer and swings open the fridge to reach for a package of shredded cheddar. "You boil the water and chuck the macaroni in. I'll heat up the vegetables."

We make macaroni and cheese Gage Cochrane–style, which is essentially what comes out of the box plus lots of extra shredded cheddar, a tablespoon of Dijon mustard, and peas and broccoli mixed in. It tastes pretty good, so I have to agree with him about his gourmet skills. We sit across the table from each other swallowing sparkling grape juice and pretending it's not weird to be having dinner together in the place he sometimes shares with his four-year-old daughter.

"So is your daughter with her mom tonight?" I ask.

"Yeah." Gage sets down his fork. "She spends a lot more time there but she has a room here too."

I nod, thinking he'll have more to say on the subject, but instead Gage goes, "I'm glad you came over. Every time I saw you at the store you looked so cute I couldn't stop staring."

"In that gross Total uniform — you have to be kidding."

"Even in the uniform," he says, eyes sparkling. "Out of the uniform's better still, but even in the uniform." Gage blushes as he realizes what he's just said, and I'm glad to see that I'm not the only one who feels self-conscious.

We wash the dishes together and then try to find something on TV. Upstairs I can hear his mother walking around, banging cupboards open. The noise really carries. "So you and your mom normally do your own thing?" I ask. Gage stops clicking the remote and lets the TV rest on a *Game of Thrones* repeat.

"Mostly. She spends a lot of time at work. She and her best friend own a hair salon together. It's their whole social hub."

I pick up one of the wooden horse figures lying next to me on the couch and run my fingers down its tail. Gage smiles and motions to the pink castle on the floor. "You can play with it if you want. She wouldn't mind."

"I better not, I wouldn't want to break anything," I kid back. The urge to kiss him is so strong that it's making my cheeks flush all over again.

Gage's stare inches from my eyes all the way down to my knees and back again. "Maybe we could come up with something else to do instead. What do you think?"

"I think I'm kind of scared to after the way things went last night," I say truthfully.

"Don't be. We just won't let things get out of hand this time." He sets his palm down lightly on my thigh. "I'm sorry I flipped last night. I didn't mean to scare you off."

Gage's front teeth peek out from under his top lip. His hand moves from my thigh to my hair. He lets a strand slip between two of his fingers before burying them in my hair, massaging the back of my neck. "I really wish …" His thought floats suspended in mid-air.

"What?" I can't catch my breath.

"Nothing." He leans in to kiss me, his bottom lip urging my mouth open. We kiss slowly, pacing ourselves. "You taste like macaroni and cheese," he tells me, smiling into my face.

"You're not supposed to tell me that." I poke his stomach. "You're supposed to say I taste good." No way did I just say that. I blush so brightly that I could easily be mistaken for a Cortland apple.

"You do," he says. "You're delicious." He cups my neck in both hands. I push my lips against his and then we're all tongues swirling, his hands in my hair and one of mine up the back of his shirt. His chest's so taut that I can't keep my hands off him. Whatever he's hauling around at the warehouse is obviously doing him a lot of good.

We kiss and kiss. Fast and slow. Deep and shallow. Soft and rough. The both of us tasting like Gage's macaroni and cheese and me filling up on a warm, fuzzy feeling that used to wash over me whenever Jacob was being especially sweet.

"See," Gage whispers in my ear, "nothing to be scared of."

We lie on his couch together and watch the rest of *Game of Thrones,* having proven to ourselves that it's fully possible to make out alone somewhere and not let things get out of hand. It makes a nice change to have someone else be more worried about that than I am. If this is hanging out with Gage Cochrane, I think I might be able to get used to it.

"You're all right," Dad says quietly. "You have no idea how worried she was …" His voice trails off.

There's nothing left for me to say. I stare past him, at the wall, and kick off my shoes and unbutton my coat. Then I edge past my father, my cheek throbbing, and stuff my coat into the overcrowded hall closet.

My parents would never know I was missing from glancing into the closet, that's for sure. My brothers' old coats take up more room in it than mine do. If Devin had to steal from us why didn't he take some goddamn coats?

"Are you going up to bed?" Dad asks in a brittle voice.

I nod without turning back towards him and stick my hand up to wave good night.

"Good night, Serena," he says to my back. "See you in the morning."

The next morning I lie in bed until my bladder's about to burst. Then I bring my cell into the bathroom with me and check messages again while peeing. I texted Nicole last night to let her know I was home and there's a reply asking for details.

I creep back into my bedroom, dive under the covers, and weave fragments of the truth into a new fiction for her. I can't tell her about Gage now. That would mean admitting my original lie, and after what happened with my parents last night I'm not ready to have my friends angry with me too. Once I've got my story straight I call Nicole and thank her for covering for me.

"I almost didn't," she says. "I was starting to think something happened to you downtown. Why didn't you call me or Genevieve back last night? Izzy called me too — said your mom called her looking for you. It sounds like she was calling everyone. I bet she even called Jacob."

"I hope not."

"I bet she did," Nicole says again. "She sounded a bit mental on the phone. And here I was thinking you were kidnapped by some psycho and that I could've been holding up a police investigation."

"I'm sorry," I tell her, the blanket pulled up to my chin. "I guess I went a bit mental myself, talking to all these homeless people and thinking bad things about what Devin could be doing. It was pretty rough." It feels wrong to be using Devin as my cover, but I did think those things yesterday, before Gage showed up and made me forget them for a while. "It got so I didn't have the energy to ask anyone else. But I didn't want to go home either so I shut off my phone, walked to the movie theatre just off Queen Street, and sat there eating fast food and watching movies until the theatre closed."

"You walked around the city at night by yourself?" Nicole says. "That must've been scary."

"I didn't think about it. I was lost in my own head. And then I caught the last train home and had to cab it back to my house." I take a deep breath as though just remembering last night is draining. "My parents freaked. My mom, she hit me." Real tears spring to my eyes.

Why did things have to get so bad between us? Why couldn't she have tried harder to talk to me instead, like she would've before Devin left?

"That's awful," Nicole says in a stunned voice. "I didn't think she was like that. I mean, I know you've said she's sort of unstable but ..."

I've never used the word *unstable*; that makes my mother sounds crazy, and I don't believe she's crazy. Severely messed up, but not crazy. A tear squeezes out of my eye, slides down my cheek and over my chin. "She was worried," I say. "Not that that's any excuse."

"I'm sorry," Nicole says softly. "Can you get out of there for a while? You can come spend the rest of the weekend at my place if you want."

"I don't have a ride. Could you phone Genevieve and ask her to pick me up?" No way am I *asking* my parents for permission to leave, but I need to get out of here. The place feels toxic and it makes me feel toxic too, like I'm being slowly poisoned.

"I'll call her now," Nicole tells me.

Forty minutes later the doorbell rings. I dash out of my bedroom, my knapsack (packed with a change of clothes, pyjamas, and my toothbrush) over my shoulders. "That's for me," I announce as I tear into the kitchen. "I'm spending the night at Nicole's."

Mom's sitting at the table in front of a partially eaten piece of toast and Dad has his hand on the coffee pot. "Hold on there a second, Serena," Dad pleads. "We want to talk to you."

"My ride's waiting." I motion to the door.

"Serena." Mom looks uncertainly up at me. "You don't know what it's like to have a child go missing."

I had a brother go missing, but I guess that doesn't count. I stare blankly at my mother. I'm not going to make this easy on her after what she did.

"I'm sorry about last night." Mom glances at her hands on either side of her plate. "Won't you sit down with us and have some lunch. It's almost twelve and you haven't eaten."

"I'll eat at Nicole's." I swivel on my heel and walk out into the hall, before I can say something I'll regret. My eyes sting as I battle with my coat in the closet. "Somebody should throw out all these stupid old coats!" I shout as I jerk the front door open.

I'm shaking a little as I throw myself into Genevieve's Honda. The car smells like warm cinnamon and my shoulders immediately begin to relax. Genevieve's long red hair looks slept-on and stringy and she's not wearing her watch, which is almost as much a part of her as her left arm. "Open the glove compartment," she commands. "I picked you up a Cinnabon for breakfast. I know you love those."

"Thanks." I cringe at the thought of how many calories must be packed into a single Cinnabon. "You're a lifesaver."

"Nicole told me what happened at home. It'll do your parents some good to see they can't walk all over you." Genevieve brushes her fingers across her lips. "No crumbs?" she asks. "I had mine on the way over."

"No crumbs. You're good."

Genevieve reverses as I bite into my Cinnabon. The cream cheese frosting floods my system with joy, almost as much as lying on Gage's couch with him last night. I wish I could share some of the details with Genevieve but I know she'd only tell me that I'm being ridiculous and will just get screwed over in the end.

"He already has a kid with someone else," she'd say. "Do you want to be the mother of his next one? C'mon, Serena, smarten up!"

I don't need to hear her say it; I'm already hearing the lecture loud and clear in my head. Gage is my guilty secret and I'm glad at least he's a happy one.

At Nicole's we play video games and eat kimchi, Nicole and Genevieve ultra-animated to distract me from my problems at home. When my cell rings I tell them to play on as I check who's calling. Hmm, big brother Morgan, who no doubt received a panicked call from my parents last night along with half of the Western world.

"Hey, Morgan," I say. "Rumours of my death have been greatly exaggerated." Mark Twain. My English teacher quoted him last year when she came back in October after being off with West Nile virus for two weeks.

Morgan laughs. "Yeah, I can hear that. I hope Mom and Dad weren't too hard on you. I tried to calm them down when they called looking for you but you know how they can be."

"Did you talk to them this morning?" I ask.

"Yeah, they said you showed sometime after one. Let me guess, was it a guy?"

I glance at Nicole and Genevieve absorbed in their game of zombie carnage. Blood and guts are spurting everywhere, intestines and eyeballs crowding the screen.

"Yeah," I admit. Since my parents know, I can't see what harm there is in Morgan knowing too. It's crucial that I keep all my secrets and lies straight; one less lie to remember can only be a good thing.

"Knew it," Morgan says, a smile in his voice. "Hope he was worth the trouble."

I think so, but that's not something I plan to go into right now. "Did Mom tell you what she did?"

"What she did?" Morgan repeats. "No, what'd she do?"

Genevieve turns and catches my eye. I can tell she overheard and is shooting some sympathy my way, even as she wastes lurching zombies.

"Ask her," I say. "I don't want to go into it now. But ask her. Make her tell you."

"Jesus, Serena, don't make me call her back. What happened?"

"I gotta go," I tell him. My mouth is dry as I hang up. I don't want to go back home to my parents at the end of the weekend. It doesn't matter that my mother apologized; it shouldn't have happened in the first place.

Nicole's land line rings, breaking my train of thought. She pauses the zombie fest and goes to answer it.

"You can sleep over at my house tomorrow night if you're not ready to go back home yet," Genevieve offers, as though she can read my mind.

"Thanks. I might."

Nicole's voice has cranked up, loud enough that Genevieve and I both turn to look at her. "She's here with me right now," Nicole says. "And that's not where she was last night so Orlando is just spreading his regular bullshit."

Nicole pauses to listen for a second. "I know you're only repeating what you heard. I'm just saying I know for a fact that's wrong.

"No, I can't tell you that either because it's personal," she adds. "Just trust me on this."

Genevieve and I exchange puzzled glances and continue to listen in. Nicole's rolling her eyes for our benefit so it's obvious she doesn't mind us eavesdropping.

"That was Renata," Nicole announces after she hangs up. "Get this, the latest is that Orlando says he saw you in some guy's car on Spruceland Avenue last night."

"The cab driver?" Genevieve guesses.

"I said that too. But Renata says Orlando never said anything about a cab." Nicole looks at me. "He said you were in this guy's front seat next to him and that while he was driving you put your head down in his lap and started getting friendly with it. Would you believe that dickhead told her he was getting ready to take out his cell and start recording? Supposedly, the light changed and you sped off, which is a pretty convenient explanation for why he has no proof."

Shit. Why did Orlando, of all people, have to spot us and go mixing the truth with his jerk-off lies. Gage and I were on Spruceland last night, when he was driving me back home, but *nothing* happened. Who would believe that, though? If I admit to being in a car with a guy lots of people will automatically think the rest of what Orlando said is true too. The funny thing is that even the part that's a lie is sort of true, only it didn't happen last night.

"You know what people would see if we followed Orlando around and taped him?" Genevieve says sourly. "Orlando jerking off alone in his car while he films other people getting off. That's the extent of his sex life. He should buy himself a wrist brace before he develops carpal tunnel."

I haven't said anything yet, and Genevieve and Nicole stare at me, waiting for me to freak out about this latest piece of bullshit. I look down at my hands, wondering why I can't figure out what I'm doing and who I'm being without everyone else having something to say about it.

"We won't let him get away with it," Nicole says. "Monday morning we're going to tear him to pieces. I bet your mom called Jacob and that when Orlando heard you were MIA he decided to run with the story."

Genevieve nods. "Don't let him get to you. No one's going to believe it anyway."

Some people will believe it all right. They'll want more details, so Orlando will have to make more crap up. I wince as I imagine the nasty things he'll say.

"And even if it *was* true — so what?" Nicole says. "It's none of his business."

"Exactly," I mutter. "I'm so sick of all this. It's nobody's business but mine what I do."

"We'll make a big joke of him on Monday, like Nicole says, and then everyone will forget about it," Genevieve advises. "There's no video. He's just being an ass, trying to see what he can get away with."

I chew my lip and think about Jacob. I know he's hooked up with at least two girls since me, but one of his friends spots me riding around in a car with someone and it instantly mutates into gossip porn. I'm ready to spill hot chocolate over someone's head again. If Orlando's alone the next time he sees me he better watch out.

Genevieve, Nicole, and I go back to killing zombies, massacring with noticeably extra gusto. Limbs go flying. Innards ooze. Brains gush blood. If I could fix everything that's wrong with my life by wasting virtual zombies, I'd be looking at outright perfection by dinnertime.

CHAPTER SEVENTEEN

SUNDAY NIGHT I COME home for extra clothes and my dad stops me in the hallway and tells me he wants me to stay home tonight. I think he's missing the point, which is that I'm currently rejecting his and Mom's authority. I say I'll be back Monday after school, grab a set of fresh everything, and jump into Genevieve's car for the second time in two days. On the way to her house Morgan calls, having heard the extended version of my altercation with my parents, and tells me Mom was wrong and feels awful about what happened. I explain that I'm taking a temporary vacation from my folks and don't really want to talk about it anymore.

Genevieve's mom has made up their spare bedroom for me. It smells like coconut, but I can't tell where the scent's coming from. The shapely vase sitting on the windowsill is filled with fake pink and orange flowers but there's no sign of an air freshener. Three paintings of various floral scenes hang on the pale yellow walls. They're the kind of decorative decision that wouldn't offend anyone, and overall the Richardsons' spare room reminds me of the hotel suite I shared with my parents when we went to the Bahamas on vacation three and a half years ago.

I mean that in the best possible way — hotel rooms are an escape from real life, and in Genevieve's spare room I feel cocooned, hidden away from anxiety and negativity. The duvet cover and matching pillowcases are a tranquil lavender and at the end of the night I lie between crisp sheets, inhaling deeply, listening to the affluent silence that echoes through the Richardsons' corner lot and texting Gage. Twenty minutes later, when the surrounding purple and sweetness have almost sent to me to dreamland, my cell rings.

I reach for it with my eyes closed and mumble into the phone.

"Did I wake you up again?" Gage asks.

"It's okay." I yawn. "It's just, this room is so much calmer than my house. I could probably lie here for fifteen hours if I didn't have to go to school tomorrow."

"So it sounds like your parents were pretty pissed off with you," Gage says. "I can't help feeling like it's kinda my fault."

"It's not your fault. It's nobody's fault." I roll over on my side, still holding my cell to my ear. "Don't worry about it, they'll get over it." I've decided not to tell him exactly what happened with my mother. There's so much serious stuff surrounding the two of us already — what we need is more mac and cheese fun and lying on his couch time. "Anyway, it was worth it." If I was wide awake I might be afraid to say that to him but in my semi-blissful, surrounded by purple state it seems like the right thing.

Gage misses a beat in the conversation. Then his voice softens and he says, "I had a good time too. Hope we can do it again sometime soon."

It's exactly what I was wishing he'd say and I murmur, "I'm sure that can be arranged."

"How about Thursday then? Do you think your folks will ground you?"

I think after what my mother did they'd be afraid to, paranoid that I'd disappear like a certain other member of my family. "That only matters if I plan on listening to them," I tell him.

"Don't say that. I don't want you getting into more trouble with them because of me. If you're grounded, we can wait."

I don't want to wait, but I'm already feeling more conscious and less likely to say anything that's the basic equivalent of *I like you a lot*. The last time I felt all excited about a guy he wanted me to suck face with Aya. I don't think Gage is like that, but if I keep thinking the best of him it'll be harder if he lets me down.

"Hey?" Gage says. "You still awake, Serena?"

I love the way my name sounds coming out of his mouth. It makes me picture myself as a better me.

"I'm here. I think Thursday should be all right. I'll call you if it isn't, okay?"

"Sounds good," Gage says. "Go back to sleep. Night, Serena."

I say good night back, hang up, and smile into my pillow.

The first person I see at school the next day is Jon Wheatley, and he acts like he hasn't heard any nasty rumours about me, so maybe Orlando's lies haven't spread as far as I've imagined. Then I get to history class and Bryant Torres, the sophomore basketball team's power forward, smirks at me as I pass his desk.

"Heard you had a good weekend," he says. "Spit or swallow?"

My jaw drops. The guys sitting closest to him laugh loudly while the girls look various shades of uncomfortable as I slide into my seat.

"He's been working on that gem all weekend," someone says sarcastically from behind me. I turn and glance at Dina Manzoor, who is destined to be a permanent resident at the top of the Laurier honour roll.

I nod at Dina to thank her. Then I stare at Bryant Torres's back like he and his buddies are so far beneath me that I might even pity them a little and say, "You left out *bite*, which I'm guessing is what usually happens to you."

Bryant smirks, but the other guys laugh out loud. "Does that trigger some bad memories, Torres?" one of them asks.

Izzy zips into the midst of the laughter and glues her gaze to mine. I've already spoken to her so she knows the rumour's a lie. "What's going on?" she asks, stopping at my desk.

"Rumours and lies courtesy of Orlando," I say in a matter-of-fact tone.

"And Bryant's penile repair surgery," Dina chimes in. Dina and I don't usually talk that much but now I see that she's her own kind of cool, which doesn't have much to do with how a lot of other people define the word but is probably a good fit with a more highly evolved, non-savage-inspired definition.

"And Bryant's penile repair surgery," I concur. "Which, as you can guess, he doesn't really want to talk about in much depth."

"Nice deflection," Bryant quips, then eyes his buddies. "But notice she never answered the original question."

"Notice how Bryant's trying to bury the topic of his penis surgery. Uh-oh." I fake concern. "Guess it didn't go so well. Next time watch out for that third option, Bry. Teeth can do a lot of damage."

Bryant doesn't have any time to regain the upper hand. Mrs. Vinicky plunks herself into her chair and takes attendance. The rest of the day goes better than I expected. Lots of people either don't believe Orlando's story or don't care whether it's true or not. I pass him in the hall with Jacob before last period, Nicole at my side. The four of us glare at each other until Jacob, in a level voice, says, "I never knew you were such a ho."

"Your friend's a liar and you know it," Nicole snaps. "Good luck with anybody getting with either of you now. The way you keep trashing girls no one will go near you."

Orlando focuses on Nicole, his eyes self-righteous and cocky. "It's not trash if it's the truth. Face it, your friend's a ho. That's not our problem."

"So you've got your version and we have *the truth*," I say, contempt oozing out of my mouth as I continue. "Why don't you guys just get a life already?" I pull Nicole away with me before the conversation can degenerate further. I still want to kill Orlando, but if he starts giving details about Gage and his car, I'm dead too. My friends could easily start putting two and two together.

"Why'd you do that?" Nicole asks once we're a safe distance from Jacob and Orlando. "We should've lain into him about his creepy mention of videotaping — asked if he was stalking you now or what the fu—"

"I could just see it wouldn't go anywhere," I interrupt. "I didn't want us all screaming at each other in the middle of the hall while everyone listens in. Besides, I just …" I clasp my hands together and fold them under my sweatshirt, skin against skin. "I'm just tired, you know? Orlando's a piece of shit and I want to break all his fingers but what's the point? It's not like he's going to admit it's a lie. We're better off spreading that news around ourselves."

Nicole's hands scrunch into two fists. She glances at the ceiling, her face heavy with frustration. "It just doesn't seem fair. We should be able to make him take it back if it's not true."

"Life isn't fair." That's something I've heard my father say countless times over the years but not, now that I think of it, since Devin left.

Nicole and I are going in different directions, and I thank her for backing me up before we split up at the library. I have to write half a page on who I relate to most for civics tomorrow: Martin Luther King, Mother Teresa, or Terry Fox. That will mean Internet research later, and thinking about research makes my mind land on Gage, who knows about good libraries. I'm already looking forward to seeing him again on Thursday.

I'm not, on the other hand, looking forward to being back at home, awash in chronic toxicity. I leave my iPod and speakers on in my bedroom so my parents will know I'm back, but pray that they'll leave me alone. Of course, that's not what happens. My mother raps at my door at 5:40 and then sticks her head in.

I'm sitting at my computer, in the middle of typing up my paper on Terry Fox. He was only twenty-two when he died, which makes him easier to relate to than Martin Luther King or Mother Teresa. We watched a movie about Terry in grade school. He lost his leg to cancer and then ran across the country to raise money for research. I don't think I could ever be that brave. If I really think about it, it makes me want to cry for this guy who has been dead for almost thirty years.

Seeing my mother's face at the door makes me want to cry too, but for entirely different reasons.

"You're back," she says, her hands hanging limply at her sides as she steps inside my room. She used to rub cream on her hands to fade the age spots but you can still see them.

"Please stop with the silent treatment," she says as she stares back at me with big eyes. "I'm so sorry about Friday. Whatever you may think, I do worry about you."

"Mom —" I try to stop her.

"Maybe you could come see Doctor Berkovich with me next time. We could talk."

"I don't want to talk to Doctor Berkovich. You're the one who did something wrong here, not me."

"You were out till all hours on Friday, Serena." The pitch of Mom's voice rises. "We had no idea where you were. None of your friends knew where you were."

"One time, that happened. One single time. I'm going to do things you don't approve of now and then." My own voice is nearly a shriek. "Are you going to have some crazy new reaction every time? Because I can't deal with that on top of everything else."

Mom presses two fingers against her forehead. "Serena, please. Calm down."

"How can I be calm, never knowing when you're going to go off on me?"

"That's never going to happen again." Mom grits her teeth and stares past me. "Your father's going to deal with you in those situations from now on. Obviously I just can't ... handle the stress."

Maybe I shouldn't be pissed off with my mother for not being able to deal with Devin's disappearance, but the truth is I'm so tired of it. Why does she get to be fragile when I still have to pull myself together?

"Mom." I start out tentative because even with everything I've just said, I don't want to be the one to kick another dent into what's left of her armour. "Can we just have some dinner? I don't want to talk about stress or Doctor Berkovich or Devin. Can't we just ..."

Mom nods readily. She doesn't do much homemade cooking anymore but that's obviously something she can handle, when she has to. "What would you like? I have the ingredients for that tuna and leek casserole you like."

"That'd be great. Thanks."

Mom stands in my room, nodding. I hate her, desperately want her to get a grip, and would do almost anything to avoid making her cry, all at the same time. Feelings should be more cut and dried than that.

Mom goes off to make dinner, and when my dad gets home we sit down to eat together and pretend we're a regular family. Dad doesn't talk about Friday night or make any reference to my absence; he just asks how school was. I humour him and talk about Terry Fox. My father reminds me that I have a special edition dollar coin with Terry's image on it.

After dinner I search out the coin, among the various other collector coins my grandmother and grandfather send me for every birthday. I should have a special case for them but instead they're lumped up inside a pine photo box. Terry's dollar coin is near the top, like he knew I'd be looking for it soon and placed it there himself. He's immortalized in mid-stride, golden with fir trees behind him. I slide the coin into one of my wallet side pockets, without knowing why I'm doing it.

By Wednesday no one at school's even mentioning the rumour about me anymore. Mom takes one more shot at trying to convince me to visit Doctor Berkovich with her and then goes back to her normal cloistering-herself-in-the-den routine. I'm not grounded, as far as I know, which is pretty much what I say to Gage when he calls on Wednesday night.

"Do they know we're going out tomorrow?" Gage asks.

"I haven't exactly mentioned that yet. I thought I'd wait until the last minute. Give them less chance to get upset."

"The last minute might make them more upset," Gage points out. "Promise me you'll tell them tonight. It's so much easier hanging out if we don't have them against us."

I sigh into the phone. "Okay, you're right." As soon as we've said goodbye I march downstairs to talk to my father, the one who's been officially appointed to deal with me in these matters. He's sitting in the living room, his feet up on the coffee table, reading a history book that has John F. Kennedy and some other guy on the cover.

My left knees brushes against the arm of the couch. "Dad?"

He looks up from his book.

"I just thought I should let you know I have plans with Gage tomorrow night," I continue.

Dad's bottom lip bulges. He closes his book and sets it down next to him. "A date?" Dad clarifies. "At least spare me the shtick about men and women being friends this time."

"All right … a date, yeah."

"If we have any repeats of Friday night, you have to know there'll be repercussions, Serena." He pushes at his reading glasses. "What was this guy's name again?"

I told Dad that last time but the info's obviously already been forgotten. Typical. "Gage Cochrane," I reply, with no hint of attitude in my voice.

"I want you to give me Gage's home phone number, address, and his cell," Dad says. "And if you're not back here by eleven, I guarantee you're going to have a problem with me that won't be resolved by walking out and spending a couple of nights at your friends'."

"There won't be any problems," I promise. Eleven is my normal weekday curfew. On the weekends I get an extra hour, but it's not like my parents were really keeping track until last Friday. If I'd lied to them from the start and told them that I was going to a party and wouldn't be back until late they wouldn't have had a problem with it. The last time I was at a party with Jacob they gave me until one o'clock, but Dad barely noticed me when I came home and Mom was already up in bed.

I have to text Gage to ask for his full address, which I didn't pay close attention to last Friday, and then jot the info out for my dad on a pink Post-it. The next evening, I'm dressed and hanging out by the front door five minutes before Gage said he'd be here so that he won't be subjected to questioning from my newly conscientious father.

I'm out the door a second after he rings the bell, skates in hand because Gage has suggested we go ice skating at Raeburn Park. The park's really pretty in the winter, a wide ring of ice surrounding the gazebo and green and blue lights lacing the trees and overhead arches. My skates are tight because I've almost outgrown them the same way I've outgrown my Rollerblades, and Gage skates twenty times better than me, but we have fun. He tries to teach me how to cross over properly when I turn (something I've never gotten the hang of) and at one point I go down with a smack and lose my breath.

Gage reaches for me with both hands and gets me on my feet again. "You all right?" he asks, leaning in to press his lips against my eyebrow.

Better now, thanks. "I'll live but *ouch*."

"You want to take a break and get some hot chocolate or something?" he asks. "There's a diner across the street. They have great chili cheese fries."

We unlace our skates and head for the diner where I sip hot chocolate and watch Gage eat chili cheese fries, munching on a grand total of three myself. "Have some more," he coaxes, pushing the plate in my direction. "You've hardly touched them."

"They're good," I assure him. "I just don't want to eat too much."

"You're not on a diet?" he says as though that would be a crazy idea.

"Not really." *Always* would be a more honest answer. "I just try to stick to eating when I'm hungry so that way I don't end up eating a lot of junk." A week ago I wasn't shy about going down on Gage, but talking about food with him makes me want to blush. Dumb.

"I try not to eat too much junk either now, especially when Akayla's around." Gage pauses and drums his fingers on the table. "Chili cheese fries are one of my greatest weaknesses."

"So what are the others?"

Gage's cheeks stretch to make room for a melt-in-your-mouth gorgeous grin. He picks up his fork and sticks it into a chunky French fry.

"What?" I urge, kicking him under the table as I smile back. "What're you thinking?"

Gage is chewing on a cheesy fry. He washes it down with a swig of hot chocolate before saying, "Just about you." His smile's back full force. "I want you to stick around for a while, so the only weaknesses I'm going to admit to are things like chili cheese fries. Sorry."

"I think I know another one already," I tell him. "Girls in need of a ride, whether they're hanging out in front of a drugstore or screaming at you on the phone."

"That wasn't even close to screaming, believe me." Gage leans over the table and whispers, "Besides, it was worth it." That's what I said to him when he called on Sunday and it's nice to hear it aimed back at me. "You could probably even get away with worse, but I guess I shouldn't tell you that."

"Because I might take advantage of the situation?" I say, cheeks bursting with another smile.

"You could." His eyes twinkle. "You could devour all these fries and I wouldn't even complain."

"Well, that situation is easily fixed. You could always order more."

"True. But again, I'm not going to point out the worst case scenarios and give you any ideas."

"C'mon." I pout at him in what I hope is a sexy way. "I can't believe you'd think things like that about me."

I can't remember anyone, ever, smiling at me in as concentrated a way as Gage has been for the last couple of minutes and I wish we didn't have this table between us. I want a second helping of last Friday night.

"I don't," Gage says, suddenly sincere. "Not really. I only think good things about you."

Our eyes lock and hold, and I know Gage is a nice guy but there's no mistaking the expression on his face; he's wishing that table would disappear too.

"So." He breaks the spell by checking his watch. "It's only ten after nine. You want to hang out here a bit longer after we're finished or maybe go someplace else?"

"Is that some kind of trick question?" I ask. "Because you know we've had trouble with that one before."

"No, I know." Gage's voice is quiet. "You're right. But we have some parameters, right? Because it's not that I don't want …" Our brassy-haired waitress swishes by and he glances sideways at her, stopping mid-sentence.

"Can I get you something else?" she asks, misinterpreting his look.

"We're fine," I say. "Thanks."

Gage and I don't resume that particular conversation until we're back at his place, making out against his kitchen counter while he's supposed to be getting me a drink of something cold. He lifts me up onto the counter and fits himself between my legs. Then he concentrates on my neck, which I never realized could feel so amazing. He kisses and nibbles until a sound escapes from my throat. It's like something you hear in a dirty movie only quieter and for a shorter duration, because I'm not used to making noises like that. It happened a few times with Jacob but never with all my clothes on. Gage slides one of his hands over my breasts, which feels good too, and I stick both my hands under his shirt and spread them across his chest.

Things don't go the way they did with Jacob, there's no predetermined end to what we're doing, just Gage burying his face in my shoulder and saying he'll be back in a minute. I nod, hop down from the counter, pour myself a drink, and take it into the family room. Today the only sign of Akayla is a red and white beaded bracelet on top of the TV. The beads are flower-shaped and I stare at the bracelet, amazed at how small her wrist is and that Gage is partially responsible for keeping this miniature person healthy and happy.

"Hey," he says when he ambles into the room a couple of minutes later, "I set my watch alarm so we won't lose track of time." He drops down next to me on the couch.

"Good thinking." I tap his knee. "What were you saying earlier, when the waitress showed up?" I feel shy bringing it up, but I need to know more about the parameters he was talking about, clues about which lines not to cross when I'm in a situation like the one in the kitchen a few minutes ago.

Gage curls his hand around the back of his neck and scratches at his hair. He hunches over, resting both arms on his thighs. "Pretty much what we've already figured out." His hand digs into his hair again. "I can't afford to mess up again. This doesn't really apply to you because you're, you know, a virgin but it's just better for me right now that I don't have sex. It's too much" — he straightens up, his eyes leaving mine for a second — "stress for now."

I know Gage says he's not good at first dates but I don't believe for a second that he hasn't been with anyone during the last four years. Maybe he's had risky experiences in the more recent past and wants to change.

"Which probably sounds like a lame speech to you," he continues. "Like it's all about me and what I want, and you obviously have your own ideas of what you do or don't want to do, which I'm sure never included having sex with me anyway."

My ideas are changeable, dependent on the moment, but I've been having a lot of private thoughts about Gage lately. "I think we should just, you know, take it slow — the opposite of what happened the first time we went out," I say, swinging one of my legs up onto the couch and tucking it underneath my other thigh. It's difficult to talk about sex like this and sit still. "And with the understanding that even then there won't be any actual sex."

Gage's cheeks are pink. "That sounds perfect to me."

To me too, only after all that I'm not much clearer on what exactly our parameters are except that Gage won't be trying to persuade me that losing my virginity to him would automatically make us closer. Even if I wanted him to be my first, which I'm not sure about either way, Gage doesn't.

Whatever else happens is up to the two of us, and my mind has already started to wander away from what the parameters forbid and towards what they include. I snuggle up to him on the couch, our arms and legs weaving themselves together as our bodies stretch out along the cushions. I don't want to know how much time we have left before his watch alarm beeps. There's no reason to think about the end when we're just at the beginning.

CHAPTER EIGHTEEN

IN MY OWN BED later I dream about Devin. It starts out like the nightmare I've had at least twenty times before, the one where Devin goes on a rampage, screaming terrible things at me and my parents. But this time the shouting doesn't come. The four of us are sitting in the kitchen in the morning light, eating scrambled eggs, when Devin announces that it's time for him to go jogging. Somehow my eyes follow him, like in a movie. I'm outside with Devin, watching him run in step with Terry Fox. The two of them smile but don't speak.

They know each other. I can tell by how comfortable they look next to each other. They've done this run before.

The film's grainy and the colour's faded and all I do is watch them run, their feet pounding the pavement as the background changes from houses to fields.

I feel strangely calm when I wake up. This is the first good dream I've had about my brother in over seven months. It could be some kind of sign that he's getting better, changing back into the Devin I knew from before. But suddenly, while I'm massaging shampoo into my scalp in the shower, it occurs to me that Terry Fox is dead and gone.

If my brother's with Terry, does that make him dead and gone too?

Terry Fox was only a year older than Devin is now when he died. He found out the cancer had spread to his lungs and had to stop his run across the country. Dread burrows in my chest at the thought. Why send me a message like this when there's nothing I can do to help my brother?

Get a grip, I lecture. *You're not making sense.* The dream's not a message, it's nothing but a mishmash of thoughts I've been carrying around in my head recently. But no matter how many times I repeat that thought, I can't rationalize myself out of the desire to hurry through my shower and rush to the computer.

I rinse my shampoo off, rub body wash over all the crucial places, and jump out onto the cold bathroom floor. In my bedroom, I pull up the Terry Fox Foundation website and fact check, my hair dripping down the back of my pyjamas. Terry stopped running on September 1, 1980, and died on June 28, 1981, almost ten months after he found out the cancer was back. Does that mean something? Do we have three more months to save Devin?

I'm losing it. *There's no warning.* No good or bad signs. No fate.

I'm just a girl who dreams about her missing brother.

I know all that with almost as much certainty as I know the earth is round, but I don't take the Terry Fox coin out of my wallet. I can be a little crazy if I want, assign my brother a guardian angel. It's better than spending hours on eBay, isn't it?

So I walk around with the coin on me for the fourth day in a row and at lunch, while I'm looking for Nicole, Izzy, Marguerite, or Genevieve in the cafeteria, one of Aya's friends catches my eye. I see her motion to Aya, whose gaze flashes up to meet mine.

She gets up from her chair and marches over to me. "Hi, Serena." Aya's shiny jet black hair used to be long, but she had it bobbed last week. The new look is more sophisticated, which I guess is the image she's going for now.

"Hey, Aya, have you seen Nicole or any of them?" Aya and I are friends these days, but I still don't feel entirely at ease with her.

"Marguerite just came in." Aya motions to the door not far behind me. "Before you go, I just wanted to ask you something — do you like skating?"

Skating? Did someone spot me with Gage last night? I knew I couldn't keep the secret forever, but I was hoping the news wouldn't break so soon. I take a breath and prepare to admit that I was in Raeburn Park with a guy last night. I'll pretend I just met him there and barely know him. No one has to know any different.

"Because there's this skating thing in Toronto tonight, one of those tours that all the pros do," Aya continues. "Anyway, my mother has eight free tickets and she said I could bring someone. Nanami was supposed to go but she's home sick with the flu."

Is that all? I run my fingers through my hair and exhale. I guess none of Aya's other friends could make it tonight. Aya and I have never really hung out on our own, but I'm so grateful that my secret's intact that ultimately I'd agree to anything. "I can make it tonight," I tell her. "Thanks."

At the Air Canada Centre later we're thirteen rows up from the ice. Aya's mom takes the aisle seat and the rest of us — Aya, her three aunts, her twin cousins, and me — file further into our row. The music's too loud to allow much talking during the show, which is full of all the triple axles and fancy footwork a figure skating fan could ever want, but at the intermission Aya, her cousins, and I spend fifteen minutes in line for fast-food chicken. Rose and Lily are fourteen and don't look anything alike, except for their perfectly straight noses. Lily's the one who does all the talking, and as we stand there she won't shut up about this guy who's been flirting with her in geography class. He's texted her four times and they were supposed to meet at the mall a couple of days ago but he cancelled at the last minute because of some family thing. It's amazing the info you can pick up within fifteen minutes, and I can see she's full-scale gaga for this guy. If I had a sympathetic twin this is most likely how I'd sound when talking to her about Gage.

"Who is this guy *exactly*?" Aya asks finally, her tone critical. "Is he sporty or smart or what?"

Lily shoots Rose an uncertain look before answering: "He's in between. But he's cute. Very cute. And funny too."

"So you want to go out with him or what?" Aya says.

"Maybe." Lily shrugs, wanting out of the conversation now that Aya's beaming a spotlight on her feelings. "I dunno ..."

"You're better off sticking to texting him and joking around in class," Aya says knowingly. "Trust me. Crossing that line isn't worth the effort most of the time. Somebody who's that cute and as much of a flirt as you're saying isn't going to want to come over to your house and do homework in the kitchen with you while your parents walk in and out."

"How do you know?" quiet twin Rose says, sticking her chin out. "You have a guy?" Even Aya's younger cousins recognize her as the good girl type, it seems. I bet they'd pay more attention to what she's saying if they knew about her make-out video.

Aya's eyes smoulder. "I don't need to have a guy to know that." Up to this point I've just been listening without comment, and now I watch Aya bite down on her lip. "*Whatever.* I'm just trying to save you some hassle, Lily. Find out for yourself if that's what you want."

Lily plays with her hair and takes another step closer to fast-food chicken — we all do (although the only thing I plan on ordering is diet pop). "I never said I wanted to go out with him."

"Yeah, but you obviously do," Rose says with a mischievous smile. "Remember what you said at lunch today about his T-shirt and how —?"

"Shut up why don't you?" Lily cuts in, giving her sister a gentle shove. The two of them lower their voices, losing themselves in their own private conversation as Aya and I stand behind them, forced to talk amongst ourselves.

"I don't want to be bitter," Aya tells me. "Is that how I sound?"

"My experiences have been pretty much like yours. So judging from that I'd have to say odds are you're right about the guy she likes." I shrug lightly, wishing I could slide some other, more recent truths, into the conversation. But I can't think how to do that and still keep my secret safe.

"Yeah, I know," Aya says, "but we can't constantly judge everyone according to our bad experiences." The two of us take another half step towards greasy chicken. "Think of guys like Joyeux Maduka. He's nice to everyone all the time."

"Yeah, but Joyeux is like a modern day saint. You can't really compare him to normal guys." I don't know which side of the conversation I'm on anymore. I think of Gage walking around with Akayla's pink heart sticker in his wallet and it melts me on the spot.

"Okay, but he's not the only one."

"I guess," I say slowly. "Maybe we just have one of those bad boy complexes." It's more complicated than that, but I'd need a degree in sociology to really understand it all. Look at what happened to Nicole and Genevieve — Liam Powers and Costas Gavril aren't typical bad boys but things still got messed up.

"Do you?" Aya's dark eyes stare at me like she means to get to the bottom of this.

The twins slide along the fast food counter to make room for us. Our fast-food chicken moment has arrived, which makes it easy for me to avoid Aya's question. It looks like the only truths I'm ready to experience tonight are citric acid, sucralose, and maybe a back flip or two by some former gold medallists. "You go first," I tell Aya. "I'm only getting a drink."

❖

Gage and I hang out a few more times. I tell him I'm getting hooked on him but I say it like I'm mostly kidding so I won't scare him. One night we end up falling asleep on his couch again, but his watch alarm saves my ass. Another time we bump into a friend of his at Starbucks, and Gage explains that Elliott is in a community teen father group he goes to.

"Does he have a boy or a girl?" I ask casually. Sometimes I wish I could've met Gage before he had Akayla, but I would've been too young for him then anyway. I'm almost used to the idea of Akayla from the evidence of her existence that I see strewn around the apartment, but when I take that further in my mind, it makes me jumpy. It's sweet to imagine things like Gage getting her up in the morning and feeding her cereal and Nutella and banana sandwiches (her favourite food, according to Gage), but his daughter's not a puppy. Gage's responsibilities are huge and they make me wonder what exactly mine could be, if I ever meet her.

I do want to meet her. Sort of. And then I don't. I want to keep my relationship with Gage just between us, but if we stay inside our bubble forever I'll never fully know him. These are things I avoid thinking about the same way I avoid thinking about Devin most of the time. I still want a baby blue scooter to whirl around Glenashton on, and I'm putting money aside for it bit by bit. That's a good thing to think about. I should be able to afford a sparkly brand new one by the summer before senior year. It might not be a 1967 Vespa but it'll be sweet. By senior year I'll be in full flair and confidence mode, with an awesome career plan and the ability to take my thinness for granted.

It's a lot to accomplish in a year and a half, but I can do it. The problem with this future vision of myself is that I can't imagine Gage next to me there, which is something I don't even realize until I spot him roaming around Total Drug Mart one Tuesday night. One of his hands is grasping a basketful of items he intends to buy and the other is holding a much smaller hand with a red and white beaded bracelet dangling from its wrist.

Akayla Cochrane's tight ringlets spill down over her puffy pink coat. Her winter boots are pink too. I'm too far away to tell for sure but I think they might have some Disney figure on them. Gage cocks his head at me and smiles but it's Ki's cash register he heads for.

I can't blame him — my line is two people longer than hers at the moment — but I still feel funny about it. My natural inclination is to stare at Akayla, because I've never seen her in real life before. But I don't want her or Gage to notice my ogling. I smile quickly and then turn my attention back to the man in front of me. I scan in his laundry detergent, antacid, and cheese slices and slip them into the cloth tote bag he's laid on the counter. Next up is a blond woman buying hair dye and a bunch of stuff from our organic line of products.

"I tried some of this the other night," I tell her as I pick up the bottle of roasted red pepper dressing. "It was pretty good."

"It should be for that price," the woman complains, dragging her fingers through her hair and looking bored with me.

What do you expect if you buy organic salad dressing? *Hello.* I smile anyway and ask her if she wants a bag. I'm loading her over-priced organic items and non-organic hair dye into it when Gage appears by her side.

"I just wanted to say hi," he says, giving me a peek at his gorgeous dimples. "I'll talk to you later?"

I glance quickly down at Akayla and then back at Gage. "Yeah, later. See you." I smile for him, wondering how I could've forgotten to insert Gage into my vision of the future, even for a moment. If I'm waiting for everything to be simple, I'll be waiting all my life. Real life isn't perfect and easy like in the movies. Real life is a great guy like Gage having a four-year-old daughter and by extension a semi-complicated life.

Gage and Akayla walk out of the store together, and I hear her high-pitched childish voice say, "Let me carry one, Dad." My back's turned, but I imagine him surrendering one of the lighter bags.

I've never had a problem imagining the two of them together; what's hard is imaging us as a group of three, which is why once Gage and Akayla are gone all I want to do is fill my mind with thoughts of senior year and my baby blue scooter again.

CHAPTER NINETEEN

༺✠༻

GAGE AND I ARE doing our lying on the couch but taking it slow thing. The irony is that I like doing that so much that I think I'd be okay with more, not sleeping with him but maybe *almost*. But we can't get close to *almost* either, and that's okay too.

Gage touches my breasts like they've been sculpted by Rodin. He tells me they're beautiful and teases me by saying that he knows I like them almost as much as he does. That's true and I laugh. If we had a robot to bring us food and stuff I could let him play with my breasts forever.

"Do you think they're done growing?" Gage asks, bending his head down to flick his tongue over one of my nipples. "Maybe we can lie here and watch them expand."

I giggle at that too. Gage makes me want to laugh at everything. "I think they're supposed to grow for four years after you first get your period," I tell him.

The first time Gage slipped my top off I worried that his mother would burst in and interrupt us on the couch, but he said they'd made a deal to always call each other first. The way he talks about his mother makes their relationship sounds weirdly formal. He said she was furious when she found out his girlfriend was pregnant, and even though she's not angry anymore, she doesn't want him thinking of her as a live-in babysitter. The bottom line is that 1) Gage doesn't want us to move our activities into the bedroom and 2) his mother is extremely unlikely to interrupt us on the couch.

"So when'd you get your first period?" Gage asks. He pulls his weight off me, sliding onto the cushion beside me. "You know, I don't even know when your birthday is."

"It's in April." I get a guilt surge as I answer him. Now he must think I'll be seventeen come April.

Gage leans over me again, nuzzling my breast and flinging one of his hands around me to fondle my denim-covered butt. "When in April?"

I stiffen, knowing that I won't be able lie to him. Gage looks me in the eye, his hand still attached to my ass. "What? You don't like people knowing your birthday?"

I open my mouth to ask when his birthday is, but what's the point of stalling? We'd only arrive back at this exact point in thirty seconds. "It's April seventeenth," I confess. "But do you remember the first time we went out and you guessed I was in eleventh grade?"

"Yeah." Gage crinkles his nose. "I still can't believe you're in eleventh grade. I feel like I'm robbing the cradle."

I freeze up again, and Gage slides his hand up to my bare back and strokes it, sensing he's upset me. "Hey, you know I don't really care. It's just weird when I think of you still going to school. I feel so far removed from that part of my life now."

The fact that he thinks he's done something wrong makes me feel guiltier still.

"It's not that," I say in a quivery voice. "I hope this doesn't really matter because it's only a few months but ..." Gage has pulled his hand away from my back, and I grab his fingers and hold on. "I'm going to be *sixteen* on April seventeenth, not seventeen."

Gage's frown is the polar opposite of his smile. You'd think life as we know it was about to screech to a halt.

"I'm in tenth grade," I continue. "Not eleventh. *That's the truth.* The rest of it really shouldn't make any difference. In a couple of months I really will be sixteen."

"Serena." This is the disaster vibe Gage gave off when he stormed out of the back seat on our first date. The line between his eyes is so deep that an expedition of explorers could be lost in there and never heard from again. "*Shit.*"

He wrestles out of my grasp and sits up on the couch, glaring fixedly across the room. "That's not something you should've lied about. I mean, look at us." He motions to my naked chest. "You're *fifteen.*"

I reach over the side of the couch for my top, thrusting my arms into it and speeding my way through the buttons. "I'm two months younger than you thought I was. That's all." I feel like crying.

"I wasn't really cool with sixteen," he snaps. "And now I find out you're not even that."

"You didn't tell me you had a kid right away!" My finger slips on the top button. I leave it open and leap to my feet. "And if my age was such a big deal maybe you should've asked how old I was before showing up at my house to take me to dinner. Did you ever think of that?"

"You look older," Gage says with an accusing look. "You must know that."

I don't know what he's talking about; I look roughly the same age as Genevieve or Nicole. "Why does it even matter?" I ask. "We're talking about *two months*. Why do you have to be so ..." My arms slice the air helplessly.

"So *what?*" Gage asks.

"It's like that night we first went out. You just ... you overreact." I'm not trying to fight with him, but he needs to see how ridiculous he's acting. "You could've just told me to stop, you know. You didn't have to leap out of the car."

Gage locks his hands around his neck and shakes his head. "We already talked about that. You don't need to bring it up again and make me feel stupid."

"I'm not trying to make you feel stupid. I'm just saying you need to keep things in perspective. It's two months!" I'm shouting, afraid he's going to break up with me for the sake of sixty stupid days.

"Can you be quiet for two seconds?" Gage demands, his angry eyes freezing me in place.

Gage sits back, his body low on the couch like I'm wearing him out. He shuts his eyes, and when he opens them again I'm still staring back, waiting for him to continue.

"I was fourteen when Christabelle got pregnant," he says. I've only heard him refer to Akayla's mother by name a couple of times, and suddenly I know that I'm going to come out of this conversation feeling even worse than I do right now. "She was fifteen. I don't know if you can imagine how fucked up that really was." The colour drains from Gage's face. "And I don't want to be in that situation again. Ever. But I especially don't want to be in that situation, or anywhere close to it, with someone who's only fifteen years old."

I blink at him and feel a lone tear fight its way down my cheek. We were never going to be in that situation together, but I can't stand here and tell Gage he's being paranoid after what he's been through. I turn my face away and bend to pluck my bra from the beige carpet.

With my fingers looped around one of the straps, I head for the bathroom. I lock the door behind me, undo the buttons on my top again, and fasten my bra into place, more tears wetting my skin. I splash warm tap water onto my face and lean against the counter, patting my skin dry. Akayla's Little Mermaid toothbrush holder set grins manically at me as I realize I left my phone in the family room with Gage and that I have no idea who to call anyway. Anyone I'd want to pick me up doesn't know of Gage's existence — my parents aren't an option.

Suddenly there's a tentative knock at the bathroom door. "Serena? Are you okay?"

I'm almost sixteen, which doesn't seem to be okay enough.

"You don't have to hide out in there," he says. "Come out and talk to me."

The suggestion that I'm hiding makes me mad. Am I supposed to root my feet to the family room carpet until he's ready to stop guilt-ing me for something I can't take back or change? "I'm not hiding," I tell him, my angry tone already losing strength. "I'm getting myself together to leave."

"You don't need to leave. Just come out. We can talk."

I don't want to listen to him talk anymore, but I can't stay locked up in his bathroom forever. I unlock the door and stride determinedly past him, Gage trailing me down the hall saying, "Have you really heard anything I've been trying to say?" We stand in front of the television, facing each other, Gage's hands in his pockets. "I can't act like it's good news that you're fifteen. I had second thoughts when you said were sixteen, more doubts when you ragged on me over the phone that time, and now … I don't know." He shakes his head like this is the final straw.

"Two months," he says in a low voice. "I'm not touching you again until you turn sixteen, so don't ask me to. We can hang out but no …" He motions to the couch, his wrist flipping sideways in aggra-vation. "I'm just not."

I part my lips and rub my left eye, which has started leaking again.

Gage reaches for my cheek, skimming his thumb across it and absorbing any dampness I've missed. "That's just the way it has to be for now, end of story."

I don't think most nineteen-year-olds would see much difference in having a sixteen- or fifteen-year-old girlfriend, but Gage does, and I wish I could've stayed calm through this whole scene so he wouldn't guess just how important it is that he doesn't break up with me.

"So what's that mean exactly?" I mumble. "You want to be friends?" No more lying on his couch? No more kisses or holding hands? I feel both starved and grateful at the suggestion. If we're friends I'll still be able to see him, at least.

"Being friends is good, isn't it?" He shrugs, his pupils growing as he stares at me. "Friends can be a lot of things to each other."

That's true, but once again I don't know what his definition permits and what it forbids.

Gage picks up on my confusion and reaches out to hold my hand. "I bet you wish you never walked into this. You think I'm crazy, don't you?"

I'm too confused to even answer, and Gage's smile is almost sad as he says, "Maybe I am. You probably have no idea how hard it is to have all these limits when what I really want to do is ..." He stops, his smile disappearing into his tired face. "But that wouldn't be a good idea anyway. You're so young."

"I'm not as young as you act like I am."

"Why?" Gage asks, cocking his head. "Because you gave some guy before me a blow job? Believe me, you're *young*, and I wouldn't want to grow out of that too fast if I were you. I mean, no matter what, even if we broke up now and you hooked up with some other guy."

"Don't talk about me hooking up with some other guy." My free hand lands on his waist, squeezing in punishment. "That's not going to happen. I'd sworn off guys before you. You're like ... you're my downfall."

This isn't a good thing to say to Gage, who already seems to see himself this way, but it feels partially true. My friends wouldn't be happy if they knew we were together and they know me better than he does. Or maybe I should say they know *parts* of me better than he does. There are other parts — the snuggling up with him on the couch and feeling like I'll starve to death if I never see him again parts — they don't know at all.

"Not in the way that you think of it," I continue. "Not because you have a daughter, which makes your life more complicated. Not because you got somebody pregnant five years ago. You wouldn't let that happen again."

"Not on purpose." Gage threads his fingers through his hair. "But that's the problem, isn't it?" He begins to tell me about the girls he's seen before me, some of whom were on the pill and some who weren't. He freaked out a little every time he slept with one of them, pouring water in the condoms after the fact to look for leaks and tracking girls' periods when he could. He says the worry was exhausting and that it reached a point last spring where it didn't seem worth it anymore unless he was really serious about someone.

"And potentially that could be even worse," he points out. "Like with you, I don't want to have to worry about what could happen if a condom broke on us or something else went wrong." By this time the two of us are back sitting on the couch together and he looks spent but maybe a little relieved to be able to be so blunt with me. "So unless someday, in the future, you're on some kind of hormonal birth control thing too we won't be together like that. It's really important that you know that."

"I know." I nod with my eyes, trying to reassure him that I really do get it.

"Okay." Gage nods too. "I sound like a broken record. So you ..." He rests his hand on my thigh. "Why'd you swear off guys? Did somebody" — he drops his voice like it's a big deal to ask — "break your heart?"

"He didn't break my heart. We just weren't right — *he* wasn't right." I explain about Jacob, the party at Wyatt's and Aya's clammy hand on my knee. I'm careful to keep my voice level, even as I insult Jacob and his friends. If Gage feels too sorry for me I might start to tear up again.

"That's really fucked up," Gage comments, his face serious. "On so many levels."

"I know." I keep Nicole and Genevieve's bad experiences to myself but mention Orlando's gossip porn rumour about me and some of the other shitty stuff that contaminates the atmosphere at Laurier.

"I didn't know you were dealing with any of this shit," Gage says, frowning. "I don't know why people bother talking trash about other people. It's not right. I wish you told me before."

"There was nothing you could've done anyway. You know how it is. School's just like that."

"I know." Gage pinches his ear. "Doesn't mean I can't drop by and throw my weight around. Make the assholes eat their words."

Gage is past the point of high school fights. I can't see that happening at all, but I still like him saying it.

"Defend my honour?" I smile at him. "It's okay. My friends got there first."

"Those are the kind of friends you want to have," he says with a slow nod.

Absolutely, but they're also the kind of friends who would disapprove of the two of us. From what Gage said earlier I know he doesn't really approve himself, and I have to wonder if there's anyone on the planet who would see us as an honest to God good idea. Even I, with my baby blue scooter future, have doubts, but I'm so glad that we're sitting together on his couch, being friends or whatever you want to call it, that I'm nearly positive every last one of us is dead wrong.

CHAPTER TWENTY

WE'VE PRETTY MUCH CALMED down, Gage and I, and are sitting on the couch watching *Ghost Hunters* with none of our body parts touching when his phone rings. On TV the TAPS teams are hanging out in a former morgue where several people claim to have spotted the ghost of a young boy in Victorian clothing. The real life noise makes me jump, which in turn makes Gage smile and touch my shoulder as he reaches for the cordless on the coffee table.

At first he sounds normal. Then his voice tenses. "So she's gone already? When did all this start?"

Gage looks at me as he listens to the voice on the phone. "Yeah, of course you can," he says. "It's just ... I have someone here right now, but of course. I'll see you in a couple of minutes. Call me later when you know more, all right? Bye."

Gage drops the cordless back on the coffee table, his eyes sombre. "Christabelle's on her way over with Akayla. Her mom was having really bad stomach pains, burning up with a fever. Her dad just drove her over to the hospital and now Chris and her brother are going too.

"I won't have time to run you home first," Gage adds. "We'll go when she gets here."

I bob my head and tell him that I hope Christabelle's mom is okay.

Gage bites his lip and grabs for the remote to switch off the TV. "Me too." His focus has shifted to a group of people I've never met. I don't really know how close he and Christabelle still are but I can't let myself start being jealous about someone who will be part of his life forever. If we're ever going to be more than friends again I need to be mature about his life and I guess that means starting now.

"Is there anything we should do before they get here?" I ask. "Is Akayla's room all ready?"

"Yeah, yeah, it's fine," he says absently. "We don't have to do anything." He fumbles around in his pocket for his cell and starts tapping out a text message. "I'm just asking Chris's brother, Damien, to keep me posted too."

I've heard Gage mention Damien before — he's one of Gage's best friends — but I didn't realize he was Akayla's uncle. There's so much I don't know.

Less than ten minutes later Gage's doorbell rings and he sprints upstairs, leaving me on the couch with butterflies in my stomach. I hear voices upstairs, but when Gage comes downstairs again less than a minute later only Akayla is with him, stepping in my direction in white socks. She's wearing two-piece yellow pyjamas under her open pink coat and carrying a pale purple knapsack in her arms while Gage has a large pink and green duffle bag slung over one shoulder.

"We're just going to dump your stuff in your room and then drive my friend home," he says, reaching down to put his hand on her hand. "You okay, sweetness?"

Akayla nods and looks me over. "Are you the girl from the store?" she asks.

"She is." Gage answers for me. "This is Serena."

"Hi," I say, smiling at Akayla but trying not to stare too much. She seems tall for four, but when was the last time I knew someone who was four? I really want her to like me and that chases all the words from my head.

"We're going to drive her home and then put you to bed, okay?" Gage repeats, walking ahead of Akayla and motioning for her to follow.

As they disappear into the hallway I hear Akayla ask, "Dad, is that your girlfriend?"

"She's just a friend, sweetness," he says after a short pause. "Like you have friends who are boys at daycare."

"Only one," she reminds him, and then I can't hear them anymore.

When they come back a few minutes later I notice Gage has put Velcro running shoes on Akayla's feet, probably because it's easier than pulling her boots back on. She yawns as she shuffles by me and I wonder if Christabelle had to get her out of bed to bring her over. The three of us pile into Gage's car, and as we back out onto the street I turn to look at Akayla. "You okay in the back?" I ask.

She kicks out one of her feet in front of her and nods suspiciously. "Dad," she says loudly. "Dad?"

"Quiet voice," he advises. "I'm right here. What is it, Akayla?"

"What's wrong with Grandma?" she asks, her face long.

"We don't know yet," Gage replies, his eyes on the road and his tone patient. "They're going to check her out at the hospital and find out. Then they can fix her up and your grandpa will bring her home again."

"Tomorrow?" Akayla asks.

"Soon," Gage says. "As soon as she's better."

Akayla doesn't have any follow-up questions for now. I watch her turn her head to gaze out the window. "Will you call me tomorrow and give me an update?" I whisper to Gage.

"If you want," he replies. "Sure" would've been a better answer, but he must be stressed out. Me being fifteen is the least of his problems tonight.

Soon we pull up in front of my house and I unbuckle my seat belt, peer into the back seat, and say, "Bye, Akayla. Nice to meet you."

Akayla points her big brown eyes at me. "Bye."

"See you," Gage says, looking at me like my presence isn't really registering. "Thanks."

For what? I don't ask. "See you," I say back.

I trudge towards my house, my head spinning with everything that happened tonight. Inside I kick off my boots and wrestle my coat into the closet. Some older, unused jackets are piled in a messy heap on the closet floor. Maybe this is as close as my mom got to the idea of cleaning out our closet.

I hear TV voices and discover my father lying on the living room couch with a glass of red wine beside him on the coffee table. An egg cup full of green olives accompanies the wine, and somehow this makes me sad. My dad's big treat for himself is an egg cup of green olives. Shouldn't there be more? Maybe he should have an affair. Live a little.

"Where's Mom?" I ask.

"In bed," he says, hoisting himself up on his elbows. "One of her headaches. How was your night?" He smiles like he's in the mood for company, but it's Genevieve or Nicole I really need to talk to.

"It was okay. Kind of quiet." I point down at his olives. "Can I take one?"

"Sure. Work away." He points to the TV. "I'm just watching NCIS here. It's a pretty good episode."

I nod at the TV. "We were watching *Ghost Hunters*."

"I thought you didn't like those paranormal shows," Dad says, arching his eyebrows.

"Gage likes them."

"Ah." Dad smiles again, and now I've really had enough.

"Gotta go," I tell him, grabbing another olive. "I owe Genevieve a call."

I scurry up to my room and sit at the foot of my bed clutching my cell and debating who will take the news about Gage and me better. I settle on Nicole, who answers on the second ring. "Do I look older than my age?" I quiz.

"You mean, like, every day or what?" Nicole says. "Because obviously if you have your makeup done and stuff you can look older. Why? Are you getting a fake ID?"

"No. Someone at the store told me I looked older."

"Some perverted old guy?" Nicole guesses.

"Not really. He was about nineteen."

"Oh, okay, but listen," Nicole says, "I was just about to call you anyway because you have to hear this craziness — Liam just got in touch with me to say he's having a party next weekend." I can hear the angst in her voice but can't tell whether it's angry angst or excited angst. I wait for Nicole to plow forward and give me another clue.

"Can you believe he had the nerve?" she huffs. "He said he didn't want me to hear about it from someone else and that I should feel free to come because he always thought it was stupid the way things ended with us."

Okay, so she's outraged. I remember the day she fell and messed up her leg and sympathize utterly. "If he thought the way things worked out was so stupid maybe he should've had your back when everyone was forwarding the video around," I say.

"That's exactly what I told him. He said every time he got near me I was shooting him bad vibes and staring at him like I wanted to saw his balls off."

I lean back against my bed and pull off my socks. "He said that?"

"Yup."

"So does he think your vibes have changed — why's he calling now?"

Nicole growls into the phone. "He's decided — just now, mind you — that maybe it was hard for me and that he should be big about things."

"He's a little late," I declare. "Or is he?"

"He's *a lot* late," Nicole says. "A *day* late would've been a lot late."

"Hmm. Yeah. Maybe next time he'll figure it out faster."

"With someone else." Nicole's voice cracks as she adds, "*Perfect.* I wasn't good enough for him to bother his ass figuring things out months ago."

"You know it's not about you. It's him." I know exactly how she feels, and I also know it's not something she feels all the time, but I wish the two of us (and maybe even Genevieve and Aya) could quit having these lapses where we blame ourselves for other people's bad behaviour.

"I know," Nicole says. "I know."

And *I know* I desperately need to tell someone about Gage, but the timing is wrong. So I keep my mouth shut until Nicole and I are done and then I do an entirely unexpected thing and dial Morgan's boyfriend, Jimmy. Morgan's safely occupied, at the MuchMusic studio doing an interview with the next Lindsay Lohan / Miley Cyrus wannabe (I saw the commercial for the interview while Gage was flipping channels earlier) and I know instinctively that Jimmy will keep my secret.

I'm blushing as I confide about Gage's issue with me being fifteen, and sweating lightly as I admit he has a four-year-old daughter. But Jimmy could be a crisis counsellor; he guides me through the conversation with unprecedented cool, pausing to ask questions and let me fill in backstory.

Finally he tells me that if I want to have a future with this guy I should think about coming clean to my friends. "And by *future* I mean whatever you want that to mean, Serena! But if you want to continue to have some kind of relationship with Gage, don't you think you should stop hiding it?"

I tell Jimmy about Genevieve, Nicole, and me — our battles with Laurier savages and our unofficial pledge to steer clear of them. I wince inside as I explain because Jimmy's a guy himself and I know he's no savage.

"It's good to protect yourself when you've been through a bad relationship," Jimmy says. "Personally, I always fell for the most savage boys imaginable during high school. Disaster, Serena! Disaster! But with you falling for Gage so soon after you'd sworn off boys, I can't help but wonder whether you're in a phase where you enjoy a bit of drama.

"Not that there's anything wrong with that," Jimmy continues. "But promise me if drama has something to do with it, that you won't *lose* yourself in it. Drama's like chocolate. Best in small amounts."

I don't think that liking Gage is rooted in a need for drama. If it's rooted in anything unhealthy it's more likely related to twenty-nine pounds of former chunk and a deep, aching craving to be wanted the way Noah wanted Allie in *The Notebook*. But I don't want just anyone to want me that way. The desire's entirely restricted to Gage. He even makes me want to watch *Ghost Hunters*, and if I thought I'd never wrap my arms around him again I'd spend the rest of my life remembering how it felt to hold him because I never want to let that feeling slip away. Even remembering it is better than nothing.

"I think I'm in love," I whisper. "I feel almost sick."

"Serena?" Jimmy's voice is as soft as down feathers.

"Yeah?"

"How come you called me instead of Morgan? Not that I mind, I'm glad you called, but you know Morgan would've been happy to talk to you too."

"I know." I can't begin to explain my reasons. I don't know how to tell Jimmy that his boyfriend's too perfect, too sure of himself, and on top of that, in some twisted way confiding in Morgan would feel like betraying Devin. "I guess you're easier to talk to. Talking to my brother about relationships, um, we're just not like that in my family."

"Mine neither," Jimmy says. "It's too bad, isn't it? But look! If it *is* love it won't burn out from not being able to touch him for two months and it won't be extinguished by your friends either. Trust me, you need your friends to talk to at times like these. They keep you from going off the rails."

I promise him I'll tell Genevieve and Nicole. I do mean it, but a revelation like that can take time and I end up seeing Gage again first. Christabelle's mom is back from the hospital after an appendectomy, recovering nicely, and Gage and I do a repeat of our skating and diner date. After he's finished his chili cheese fries he says he'll drive me home and I ask if he's afraid to be alone with me now that he knows I'm fifteen.

Gage gives me a pointed look. "If we're just friends we don't need to be alone, do we?"

Friends can cuddle, maybe. But I'm scared to say it in case he thinks I really mean something else.

I grab the ketchup and flip the lid open for no particular reason. "I just miss being close to you," I admit at last. "I didn't mean anything else."

Gage spreads his legs out under the table so that they're touching mine. "I miss that too." I feel the full weight of his stare on me. It feels like sunshine. He reaches out to hold my hand on top of the table and he's warm like sunshine too.

I squeeze his fingers and say, "If you start going out with someone else during the next two months I'm going to kill you."

Gage flashes a broad grin. "Where am I going to find someone who'll put up with me?"

"Good point, but what do I know, I'm not even old enough to drive."

Gage groans and covers his face with his fingers, smile still visible between the cracks. "Thanks for the reminder, Serena. Am I going to hear about how young you are every time I see you for the next two months?"

"I'd actually prefer if you forgot about that but I guess that's not going to happen any time soon."

"Nope," Gage says confidently. "It's not."

"You never told me when your birthday was, you know."

"September ninth," he says.

That means there's three and a half years between us. The number doesn't sound like that big of a deal to me, but if you're the kind of person to worry about numbers I guess I could see why three and a half would ring more alarm bells than two.

I grab the bill from the middle of the table and announce, "It's on me this time."

"No, it's not," Gage counters, reaching for the bill too. "C'mon, you didn't even eat anything."

We both cling stubbornly to the diner bill, which doesn't even amount to ten dollars, like it's profoundly meaningful.

"You always pay," I tell him. "It's not fair." So he's older than me and he's a guy; I'm not going to allow those things to define every single aspect of our relationship. "I'm not planning on letting go, so unless you want to sit here all night ..."

Gage looks me in the eye, judges me serious, and releases his hold on our bill. "All right. Thanks."

There's still another hour before I have to be home and Gage says if it wasn't so cold we could just walk around or something. "I wish people would keep Christmas lights up all winter long," he adds. "Not the reindeer and other decorations, just the lights. Maybe then winter wouldn't seem so long."

"You don't like winter?"

"I don't mind the cold," he says. "I just don't like the short days. By the time I get off work the sunlight's gone."

"I hate that too, but we can walk for a bit if you want. It won't be any colder than skating."

Gage nods but says, "We can go back to my place and hang out there if you want — just, you know how it is, right?"

I nod solemnly, but I guess part of me thinks he'll back me up against the kitchen counter and kiss me until my lips are numb anyway because I'm surprised when it doesn't happen. Instead we sit on the couch and flip channels. Gage is different from other guys I've known in lots of ways but he's exactly the same when it comes to the remote.

He says it's because there's nothing good on and hands the remote over before heading off to the bathroom. There's an open DVD case on top of the TV stand and I amble over to check out what it is. Someone has printed "AC-JAN" on the DVD in black marker. Akayla Cochrane? Curious, I slide the DVD into the player and it immediately starts playing.

Akayla's standing in her bedroom, her hair in twin braids, grinning toothily at the camera. Her room, which I've never seen in real life, is decorated with perfect painted likenesses of Babar characters — Babar, Celeste, Zephir, Pom. I'm surprised I remember their names, and now that I've seen their images on screen I know I won't be able to resist taking a real life peek at the bits of the room I can't see on the DVD.

"I don't know what to sing," Akayla squeals, hopping up and down. "You sing with me, Dad! You start."

Gage laughs from behind the camcorder. "I'm the cameraman," he says. "You do the singing. You're better than I am."

"But you sing with me," Akayla insists, and that's all it takes to get Gage (invisible behind the camera) to sing a duet of "Nobody Likes Me (Guess I'll Go Eat Worms)" with his daughter. Akayla does an uncoordinated little dance as she sings, stretching her arms out to suggest the girth of the big fat ones and later dangling tiny invisible ones into her mouth and chomping down on them.

By the end of the song she's collapsed, face down, into giggles on her bed and Gage is laughing louder and saying, "That's a gross song. Who wants to eat worms? You don't even like to look at them. Sing something nice."

"Like what?" Akayla looks up at the camera. "I know!" She begins singing "On Top of Spaghetti" substituting the word *poopses* for *meatball.* I start to giggle at the ridiculousness of it myself, and by the time Gage joins me in the family room again I have tears streaming down my face from watching Akayla sing her icky but hilarious poopses song. It's not so much what she's saying that's funny, but how much it's cracking her up.

Gage shakes his head as he sits down next to me, the trace of a smile on his lips. "She's obsessed with everything related to poo," he comments. He doesn't seem to mind that I've stuck in the DVD and adds, "The next part is actually good. Here ..." He swipes the remote from the coffee table and fast forwards a bit.

"This time something sweet, okay?" off-screen Gage suggests from the TV. "What's the sweetest thing you can sing?" He answers his own question. "Okay, I got something. I'll get you started again."

Oh, I know this one too. He's started into "Sing," which is one of those songs you grow up feeling like you've known all your life. He's right; it probably is the sweetest thing *anyone* can sing, and when Akayla joins in she does a good job, like she's taking this one seriously. She sways gently on her heels, tilting her head as her big brown eyes stare earnestly into the camera.

The two of them sound so adorable together that I want to throw my arms around Gage and crush him in an everlasting hug. He stops the DVD just after he and Akayla deliver the last line. "She's really cute," I say, restraining myself admirably, "even when she's singing about poop."

"Believe it or not, that does get old," Gage says, making a face. "But yeah, she's cute."

"I guess she must get that from Christabelle," I tease.

"She must," Gage agrees, but his eyes are sparkling. "How come I'm getting the feeling the next two months are going to be the longest on record?"

CHAPTER TWENTY-ONE

GAGE DID KISS ME good night but it was short ... and different, like he was making it clear there was no chance it would get out of hand. He let me look at Akayla's room too. Her ceiling's painted with puffy white clouds against a blue sky backdrop, and the walls, like I described before, are filled with Babar characters and a landscape of mountains and trees. Gage told me Akayla's uncle, Damien, did it for her and that he's in his second year of art school.

Later I dream about that blue sky, but the second I wake up the rest of the dream is swept away, only that single image remaining. This is the day that I'm going to tell my friends about Gage; somehow I know it when I open my eyes, a corner of my mind still meditating on calm blue skies.

No excuses. Today I'm not coming home with my secret.

The first person I see at school in the morning is Aya, and I want to troop over to her and start blabbing my secret history of the past thirty days, just to get the initial telling over and done with. But she's not alone. Aya and Joyeux Maduka are strolling down the hall together, looking like shiny happy people, and I wave at them as I pass, not wanting to interrupt. Izzy's in my first period history class, but telling her before Genevieve or Nicole doesn't seem right so it's lunch before I get anywhere near the subject.

I hang out by the cafeteria door and nab Genevieve when she approaches. "I have to talk to you," I yelp. "Have you seen Nicole?"

"No." Genevieve squints as me. "Are you okay?"

"I'm good. I just want to talk to you two — alone."

"Sounds serious," Genevieve comments, flicking her hair back behind her ears as her eyes try to pin me down. "What's going on?"

"Let's wait for Nicole. I just want to do this once."

We don't have to wait long for Nicole, whose deep frown doesn't disappear at the sight of us lounging around outside the cafeteria. "What?" she asks in a wary voice. "Why are you guys looking at me like that?"

Genevieve shrugs and glances at me. "Serena has something she wants to talk about."

"Can we go to your car?" I squeak, focusing on Genevieve.

The three of us zoom towards her Honda, Genevieve and Nicole eyeing me carefully, like they expect me to burst into tears. We climb into the back seat together, because it seems like the easiest configuration for conversation. Then Nicole, her frown replaced by an expression of concern, says, "Is it Devin? Did you hear something?"

"It's not Devin." My lips feel like they're cracking. If my friends weren't staring at me with such high-definition intensity I'd ask whether either of them had lip gloss. "And it's not something bad."

Genevieve and Nicole swap confused looks.

"I met a guy," I confess. "At the store. And I know we had this thing about not seeing anyone because most of the guys we know happen to be dicks but he's not like that." I can't seem to stop talking. "At all. He's really nice. And he's not even interested in having sex. In fact, he *won't*. And we're at a point now where he'll barely even touch me so —"

"Back up," Genevieve commands. "What do you mean you're *at a point now*? How long have you been seeing this guy?" Her blue eyes are a frosty match for her tone, and Nicole, on Genevieve's other side, is staring at me with her mouth open.

"Not that long."

"*How* long?" Nicole asks, clenching her lips shut as soon as she gets the words out.

"About a month, I guess."

Genevieve slides her right hand under her chin and says, "So that means you were single after Jacob for an entire two months."

I fold my hands tightly over my abdomen. "I knew you'd say I told you so. Why do you think it took me a month to mention it?"

"It's a bit hard to avoid saying I told you so when you turn around and act like a cliché," Genevieve retorts.

"Wait!" Nicole exclaims. "That guy in the car! Orlando was telling the truth and you let me stand there and go off on him for no reason. You let us stick up for you, acting all self-righteous when you knew all along he was telling the truth."

"He wasn't telling the truth," I protest. "We were in Gage's car but nothing happened. Seriously. Orlando could've spotted us together but he didn't see anything else."

"That's kind of beside the point anyway," Genevieve says to Nicole. "Even if she did blow him in the car it doesn't give Orlando the right to make her sound like a slut. You, of all people, should know that."

Nicole's eyes blaze. "Me of all people? Who put you on your pedestal? God, Genevieve, you really think you're miles above us all, don't you?" This isn't the kind of thing Nicole would normally say to Genevieve but she's clearly pissed.

Genevieve tosses her hair back and levels a *don't bother screwing with me* look at Nicole. Then she slings her gaze back to me and says, "Did you just say Gage? Gage *who*?"

"Gage Cochrane," I reply, my fingers cold and my stomach sinking. "He used to go to school here. He graduated a few years ago."

"I was afraid you were going to say that." Genevieve blinks steadily at me. "Do you know he has a kid?"

"I know." My stomach gurgles.

Genevieve's face crumbles like I'm beyond hope. "You *know*? You know the *oh so amazing perfect gentleman* you've been talking about has a kid with someone else and you don't see that as some kind of issue?"

"I never said he was perfect. But you don't know him — he's a really nice guy."

"I know *you*, and after Jacob I would've thought you'd know better than to hook up with someone that's only going to dump a whole other set of problems on you." Genevieve shakes her head. "A *nice* guy who barely sees his kid for years — uh, I don't think so, Serena. Sorry, but it doesn't sound like you have a clue what you're talking about."

"You don't know him," I repeat, but now I'm not so sure. Genevieve and Gage would've had a year's overlap in school and obviously she's heard certain things. Bad things.

"I don't care about him," Genevieve says. "You're the one I'm worried about."

Nicole wriggles abruptly in her seat, her forehead flushed. "I've heard enough. I'm getting out of the car."

"Nic?" I swing the door open and follow her. "Don't be mad. I wanted to tell you earlier. I just ... we've been so ..."

"*We* haven't been anything," Nicole says. "You've been off doing your own thing, which is ... *whatever* ... you still could've said something."

Genevieve catches up with Nicole and the two of them stalk off across the parking lot leaving me in the distance feeling lost and alone. Eventually I end up back inside the cafeteria where Nicole and Genevieve are sitting with Izzy and Marguerite, giving me heated looks.

I scan the room for somewhere else to sit, knowing that I won't be able to eat a bite. Aya waves at me from a table near the middle of the cafeteria, tossing me a life preserver, but I'm not emotionally prepared to spill my story all over again. I bolt into the hall and head for the only truly quiet spot I can think of.

A clump of people are sitting near the library sign-out desk and I hurtle past them, grab a horror paperback, and plunk myself into a chair near a window. I knew telling Genevieve and Nicole the truth would be hard. I guess I even knew it could be *this* hard, but then I think about what Genevieve said about Gage barely seeing his daughter for years, and I have to wonder, once again, if I really know a damn thing.

After school I curl up in the high-backed office chair in Mom's den and stare at her army of Swarovski figurines. Maybe if I'm still sitting here when she gets home she'll ask what's wrong and I'll actually tell her. I cradle a crystal Dalmatian puppy in my palm and try to imagine how possessing it, or hundreds like it, could fill the hole inside me.

Some days the hole seems bigger than others. I used to think that if Devin came back it would seal up instantly, but now I think it was there before he left. I miss him, but he didn't create the emptiness inside me. Maybe he just recognized it better than other people did.

I get restless waiting for Mom and slip my cell out of my knapsack to check for messages. Nobody's called, and for the second time in less than a week I dial Jimmy on impulse. "Hey you!" he says brightly. "You know, I was just thinking we should have you over for dinner soon. What's your favourite food?"

"Italian stuff I shouldn't really be eating," I tell him.

"You can indulge for one night. I'm not going to be pushy and suggest you bring Gage but how's that going?"

I bite my nails and repeat my earlier conversation with Genevieve and Nicole, complete with Genevieve's comment about Gage hardly seeing his daughter for years.

"Oh dear!" Jimmy says. "They're incensed you didn't share with them earlier."

"Just a little." What would I do without sarcasm?

"But about his daughter," Jimmy begins. I hear another voice in the background, and then Jimmy says, "Morgan just came in. Have you told him any of this yet?"

"It's like I said before, we just don't talk like that, Jimmy. He knows I'm seeing someone, but I haven't shared the details."

That's the moment when my mother strides into the den and stares down her nose at me. I'm holding my cell in one hand and her precious crystal Dalmatian in the other and I glance at her displeased expression, pull the phone away from my ear, and tell her I'll get out of her way. "Here," I say, pressing the Dalmatian into her hand.

I feel like crying as I walk away, which is how I've been feeling on and off for the past few hours only I've made up my mind that I won't let myself break over a difference in opinion. If my friends are my friends they'll get over their anger, and if they don't, they never really were. And if Gage isn't the person I think he is all the hoping and wishing on my part won't change him. Maybe being a better version of myself means caring less about all of them and how they see me.

"You'll come over, though?" Jimmy asks. "If I suggest having you over for dinner to Morgan?"

"I'll come," I promise, taking the stairs to my room two at a time. "But please don't do Italian food unless it's chicken breasts or salad, okay? I'll only eat too much and then be mad at myself later. And don't tell Morgan anything about Gage."

"I won't breathe a word! And we'll be good and have low-fat everything if that's what you want."

Apparently that's what I want. Maybe I should be okay with being fat again too, should that happen, but I'd really rather not. I'm not sure whether the hole inside me is a result of being chubby for years and feeling people judge me for it or vice versa. When you spend so long inside a situation the facts surrounding it blur and swirl so that all you can see is haze.

I tell Jimmy goodbye, and when I turn around my mother's standing in the hallway in a long burgundy cardigan she bought on sale last winter. "Are you all right?" she asks, studying my face. Mom's already put on her cozy slippers and I stare down at her feet and nod. Aside from her ever-expanding crystal collection she hasn't bought anything new for herself since June. Doctor Berkovich should advise her to go shopping.

"You're not still angry with me, are you?" she ventures. I spy the apprehension in her eyes, and I can't remember the last time I gave my mother a hug for no special reason. Surprising myself, I step into the hall and wrap my arms around her back.

She sensed I was upset and followed me out of her den today. That's occasion enough.

CHAPTER TWENTY-TWO

IZZY SIDLES UP TO me as I leave history class the next day and asks when I was planning to tell her the news. She says she knows we're not as close as before I started hanging out with Nicole and Genevieve but she thought we were still friends.

Of course we're still friends. At least, I hope so.

I spend most of the day wishing I'd kept my relationship with Gage under wraps. Marguerite ignores the topic entirely but acts like she's semi-pissed with me anyway. When I try to talk to Genevieve about it she tells me she doesn't think there's any point because the subject will just make us fight, which is true but doesn't make me feel better because the strain between us is just as strong as it was yesterday. Nicole's communication with me is as minimal as possible, and even Mr. Cushman, who couldn't care less who I'm dating, is extra mean to me, complaining that I'm obviously a million miles away and that he's tired of seeing the "keen disinterest" in my face day after day.

"What did I just say?" he demands. "Would you care to prove me wrong and quote what I said to your classmates while you were zoning out moments ago?"

"Sir, we weren't listening either," Jon Wheatley quips.

Most of the class laughs, but the most I can manage is a smile, which I direct at Jon Wheatley as a kind of thank you.

By the end of last period I'm so drained that I could curl up at the foot of my locker and take a nap, either that or devour a six-slice Bacon Chicken Mushroom Melt pizza solo.

Aya's leaning against my locker when I get there, which means the napping idea is out. "Hola," she says with a smile.

"Hi." I haven't had the Gage discussion with Aya yet, and I wish we could skip it entirely.

"I just thought you should know that Joyeux and I are going out this Saturday," she says. "So you're not the only one who hasn't re-formed herself."

"You and Joyeux? Are you serious?" I flash a smile back at her. "What are you going to do about the height differential?" I knew something was up when I saw them together yesterday. They looked abnormally happy in each other's company.

"What can I say, I like tall guys."

"You and Joyeux," I repeat. "That's good news. You see?" I bump her arm. "You're not bitter."

"I think I still am a bit," she confesses. "Just not with Joyeux. And you" — she raises one eyebrow — "you can really keep a secret, can't you?"

"It looks that way. Did you hear about Gage's daughter and everything too?"

"From Nicole," Aya tells me. "She wasn't badmouthing you or anything, just filling me in."

"Hey!" someone booms from behind me. I know the voice too well to be pleased to hear it address me. Aya's eyes sharpen as she casts a cutting stare behind me.

Jacob leans his shoulder against the locker next to mine and lowers his voice. "With all the shit I'm hearing about you lately, I don't know where your head is at. But I didn't think you were the type who liked to share, so maybe you want to talk to your boyfriend about his habit of hooking up with his ex." Jacob smirks, pushes his weight off the locker, and struts away from us.

"I'm sure that's complete B.S.," Aya tells me. "Jacob's been mad at you ever since you dumped him. He probably doesn't even know Gage."

"I know. I just wish everyone would stay out of my business." I realize how that could be misconstrued and backpedal. "I don't mean you. I mean people who want to tell me what to do."

"Like me with my cousin the other day," Aya says wryly. "Sometimes people are just concerned. Not Jacob, obviously!"

"Obviously," I repeat. I'd never take Jacob's word for anything, and I hate to admit it, but doubt is lining the bottom of my stomach. How do I know Gage hasn't hooked up with his ex recently? He sees Christabelle all the time. Her brother is his very best friend. But would they still be best friends if Gage hadn't seen his daughter for years? That doesn't seem likely. At least *some* of what I'm hearing has to be a lie.

Work's the best cure for my racing head. The weekend shifts can get pretty crazy, and on Saturday Ki jokes that they should provide us with free adult diapers so we can skip bathroom breaks. "And hook us up to an IV," I suggest. "That way they can eliminate the concept of breaks altogether."

Mr. Lapatas shows up in my line in mid-afternoon and buys paper towels, mouthwash, and echinacea. "I didn't know you worked here," he says, smiling like he's glad to see me. He's got what has to be at least day-old beard growth on his chin, and it looks good on him.

"Since before Christmas," I tell him, holding up his echinacea. "Are you getting a cold?"

"It feels that way, but I'm not giving in without a fight." As he grabs his bags he adds, "I'll let Nicole know I ran into you."

"Tell her I say hi." I could call her anytime myself — I don't think she'd hang up on me or anything extreme — but I don't want to have to fight my way through her disappointment in me.

My Total Drug Mart shift's over at eight, so it's still early when Dad picks me up. Gage and I aren't seeing each other until tomorrow, and I haven't made any other plans. I lie on the couch and watch *Mamma Mia* on MuchMusic. In the movie nobody really cares that Meryl Streep slept with three different guys within the space of a few weeks and therefore doesn't know who the father of her daughter is. Everybody dances and sings while looking blond, gorgeous, and like they know with absolute certainty that everything will turn out okay in the end. If Nicole were watching with me she'd make me get up and dance too.

Even without her, *Mamma Mia* puts me in a good mood and I'm sure I sound happy when I answer my ringing phone. "You must be watching Much," Morgan comments. "I can hear ABBA in the background." I guess my brother knows the MuchMusic schedule by heart.

"They're not bad," I tell him.

"Of course they're not bad, Serena. They're ABBA." Morgan chuckles at my adolescent ignorance. He probably figured out ABBA were good just after he stopped wetting the bed. "Listen, Jimmy was suggesting we have you over for dinner, but I was wondering if we should try to rope Mom and Dad into coming along too. You know, get them out of the house for a change. Hit a restaurant in Yorkville or something."

"Sure, if you think you can convince them to go."

"I'll give it my best shot. Unless you'd rather keep them out of it. How're you getting along with them these days?" Morgan and I had a similar conversation about ten days ago, during which I explained that my parents and I were back on an even keel, but now my assurances are followed by a more challenging question. "And what about that guy — you still hanging out too?"

I tighten my grip on my cell. "That's kind of a nosy thing to ask, don't you think?"

"I'm just making conversation, Serena. Sometimes I get the feeling you don't want to talk to me."

Poor baby. Excuse me if I don't idolize Morgan the way everyone else seems to and make things feel like work for him from time to time.

"You're touchy today," I tell him, my voice brightening so he'll sound like the one with the problem instead of me. "If you really want to know, I *am* still seeing him. I even met his daughter the other day." I've decided to go with the casual approach, as in *doesn't everyone have a kid with their ex these days?*

"His daughter?" Morgan repeats. "How old is this guy?"

"Nineteen."

"Okay," Morgan says after a moment. "Is that weird? I mean, for you?"

"I haven't really seen her much." My palms have broken out in a sweat. "She's not with him all the time." Time to bail out with a little white lie before the questions can get any tougher. "Anyway, Morgan, I should get off the phone. My friends are on their way over to pick me up. Let me know what's going on with the dinner plans."

"Yeah ... will do," Morgan says, like he's still trying to catch up with the conversation.

I hang up and evaluate Morgan's reaction. It was light years better than Genevieve's and Nicole's, but still, why does everyone have to get weird about Gage being a father? It's not like he's setting me up to be Akayla's stepmom or something. We're only hanging out with each other a couple of times a week max, and no one but Jimmy knows how I really feel about him.

I'm not altogether sure I know how I feel myself. Everything's so confusing that part of me wants to stop thinking about him period. That same part wants to call Genevieve and Nicole to come pick me up like the past few days never happened.

Then there's another part that makes me drag Gage into the house to meet my parents when he rings the doorbell on Sunday afternoon. Up until now I've made sure I was the one to answer the door every time, and if I subtract sex (which we pretty much ruled out after the first date) so far it seems as if most of the angst has been on my side. I haven't even told Gage what my friends have been saying about him because I haven't worked out a way to soften the negativity.

On the upside, Gage is good with my parents. He shakes my father's hand and says that it's really icy on the road today. Mom says that she hates the way winter gets into your bones, and Gage agrees that it's awful and says he thinks the entire country must have a mild form of seasonal affective disorder. Dad wants to know if Gage has snow tires, and they start discussing things like treads and stopping distances. That could go on forever, and after a few minutes I'm forced to interrupt and say we should get going.

We're only heading over to the mall, but I don't want to thoroughly turn Gage off with overexposure to my parents. I'm pretty quiet in the car, but when we're crossing the parking lot Gage starts talking about how hungry he is because he overslept and skipped breakfast. Seems like he was at Denny's half the night with Damien and some other guys, eating burgers and steaks after a late-night hockey game.

"I didn't know you still played hockey," I say. I thought he was all about soccer these days.

"Pick-up hockey. Yeah, sometimes."

I can't stop going over more important questions in my mind, and I suck in my cheeks and look away. "Are you okay?" Gage asks.

"I'm fine." I toss my hair back, faking confidence. "I'm just having stupid issues at school, people saying stuff about us."

"About us?" Gage echoes. "Is that asshole spreading rumours again?"

"Not him." By this time we're inside the mall, wandering past Tim Hortons. "My ex and my friends." Why did I drag Jacob into this? Damn. "My friends are just concerned, with you having a history."

"A history?" Gage stops walking. His eyebrows leap towards each other, his arms knotting in front of his chest. "What exactly do you mean? What are people saying?"

I've stopped too. I turn to face him. "My ex, who you know is a complete prick, said you still hook up with Christabelle, and one of my friends said you barely saw your daughter for years." I feel my face drop, weighed down by tension and a gnawing sadness I haven't been able to shake since I sat in the back of Genevieve's car with her and Nicole. "My friends were pissed off that I didn't tell them about you earlier too — well, most of them were. So now things are weird between us."

Confusion whips across Gage's face. He glances down at my feet in silence.

"And I'm confused," I admit. "Because I don't want to believe those things and I know they're just repeating stuff they've heard. But where did it all come from?"

Gage's eyes zoom up to meet mine, his arms springing apart to hang awkwardly at his sides. "So what if it's true?" His pupils are solemn, and I watch him fill with a tiredness that spreads from the inside out.

"It can't be," I mumble. Hearing it from his own mouth, I still can't quite believe it. He wouldn't do this to me.

"Not exactly in the way that it sounds, maybe," Gage says, "but I wasn't around for Akayla as much as I should've been until last spring. For a long time I just couldn't deal with it. And then when I could, Christabelle's folks were still mad at me and didn't trust me. I don't blame them either. It's not something I'm proud of or like to think about. It took a while to convince them I really wanted in on all the child care stuff."

Gage's hands lose themselves in his pockets. "I don't see what any of that has to do with you, though. Unless it's just blown your image of me." He searches my eyes for confirmation, and when I don't say anything he adds, "Christabelle and I aren't together like that. We haven't been in years."

"How many years?" I ask in a thick voice.

"Two," he says with a sigh. "I can't believe the way high school has come back to haunt me." He shakes his head, his cheeks reddening. "It was only for a couple of weeks, years after we'd broken up. But when Christabelle saw I still wasn't ready to be a father, she stopped things. And it was for the best. She's great, but we weren't right for each other. We were only kids when we were first together; we hardly knew who we were ourselves. Everything's changed since then, including me. Christabelle isn't something you need to worry about — we're over with for good."

Gage turns and begins walking again. "So much for not getting serious," he says over his shoulder. "Now you know my whole life story."

I haven't moved from my space just beyond Tim Hortons, and Gage twists to look at me. "You're upset."

"You're the one who seems upset. You can't blame me for wondering about this stuff."

"I don't," he says sheepishly. "I just don't want you thinking bad things about me, even if some of them are true. I wish I'd had the chance to tell you all of this in my own time. To build up to it in a way that would make it sound less shitty, if that's possible." He takes two steps towards me, flinching as he stops. "All of that is in the past. This is *now*, right? Us." He holds out his hand to me.

I meet him halfway and take it, relieved to know the truth even if he didn't want me to hear it yet. There's nothing he's told me that I can't handle. We stroll towards the food court, Gage bending to kiss my hair as we pass the dollar store. I release his hand and snake my arm possessively around his waist. It's lean and hard, unlike mine, and I really have no idea how I'm going to get through the next two months on this starvation diet of abbreviated kisses.

I like Gage too much to try to tempt him, but as we walk in the direction of food I can truthfully say that I'm more than ready to be sixteen.

CHAPTER TWENTY-THREE

GAGE DOESN'T UNDERSTAND WHY it took so long for me to tell my friends about him. My explanation — in our noisy corner of the food court where three young boys are running around a nearby table and trying to tackle each other — makes him take a long gulp of his soft drink and worriedly say, "I hope they haven't already made up their minds not to like me."

My friends' reservations about him are partly my fault, and I want to fix that. I tell Gage I think he should meet them so that they can all give each other a chance. He swigs more of his drink before agreeing and suggesting that I invite them to a party his friend Elliott's having next Friday.

Now I'm nervous about meeting *his* friends and even more nervous that Genevieve and Nicole will tell me they don't want to go. I'm not going to break up with Gage because they don't like the idea of him without having even met the real person, but I don't intend to be one of those girls who ditches her friends for a guy either. As much as I care about Gage, I know we could combust in a hundred different ways and where would that leave me?

Genevieve's not around for lunch on Monday so I wait until the three of us are trekking across the parking lot after school to start recapping what Gage told me about Akayla and Christabelle. I know it's none of their business, but it's not fair that people are talking behind his back. This one time only, I'll set things straight for him.

Genevieve and Nicole climb into the front seat, their bodies swivelled towards me in the back. None of what I reveal changes Genevieve's face. Her Gwyneth Paltrow/Nicole Kidman composure makes me frown. "I think the three of you should meet," I continue. "He wants you to come to his friend Elliott's party on Friday."

Nicole's lips curl in what I assume is irritation. "He thinks we don't like him now," she says. "Do you know how awkward that will be?"

"You don't have to stay if you don't want. Just drop by and say hi to him."

Genevieve looks skyward, or at least it would be skyward if we weren't sitting in her car. "I'm glad you talked to him and found out his version of things. But please don't tell me he's going to become some kind of appendage now and we'll have to go out with him all the time."

"I never said that," I snap. "I get that you're mad at me, but going out with Gage doesn't automatically change everything else about me."

Genevieve smoothes her lips together. "I thought you wanted to figure out how to be your own person."

"So if I want to hang out with someone but *don't* because you don't want me to, how does that make me my own person?" I ask, my ears burning. "I'm not saying everything I do is perfect and that I have no issues, but God, we're talking about someone I see maybe twice a week. It's not like I've packed up my stuff and am moving in with him."

"I'm not trying to be harsh, Serena." Genevieve bends her head, volumes of red hair spilling forward. "Honestly, I guess I feel like I don't know you as well I thought. You were so adamant about being on your own before. It seemed like a core thing about you." Genevieve's thin fingers part her hair. She stares at me as she says, "And in a way this is about me too. I'm friends with *you* because I want to be, and maybe it sounds selfish that I don't want to automatically include another person into our friendship. I've done that before, with other friends' boyfriends, and it didn't work very well.

"But anyway," she continues, "of course I'll meet him if you want me too. Although, I think, like Nicole says" — she points to Nicole next to her — "that he's not going to be really happy with us after what he must have heard. Not that I blame him either."

Nicole's gaze rockets over to Genevieve. "So you're going to the party?"

Genevieve nods slowly. "It sounds like we should."

Nicole groans to herself. "If any of the guys there have seen Liam's video I'll be a magnet for losers." No one at Laurier even talks about her video anymore. It's old news, and together the three of us have had it out with anyone interested in hassling her. But we won't know any of the guys at Elliott's party, so she might be right. It could be like starting from square one again.

"I'm sure no one will recognize you anyway," Genevieve says. "But we can do your hair and makeup differently if you want. And like Serena says, we don't have to stay long." Genevieve glances at me for confirmation.

"Only as long as you want. I just want you to meet him, at least, so we stop feeling like some deep dark secret."

"Hey, what about your parents?" Nicole says suddenly. "Do they know?"

"They've met him, but they don't know about Akayla. I can't figure out how to get the news out there without it being this huge thing." I rub my chin, which is stone cold because Genevieve hasn't started the car yet.

"They met him?" she repeats, and in an instant I feel like we've leapt from Nicole being angry with me for going out with Gage in the first place to being irritated that she didn't have the opportunity to look him over before my parents did. "Do you think they liked him?"

"From what I could tell, yeah. But it was only once. They talked about the weather."

"And his daughter's name is Akayla?" Nicole adds. "That's really pretty."

Finally Genevieve starts the car, remarking that her tits are freezing. More often than not Genevieve sounds like someone who read and understood *The Communist Manifesto*, so whenever she comes out with something remotely raunchy about herself it makes Nicole and I smile, which we do in the front and back seat respectively as Genevieve backs out of her parking spot and heads for Nicole's house.

My party curfew is still one o'clock, and Genevieve and Nicole have promised to swing by and pick me up, but my parents know that Gage will be the one dropping me home in a taxi later. Thankfully the warning look that used to be in Dad's eyes before I left with Gage has dimmed recently.

Over takeout chicken beforehand my mom reminds me that we're having dinner with Morgan and Jimmy downtown tomorrow. Mom's eyes glaze with anxiety at the thought. My life has changed a lot since Devin left, but Mom's is still on pause. She'd rather spend tomorrow night in the den, just like any other night. The conversation during the rest of the meal is minimal, and I wish there wouldn't be so much quiet between me and my parents. Even when we do talk it feels like we're not really saying anything.

There's plenty of time for me to help with the dishes before my friends show up. Then I pour myself into a pair of newly purchased jeans with a bronze metallic sheen on them and a blue sequin halter top. I paint my toes a shimmering grey-blue to match the top and, once they're dry, slip my feet into silver heels. There were plenty of other outfits I considered wearing tonight but ruled out as too casual, too slutty, or too glamorous for the occasion.

When Genevieve and Nicole roll up Genevieve makes me feel like I'm overdressed anyway. She's wearing a big navy hoodie and tan cargo pants, which she looks fantastic in because Genevieve looks gorgeous in everything. Nicole, on the other hand, has three different shades of blue Manic Panic in her hair, purple lips and is wearing a skull and crossbones T-shirt, studded bracelet, and a loose black skirt that would drag along the floor if it was half an inch longer.

"I thought I might as well have fun with it," Nicole says as my eyes take her in. "You look good."

"And you look like a whole different person!"

"Yep. I'm going to stand in the corner all night and snarl at people." She winks at me. "Except Gage. Don't worry, I'll be nice to him."

"Me too," Genevieve chirps. "Best behaviour."

Gage warned me that Elliott's family is rich, so the three of us are fully expecting the regal-looking gate with empty planters topping either side that greets us at Elliott's address. I recite my name into the intercom and say Gage Cochrane invited us. Bingo. The gate swings open. We drive through and park the car with the thirty or so others strewn along the winding driveway. Elliott's house is a bona fide mansion. If I saw a picture of it I'd have guessed it was a Mediterranean hotel. Two teenage guys walking about twenty feet ahead of us stroll through the middle of three arches and open the front door. We follow them inside and through a long hallway decorated with boring but picturesque pastoral paintings. At the end of the corridor there's a single door, which the guys push open to reveal a screening room that's roughly the same size as the second smallest cinema in our local multiplex. Gage told me that Elliott's screening the *Godfather* movies but that there'll be other places to hang out if we're not interested.

I passed the information to Genevieve and Nicole too, but I guess they were imagining more of a home theatre vibe because they both aim incredulous looks at me. Some of the standard theatre seats are already filled, and I catch sight of Gage in the third row with his legs stretched out over the chair in the row in front of him just as Nicole points at the back of cinema. "This guy's even got vending machines," she says. "What did you say his father does?"

"Mafia godfather," Genevieve jokes. "Isn't it obvious?"

Gage is on his feet, weaving his way through pockets of people. Seconds later he edges in behind me and squeezes my elbow. "Hey. I hope you guys didn't have any trouble finding the place."

Nicole, not realizing Gage was about to make an appearance, has wandered off to examine one of the snack machines.

"It's practically the only house on the block," Genevieve says with a smile. "Serena said your friend was rich, but I guess we didn't realize quite what that meant." We glance over at Nicole, who is pushing buttons repeatedly, letting the vending machine supply her with free chocolate bars.

"This is Genevieve," I say to Gage as I lean into him. Part of me still feels like I shouldn't snuggle up to him in front of her but I'm happy to see him and refuse to listen.

Gage returns Genevieve's smile and asks if she's ever seen *The Godfather*. "If you don't want to watch there's a pool room too, and they have a place set up for gaming and another one for dancing."

"Don't tell Nicole that," Genevieve says. "We'll never get her out of that room."

"Don't tell me what?" Nicole asks, but it's Gage she's looking at. "You must be Gage. I'm Nicole."

"Good to meet you," Gage says. "Do you guys want any food? There's some stuff set up in the kitchen and I can introduce you around."

Gage leads us to the kitchen, where we grab beers (except Genevieve who, as the driver, takes a Sprite) and pick through the hot and cold buffets. I take some strawberries, smoked salmon, and two mini quiches while Genevieve and Nicole weigh down their plates, which are white with blue trim and not made of paper the way they normally are at parties. I listen to the three of them make small talk, Genevieve and Nicole going out of their way to catch every word Gage says. I never realized that we had some of the same teachers at Laurier. I also never realized that Genevieve knows a fair amount about soccer and is kind of a Toronto FC fan herself.

Afterwards Gage shows us the pool room, which Genevieve is disappointed to find doesn't feature a swimming pool but a pool table, and then the gaming area. The family room's supposed to be for dancing but at the moment there are five people sitting around and talking over the din of the music, white and blue plates spread across their laps. Icona Pop are singing "I Love It," and I look at Nicole, who is bouncing on her heels, dying to throw the rest of her body into the song.

"Okay," Genevieve says, "let's do it. But I want to catch the movie later."

The three of us dance while Gage smiles but refuses to join in. He sits there watching us while nursing his beer and chatting to a couple of the other guys lounging around. When another girl gets up to join us, during the third song or so, he wanders over and says he'll catch up with us later. Eventually we all end up back in the screening room, where the movie's already started. During the intermission between *The Godfather* and *Part II* Gage introduces us to Elliott (whom I already met that time at Starbucks), Damien, and a few other people.

Damien towers over me at what must be about six-four. I talk to him about art and mention a bit about Jimmy's gallery show downtown. When I look at Damien I can't help but wonder how much he looks like Christabelle. Is she super tall too? Damien says he wants to get into the Toronto Outdoor Art Exhibition this summer so he can get exposure and hopefully sell some stuff. I'd like to see his artwork, but it feels too soon to suggest that, so I just tell him that would be cool.

After a few minutes Nicole and Genevieve sidle over to me and say Nicole wants to dance for a while and then they'll probably take off, unless I need them to stay. I give them the okay to go and thank them for coming. As it is, I have to be home in less than an hour myself.

I zip over to Gage and whisper in his ear that it might be easier if I just left with my friends. Then he won't have to miss any of the party. "Stay," Gage says, his palm resting on my back. "I'll make sure you're home on time."

We find a quiet corner to hang out in at a room near the back of the house which is part dark wood library and part old toy resting place. Board games like Mouse Trap, Gumball Rally, Pictionary Junior, and The Incredible Hulk Smash Game line the shelves along with hardcover copies of Charles Dickens and Jane Austen novels and random science and arts and craft sets.

We slump down on the maroon leather couch together, and Gage says, "Did I tell you how great you look tonight?"

I smile and clasp his knee. He looks like his regular self, which is more gorgeous than I'll ever be. "So, I'm glad you got to meet Genevieve and Nicole."

"They weren't what I was expecting," he admits.

"How?"

"I guess I thought they'd be more like you. The three of you seem so different." He grins. "I wouldn't have expected Nicole to be into hip hop and pop either, judging by how she was dressed, which I guess shows you why that's a bad idea — thinking you know something about someone because of what they look like."

"She doesn't always dress like that either."

"Chameleon, huh?"

"Sort of." I bend to slip my shoes off. Then I swing my feet across Gage's thighs and stretch out along the couch. "Don't let me fall asleep," I tell him.

"I won't." Gage grabs one of my ankles. His other hand fits over my toes and begins to rub. He works his way down my foot, massaging the length of it, the instep, and then my individual toes. Now he has both hands at it, one of them working my heel and the other sliding slowly up into my pant leg, sensually stroking my calf.

This is something that's okay to do to someone who's almost sixteen, I guess, and I dig my toes into his thigh and complain that he's evil.

"How is this evil?" he asks with a devilish grin. "You don't like massages?"

"It's not really fair though, is it?" I say with a flirty look. "I can't do anything back." Panic streaks across Gage's face. Just for a second, but I see it anyway. "I don't mean *that*. I mean, you know, like a back massage or something." Ever since the revelation about my age I've been doubly aware of the boundaries Gage wants to keep in place, which means keeping my hands to myself even more so than I would've a few weeks ago.

"No, I know," Gage says, his jaw relaxing.

He really has to chill a little. We both know we're not working our way up to full-blown sex. Not now and not in two months. I want to ask him to trust me, but that's not how trust works. You can't ask for trust and expect to receive it, like a cheque in the mail or something. It needs to evolve over time.

"Can I tell you something?" I ask, shivering a little as I sit up.

"Sure." Gage has begun to look vaguely nervous again.

"It's just that I guess I'm kind of relieved that you're not in a hurry to have sex." I feel a blush work its way out from my nose all the way to the tips of my ears. "Because I don't think I'm totally ready for it anyway, even though I really like you." I'm not sure any of that came

THE SWEETEST THING YOU CAN SING

out right. I'm riding the charge of emotion I got from watching him tense up, speaking before I can think.

It's not that I haven't imagined us doing it — I think about that multiple times a day — but there's a gap between thinking about something and actually doing it. When it comes right down to it, I think I want to hang out in that gap with him awhile, just having some fun with each other in ways that won't make either of us too nervous.

Gage's stare is infinitely quiet. "I really like you too," he says. "I'm glad you didn't leave with your friends. It wouldn't feel right if we never had a chance to be alone tonight."

"Yeah." That wild pulse of emotion's still there, dancing under my skin. I'm like a volcano waiting to blow, and I probably shouldn't say this next part at all but Gage does something to me that's hard to ignore. "Maybe I shouldn't think this way, but sometimes I wonder if you'd think that if you met me before."

"Before what?" Gage wants to know.

I curl the hem of my top around my fingers and tell him about the twenty-nine pounds that seemed to change everything. Guys who had never really bothered with me before smiled at me in the halls or stopped me on the way into class to say hi, even though they knew I was with Jacob. Guys I didn't know at all turned and stared, like they didn't even know they were doing it. Twenty-nine pounds ago I was only attention-worthy because of Morgan, but now something else entirely deemed me worthwhile.

I stop talking and wait for Gage — who has been watching me with an intent expression — to say something. He slides his hand around the back of my neck and gives me a long, unbroken look. "It doesn't sound like a lot," he says. "Twenty-nine pounds. I don't think it would make that much difference to me."

"Like when you came into Total and *even* thought I looked cute in the uniform?" I say cynically. "You seriously think that would've happened if I was chunky?"

Gage's eyes zoom back towards the shelves full of old books and board games. Then he raises his chin and shines all his focus decisively back on me. "Honestly, maybe not, but it wouldn't matter to me now that I know you and that's the truth."

I think I believe him.

"Are the tough questions over?" Gage asks, swivelling away from me as he pulls his crewneck clean over his head and tosses it to the ground. "Because I'm thinking I might take that back rub after all if you don't mind."

The fact is I've never seen Gage shirtless — with his shirt or sweater pushed up, yeah, but not *off*. The only chest completely exposed before this moment was mine. Now I stare at Gage's bare back, from his belted jeans all the way up his spine to the light brown locks of hair resting against his neck. I lean in to plant a quick kiss between his shoulder blades. My fingers rest on his shoulders while my thumbs move in deep, slow circles, communicating without words, dissolving any remaining doubts between us.

CHAPTER TWENTY-FOUR

❧

MY TOTAL DRUG MART shift the next morning starts at eight, which feels ridiculously early not so much because of Elliott's party (I made my curfew with six minutes to spare) but because of the time I spent in front of the TV afterwards, thinking over a lot of things as it hummed in the background. I thought about Akayla and how in the future, when the timing seems right, I'd like to go over to Gage's and hang out with them both one day. If I were him I wouldn't want my girl-friend hanging out with my daughter a lot in case she gets attached and things don't work out, but maybe every so often would be all right.

More than that, though, I thought about how relieved I was that Genevieve and Nicole were willing to meet and make an effort with Gage. And I thought about how I haven't been fair to Izzy and Marguerite, who were my friends — and good ones — before I ever got to know Genevieve and Nicole. It's weird when you get really excited about people — whether that's Genevieve, Nicole, or Gage — you just want to be around them all the time, especially when you feel like you're on the same wavelength, which is how I feel about all three of them.

Still, that's no excuse to neglect my old friends, and I plan to spend a bit more time with Izzy and Marguerite from now on, if they still want me to. I also realized, as I lay in front of the television with some semi-dirty old movie on low, that I could hardly feel that emptiness inside me anymore. Not that I thought I was cured. The hole shrinks and grows at different times, I guess. Maybe it's the same way with other people only they don't say. I think it must have been the same, only much worse, with Devin, and I wish he could've talked to me about it before his drug problem spiralled out of control.

Some of these thoughts spill over into the next day, when I'm standing at the Total Drug Mart checkout, offering early morning customers a sleepy smile. We're not usually busy early so there's time for me to think and to wander over to the cosmetics department to talk to Angela about the new plaza they're building just behind ours and what will be in it. Somehow Angela knows Gage and I are seeing each other, although I never said anything. Anyway, Angela tells me Gage is a good guy, which by now I know for a fact.

While Angela and I are chatting by the Elizabeth Arden products, a girl about my age wobbles into the store with the remains of her mascara draining down her face. Her eyes are bloodshot, she's teetering on spiky-heeled brown ankle boots, and she smells like cigarettes. If I had to guess I'd say she hasn't been home since last night. The girl notices me looking her over and glances blearily back like she's so tired that she doesn't care who sees her crying.

I have no idea what happened to her, sometimes just drinking too much is enough to make people cry, but she makes me think of myself that night in November when I left Wyatt's party and walked home alone in the dark because that seemed like a better thing to do than listening to Jacob and his friends scream at me to kiss Aya. The girl doesn't just remind me of me, though. She reminds me of Nicole's skinned leg filled with pebbles because of the lanky junior who wouldn't quit watching Liam Powers's video on his phone and of how last night, even after months, she's still worried about people recognizing her and making trouble. There's Aya too. No one would dare say a word against her while Joyeux's around, and I get the feeling he'll be around a lot, but she had it pretty bad for a while.

All of it starts to make my brain work overtime, wondering what we could do to stop all this nastiness in its tracks. Would it be crazy to try to start some school club, some anti-bullying, anti-harassment thing? It's something I should really talk to Genevieve about. She was student council treasurer last year; she knows all about how Laurier operates. We'd need a teacher as a club advisor. Maybe Genevieve would have ideas about that too. Or we could make a Facebook group. Or do both. As the stream of Total customers picks up the thought gets pushed to the back of my head, but it's definitely something to look into.

The afternoon rushes by, and before I know it my father's picking me up, chauffeuring me home so I can change out of my uniform and reapply makeup. The LeBlanc family dinner outing has been pinned down to a seven o'clock reservation at a Toronto restaurant called Hi-*Lo*. We meet in Yorkville, which is a swank part of town full of high-rise condos that no normal person could ever afford. I think I spot Rachel McAdams when we walk into Hi-*Lo*. She's talking to an Asian woman with a buzz cut who could be famous too, but I don't happen to recognize her.

The model-gorgeous hostess leads me and my parents to Morgan's table. He and Jimmy have already started a bottle of wine and they look relaxed but happy to see us. I drop myself into the chair next to Jimmy's and wish we had a moment alone so I could update him about Gage and my friends.

As usual, my dad doesn't have much to say to Jimmy. He talks politics with Morgan while Jimmy engages Mom in a conversation about her work with the museum. I peruse the menu and keep an ear on both discussions. Soon the waiter drifts over to take our orders, and while Mom's busy ordering Jimmy leans closer to me and asks how things are going. "Actually good," I tell him. "After all the earlier drama everything's pretty much worked out now."

"Terrific!" Jimmy says, his shoulder nudging mine.

I glance covertly at my family and whisper, "If you text me your email address later I can fill you in."

"Definitely!" Jimmy says. "I love happy endings." Morgan does too. He's not into crime shows or tragedies; he'd rather watch something guaranteed to keep a smile on his face.

In fact, my brother tries to work his famous Morgan LeBlanc magic as we sit awaiting our drinks and appetizers. I know precisely what Morgan's plan is — a few days ago he explained about presenting my parents with a Toronto theatre company subscription for their upcoming twenty-fifth anniversary.

Morgan reaches across the table and hands Mom a small beige envelope. "That's a little something for the both of you, from the three of us." Morgan wouldn't let me pitch in with any cash but he signed my name to the anniversary card, which he now passes to Dad. Mom, especially, used to be a big theatre fan, and up until last summer my parents would hit a production every month. Dad rips open his envelope, reads the card, and jokingly says he hopes whatever's in the other envelope doesn't set the bar too high for him. The four of us face Mom, who is peering at a sheet of paper that was folded inside her envelope.

"You can choose any ten of the twelve plays the company will be performing this year," Morgan explains.

"Yes ... I see," Mom says, sucking in her cheeks. "Thank you."

"Here." Morgan reaches down beside his chair, waves a colour brochure in the air, and passes it to my mother too. "It was too big to fit in the envelope."

Mom sets the brochure down next to the tiny envelope without opening it. She attaches her stare to the table in front of her, blinking quickly. None of us seem able to speak. All eyes are stuck on Mom, waiting for her to offer some sign we can move on from this jagged, uncomfortable moment.

Morgan's heart is in the right place, but I knew my mother would balk at the idea. Too many nights away from home hang in the balance. She's not supposed to enjoy herself anymore. I know this without her having to say it, and suddenly I also know what I didn't foresee before, that taking my parents out to dinner and springing the anniversary gift on them has increased the pain associated with the occasion. My mother had a chance to steel herself against Christmas and birthdays because she knew they were coming. She didn't guess tonight would be special, and now it's become a special night without Devin.

The second I realize that I try to fix it. "It's okay, Mom," I say. "You don't have to use them all."

A fat tear squirms its way down my mother's cheek. "It's not okay."

Dad pushes his chair swiftly away from the table and stumbles to his feet, obviously unwilling to deal with the melancholy turn our dinner plans have taken. He strides away from us without looking back. Morgan wrinkles his forehead. He frowns and squints at Dad's back receding into the distance. "*Shit*." Morgan's eyes dart to mine. "Should I go after him?"

"Go," I advise.

But left with my mother, I don't have a clue what to say to make her feel better. I suppose the only one who could make her feel any better right now is Devin.

I hate him for that.

Jimmy cocks his head to indicate the approaching waiter. "Our drinks. We could certainly use them around about now, couldn't we?"

Jimmy pats the table in front of my mother. "Do you want something a little stronger, Tessa? I was thinking of moving on to cocktails myself."

"Sounds good to me," I kid, trying to give the atmosphere a shove in the right direction.

"You go ahead," Mom tells me, and at first I think she doesn't mean it. "I don't want to spoil everyone's night." She pinches the bridge of her nose between her fingers and tilts her head forward. "Whatever you want, Serena. It's fine."

"There's plenty of night left, Tessa!" Jimmy insists. "Nothing's spoiled. Don't you worry about it." Jimmy takes the liberty of ordering two margaritas for them.

My mother glances at me and adds, "Make that three, please."

I've never had a real cocktail before, just rum and Coke or screwdrivers. As soon as the margarita arrives I take a sip and decide I don't like it but continue to drink it anyway. By then Jimmy's begun to entertain us with stories about his own dysfunctional family, including his alcoholic, homophobic middle-aged uncle who has a habit of ranting drunkenly at Jimmy to at least consider trying to sleep with women ("Some of them look almost like boys, anyway, Jimmy, and lots of young women are up for *experimental* sex").

"My own explanation of what I'm looking for in a partner bounces off him each time," Jimmy muses. "But when he gets good and tired of listening to it, he decides it's time to berate my father for failing to turn me into a 'real man.' And my father, the poor man, I think silently half agrees with him so doesn't know which one of us to argue with and gets very quiet until my uncle passes out cold." Jimmy picks up his margarita glass and gives it a gentle shake. "At which point he complains about him bitterly. So this is all very civilized in comparison."

"That's terrible," my mother says earnestly. "People have to let you be who you are."

"Live and let live." Jimmy smiles sagely. "I completely agree with you, but at the same time I think we're most comfortable with people who are our mirror images."

That feels like the truth, and I nod at Jimmy and swallow more of my margarita. Dad and Morgan have yet to reappear, but somehow the upset seems more easily handled without them. I'm really starting to hope that Morgan and Jimmy get married one day. Jimmy would be such a good thing for our family, and he's not easily fazed by our shortcomings either. I feel an undiluted burst of affection for him and wonder whether Devin would like him too.

At last our food shows up, followed by worn-looking versions of Morgan and my father. No one mentions their absence or what brought it about; Mom ogles Dad's basket of exotic mushrooms appetizer and remarks, "That sauce looks tasty, Peter."

Dad spears a mushroom and pops it in his mouth. "Rich," he comments. "But very, very good."

And this is the way our dinner continues, with no further discussion about the theatre tickets. We talk about the weather (the importance of snow tires again), a guy who jumped onto the TTC subway tracks to save an old woman who fell from the platform as a train approached, hockey (which really only Morgan and Dad know anything about), and pets (Morgan and Jimmy are trying to decide whether they want a kitten or a bird).

When the bill arrives Morgan and Dad haggle over their portions, which I guess means everything's back to normal, or as close as we get in my family these days. Morgan and Jimmy cabbed it to Hi-*Lo*, and Dad offers to drop them off at their apartment. The group of us troop out to the sidewalk and head for the nearby parking lot where we dumped the car earlier in the evening.

I don't know what it is that makes me turn and glance across the street, but the moment I do my eyes latch on to a green shell coat. This time my mind's doubt-free. My brother Devin's rambling across Cumberland Street with a brunette in skin-tight white pants. Her hand is wrapped in his, and now I know there is such a thing as a sixth sense because Devin sees me too. He pulls the brunette along faster as his head jerks away from me.

I don't care if he wants to escape us. This time I'm not letting him go. I roar his name across the traffic streaking between us. Morgan's walking next to me, and I see his eyes snap to Devin's form in the distance. A few more seconds and he'll be gone, lost all over again.

My heels aren't as tall as last time and I sprint forward, weaving in and out of oncoming pedestrian traffic. Devin sees me coming and he's nearly running too, that pasty, unfamiliar brunette still attached to him. "Stop!" I yell to him across the street. "Devin, wait!"

The girl's gaze races to meet mine for the first time. I wonder if she even knows his name is Devin. Who is she?

Devin doesn't stop. He makes a sharp left and darts down into the nearest subway station entrance. Saved by Toronto transit once again! Only I don't plan on stopping either. I fly over the curb, my heel catching the tiniest mound of black ice, which flips me over, turtle-like, and forces all the oxygen from my lungs. For the first few seconds the only thing I can do is lie there motionless on the sidewalk, gasping for breath and feeling my back ache.

Morgan appears over me, and I shift my body into a seated position. None of my parts are broken. They just hurt in a way you don't usually encounter in everyday life.

"Are you okay?" Morgan asks, hunching down next to me. "That was some flip."

"I'm okay."

Morgan holds his hand out to me and pulls me gently upwards. "You positive you're all in one piece?"

"My back hurts." My hand flies to my bruised spine. Then, in a millisecond, my brain leaps back to the moment before I fell. "Devin! Where is he?" I've started shouting again, my voice made hoarse by the pain from my fall. "Go after him!"

Morgan gazes in the direction of the subway entrance across the street. "He's gone, Serena."

"Not necessarily. We can follow him. C'mon." I grab Morgan's coat sleeve and pull him along with me, almost the way Devin was doing with the brunette.

Morgan doesn't fight me. He scurries towards the subway, matching my steps, and I think this is it: we're finally going to be reunited with Devin again, whether he wants the same or not. This is the moment four out of five of the LeBlancs have been waiting for.

But that particular subway entrance is the unmanned kind, and worse, the type they call an iron maiden — metal bars in a revolving door. Without subway tokens Morgan and I aren't going anywhere, and there's no way to buy one at this entrance. We're stopped dead because we don't have access to a stupid three-dollar subway token.

"Bellair Street entrance!" Morgan shouts to me. "Let's go!"

We jog off towards Bellair Street, Morgan holding on to my sleeve, partly to speed me up and partly, I think, because he's worried I might fall again. We stomp into the Bellair Street subway entrance and dart downstairs where, miraculously, the booth attendant is alone with no line to slow us down. "Two," Morgan snaps, sliding a bill towards the attendant and not waiting for change.

Morgan runs towards the platform, his long black coat flapping behind him. I run too, as fast as I can without wiping out again.

The east- and westbound subway trains board from a central platform, meaning Morgan and I are in luck again. We stalk off in opposite directions, patrolling the subway platform. I pass a teenage couple making out, the guy grabbing handfuls of the girl's ass, and then an old guy in a tweed cap, coughing into his palm. The sound of an oncoming train electrifies the air. Morgan and I don't have much time left. We have to find him.

I'm running again, scanning faces and forms, and then turning to race back in the other direction, rushing towards Morgan, who is holding up his hands, looking as frustrated as I am. The eastbound subway squeals to a stop next to us. Morgan and I stand in place and continue to scan the passengers desperately as they board. I already know we missed Devin somehow. There just aren't that many people on the platform. If Devin were still down here we'd have run into him already. He must have hopped on an earlier train while we were stuck at the other subway entrance.

For the second time this year, Devin's been rescued by public transit, and for the second time this year, Toronto's transportation system has let me down, swallowed up my missing brother as though he doesn't matter to anyone.

Morgan and I stare at each other in the quiet of the now empty subway platform. His eyes are tired and anxious.

"It was him, right?" I say. "You saw him this time."

"I saw him," Morgan confirms. "It was definitely Devin." Morgan's hands magnetically attach to his waist. He bows his head before straightening it out and meeting my eyes again. "I'm not ready to face them yet." *My parents.* Our family dinner didn't start out well and this is another turn for the worse. Much worse. Last time I spotted Devin Morgan didn't really want to know and warned me about Devin dragging us all down with him. But a couple of minutes ago Morgan was running as fast as I was. Today it seems we're in this together. "Can we take a couple of minutes?" he asks.

I nod, my hand winding around my back, reaching for my spine.

"It still hurts?" Morgan asks.

"Yeah."

Morgan sighs. His hand reaches for his hair, as though he's about to drive his fingers through it. Changing his mind, his arm drops back to his side. "It seemed like a good idea at the time," he says. "The dinner, the theatre tickets, all of it."

This time I do feel sorry for Morgan, my perfect brother trying so hard and still not getting tonight right. "It was a good idea," I tell him.

"Uh-huh," Morgan says wearily. "Good idea, bad execution."

"The execution wasn't up to you." I smile a little. "That's where it went wrong."

"Mmm." Morgan presses his lips together and nods. "You sound a lot like Devin sometimes, you know. The two of you always …" He abandons his sentence to the eerie silence of the subway.

"What?" I ask.

"You were always setting up comparisons between yourselves and me, trying to make me feel like I was doing something wrong just by being myself." Morgan shakes his head dismissively as if to suggest it's all in the past, but Jimmy's words come back to haunt me. *I think we're most comfortable with people who are our mirror images.*

We always felt Morgan was too good for us, Devin and me. I don't know if I believed that because it was what Devin believed or if it was something I would've thought all on my own. Devin was the one who always listened to me and gave me his time, but I could've given my older brother more of a chance, there's no question.

"I didn't mean to … be like that," I stammer. I hate regrets. On their own they're like parasites. There's no point to them unless they provoke some kind of change. It looks like the new, improved me still has lots more evolving to do.

"I know, Serena." Morgan nods lightly. "It's okay. Tonight has just …" He throws his hands into his pockets. "I don't have a clue what to do with them." He means my parents again. "What do we tell them?"

They would've heard me shout Devin's name, definitely. Choice is an illusion. "Just the truth, I guess. What else do we have?"

"You're right," Morgan says resolutely. "There's nothing else for us to work with."

I reach out and squeeze my big brother's arm. We walk slowly in the direction of the nearest exit, in no hurry to reach our parents and get on with the job of revealing the unhappy truth.

CHAPTER TWENTY-FIVE

✦

MY PARENTS ARE EERILY quiet when we materialize back in front of Hi-*Lo* and explain about chasing Devin down the street. Morgan wants me and my parents to come back to their place for coffee so that we can discuss things further, but my father complains that he's tired. We drop Morgan and Jimmy off at their apartment building, and as we pull away from the curb Morgan waves to me, forming a phone with his fingers and mouthing, "Call me."

I've been wrong to be jealous and angry with him. I didn't think he even really knew because we've never fought in the almost feral way some brothers and sisters do. Even now I know the jealousy hasn't been fully vanquished, but my new awareness has shrunk it, changed it.

In the car Mom finds her voice and starts firing Devin questions at me. What he looked like. Whether he seemed healthy or not. If the girl he was with appeared to be his girlfriend. Why he would run from Morgan and me.

My answers are incomplete and vague. He looked okay. Not much skinnier than when he left home. I have no idea who the girl is, not anyone I've seen at our house. Devin ran because he doesn't want to talk to any of us, but I don't say that to my mother, and anyway, it's obvious. At first I'm surprised that my mother's as composed as she is — maybe deep down she believed Devin was dead and the fact that he's striding around Toronto hopping on subway trains sounds like good news. But later that night, when I'm trying to sleep, I hear crying and ragged voices from my parents' bedroom.

I wait for it to stop. It doesn't. I dial Morgan, who immediately calls our land line. After a few minutes my parents begin to quiet down, so this time my big brother can be assured he did something right. Then Morgan calls me back on my cell and chats about nothing like he's trying to distract me.

After a bit I ask if Jimmy's still awake too. "He went to bed a couple of minutes ago," Morgan says. "While you and I were on the phone."

"I was going to text him my email address but I guess you can pass it on to him."

"Sure, I'll do that," Morgan tells me. "And next time we'll just have *you* over for dinner like the original plan. I'll leave it to you whether you want to bring someone or not."

"You mean *the guy*, don't you?"

"Exactly," Morgan says. "*The guy*. Or not, whatever you prefer."

"Okay, I'll think about it." I yawn into the phone. "I'm about three seconds away from unconsciousness so I better say good night."

"Good night, Serena," my brother says, and I feel like I know him a bit better than I did before Devin left last June. Is it awful to think there may be some good things about Devin's disappearance?

I put my cell down and snuggle into my pillow. After spotting Devin earlier I'm positive I'll have one of my two dreams about him, but when I wake up to the sound of my alarm at eight o'clock the next morning I can't remember dreaming at all. No one else is awake yet, and normally I wouldn't be up this early on a Sunday unless I had to go to work either, but I made up my mind what to do next just as I was dozing off last night and it can't wait.

I'm going on a Devin quest again. A quest I won't quit until he speaks to me. Just me.

Morgan might help, if I asked him, but when I do find Devin I don't want him to feel like we're ganging up on him, ready to play the home version of *Intervention*. I just need to know that he's okay, or that he will be, eventually.

I eat a bowl of Raisin Bran, leave a note for my parents, and creep out of the house. Then I text Genevieve to inform her she's my alibi and that I've gone searching for Devin in Toronto. It takes me longer than ever to get downtown because the local bus that hooks up with the commuter train to Toronto's running on a lame Sunday schedule.

There's no wind or snow today but the temperature's bleak and I shiver in my hat and layers as I retrace last night's steps along Cumberland Street. If I were skating I wouldn't feel the cold so much. Of course, if I were skating there'd be hot chocolate too. So I pop into Starbucks for severely overpriced hot chocolate and scan the faces of the other customers. The old Devin usually preferred independent coffee shops, but if I want to maximize my chances of locating him I'll need to stop in to every coffee shop and fast food restaurant between here and Queen Street West.

I'm under no illusions that I'll find him today, but he can't hide out forever. I'll come back to Toronto whenever I can, for however long it takes. In Starbucks I dole out my change with one hand and hold my phone out with the other, pushing it under the barista's nose and asking if she's seen my missing brother. She barely gives my cell a glance before shaking her head and telling me no.

I put my gloves back on and slip back outside with my hot chocolate. The city rapidly becomes a blur of greasy food, ground coffee, and people replying that they've never seen my brother. Questioning the service industry people works best because they can't shake me off and are more likely to have noticed Devin in the first place. I know I remember the customers that stop in regularly at Total Drug

Mart — I probably remember some of them better than they remember me because normally people just want to fast-forward through the transaction and jump to more interesting moments in their lives. Me, I'm stuck behind a counter for hours at a time.

Some of the people I show Devin's photo to stop and take the time to absorb the image and search their memory. Others couldn't really care less but look at it anyway. In between my fast food stops it's so chilly outside that I think about Bucky and his owner on Queen Street. I hope they're not out in this, but if they are I have another five-dollar bill set aside for them.

When I lose feeling in my fingers, despite my thick gloves, I decide it's time for lunch. After inhaling the scent of so much grease and sugar, the only thing I can handle the thought of is rabbit food so I buy a fresh fruit tray at Cultures and stay awhile to get warm. Back out on the street afterwards, I begin the whole cycle over with a fresh hot chocolate and a string of fast food restaurants.

I skip most of the clothing stores and lurch past a strip club. The sign's top line promises: "THE BEST ALL NUDE DELICIOUS HOT GIRLS." The second reads: "VISIT OUR VIP ROOM. WELCOME TOURISTS!"

Wandering by the Eaton Centre shopping mall, its warmth tempts me. But for some reason I think I'll have better luck out on the street so I keep going, popping into any place that will feed a person for less than five dollars. That makes the Golden Arches top of the list, and I stumble into McDonald's, reaching for my cell in my back pocket as I join the line. My eyes scour the customers — a family of five, two young Asian women grabbing a table by the wall, a trio of teenage guys in gang colours. I can't explain, but when my gaze lands on Devin, gulping down a jumbo-sized drink near the window, the sight doesn't come as a shock. It's as though on some level I already knew I'd find him here.

That's the way it seems for a moment or two anyway. Seconds

later my heart's up in my mouth and I'm welded to the spot under my feet.

Now. Before he sees me. I wrench my left foot up and then my right. My legs obey and rush me over to Devin's window seat. He doesn't even see me coming.

I stand directly in front of him so he can't run without pushing me aside.

Shit. That's what he's thinking when he looks up at me. I read it in his face. He screws up his eyes as he stares at me, cringing in his seat. Then he clamps his lashes shut and lets his mouth fall open.

My brother's hair is the same colour as mine, but it looks as though he hasn't washed it in a few days. He has the kind of scalp that gets oily fast; that's like mine too. His eyes are deep-set, like my father's. If you look closely enough you'd recognize bits of all the other LeBlancs in my brother Devin. To my eyes he seems overly skinny for his frame, but people who don't know him may not think so.

"So sit," Devin barks. "Stop staring at me."

"You'll take off," I tell him, my voice unnaturally intense for such a mundane location. Drama must happen all the time at McDonald's, but stupid reality show type melodrama. Devin and I shouldn't have the crucial conversation we're in for at a place whose mascot is a clown.

"I won't," he mutters.

I don't believe him.

"I won't," he repeats with an ultra-sharp edge. "*Shit.* Sit, Serena!"

I angle my body towards the chair next to his and drop reluctantly into it.

"Shit," he says again, both hands rubbing at his hair. "What're you even doing here?"

Duh. "Looking for you." I stretch my legs out a bit under the table and accidentally knock one of them against his.

Devin doesn't move to accommodate my legs. He glares at me

in silence. That green shell coat I've spotted him in before is slung across the back of his chair. He's wearing a blue polo shirt with the number 15 on the front and grey pants, and I can't stop staring at him. "Morgan and I went after you yesterday, you know," I continue. "Even after you went down to the subway. We were on the platform, searching for you." I push my chair back to make room for my legs. "I've been looking for you all day."

Devin's expression is disinterest mixed with irritation. "You're wasting your time."

"I get to decide what's a waste of my time," I tell him.

"Okay." Devin yawns and rubs his eyes. He has dark circles under them, something he was always prone to, only now they're more pronounced. "Whatever."

"*Whatever*? Do you have any idea what you've done to Mom and Dad?" Devin's soul has been sucked out of his body. He doesn't look like the Devin from my zombie dreams but the vibe surrounding him is the same. It's like he's not even hearing me. "Mom's been an inch away from having a complete breakdown since the moment you left," I explain. "All she does is visit her doctor and haunt eBay. And Dad, there's nothing he can do about it so he pretty much just sits around too. Their whole lives revolve around staying home in case they hear news about you."

I straighten my back against the uncomfortable McDonald's chair and spit out, "At one point we thought you might be dead. Somebody found a body in Newmarket. Mom called the police because it could've been you."

My neck cranes forward. "Every single day at our house is a day you're not there, a day where we have no idea what's going on with you."

Devin smiles bitterly, his hand rhythmically tapping the table. "Dad and Mom did that to themselves. They're the ones who kicked me out, if you remember. So why don't you lay the blame where it belongs."

"What else could they do but kick you out with the way you were acting?" I'm not getting through to him at all. "You *punched* Dad. You were stealing things, fighting with everyone." Bringing weird people home. *Using.* I stop myself before adding the last two to the list, but I could go on and on.

Devin's mouth puckers. "They've done a number on you — you're brainwashed through and through. Seeing everything from their side."

"You honestly think it was different than that?" I ask him. "Don't you even remember what you used to be like before you started with the ..." I can't bring myself to put a name to his problem. *Meth* is such an ugly word. I never realized that before last June.

"Serena." Devin holds his sides as he hunches over the table. "I'm not going to sit here and listen to you romanticize the past like it was so perfect. You know what I felt like before? Like shit. Like *nothing.*"

He reaches for his shake, closing his fingers around it but not picking it up. "So you think you can come looking for me and change my life? I already did that. It's *done* and this is it. I'm not changing back to the person I was before, and it sounds like you're the one who needs to learn to deal with that — you and Mom and Dad." He yanks his legs towards him under the table. "I have places to be. I need to go."

"Places?" I repeat. "Where?"

"*Oh.*" Devin forces a laugh. "Don't we sound like Mom now?" The contempt in his words throws me off balance. It's not fair for him to hate Mom so much after all the worrying she's done about him. He must be frozen on the inside, his heart and mind a solid block of ice.

"Right," I say sarcastically. "How embarrassing for me to actually give a shit about you and what you're doing with your life. How embarrassing for me; how embarrassing for Mom."

"Sweet Jesus," Devin grumbles as he gets up. "Do we have to be so melodramatic?"

I stand too and watch him tug on his coat. It has a zipper around the back of the neck that suggests a missing attachable hood and one of the sleeves bunches partway up his arm. He yanks it down to cover his polo shirt as he looks at me sideways. "I'm cool," he mutters, bobbing his head as an afterthought. "Really, okay? And you'll be okay too if you just stop worrying so much. I don't even know why you …" His hands comb restlessly through his hair again.

"What?" I ask him. "What?"

"Why you bothered," he adds. "This is the way things have to be." He shrugs.

I put my hand out to stop him, thinking he's about to move. I'm not ready for him to disappear on me again. Even this shitty, hollowed Devin is better than none at all. "You can't just leave like this. Give me a number to call you at — a cell or your land line. Something."

Devin stands in front of me, his head tilting slowly to one side. "I think with the way things are now it's better that I don't." He edges past me, turning to add, "I have to go. Take care, okay?"

I follow instinctively, just a step behind him. Out on Yonge Street, Devin turns and looks at me, his breath lighting up the cold air. His hands find their way inside his pockets as he frowns. "You can't follow me forever, you know."

He doesn't know about the dreams I've been having about him. He doesn't know about Gage or my friends or Total Drug Mart. He hasn't asked me one single question about myself and what I've been doing all these months. "Don't you care at all?" I ask him. "Would it matter if I dropped dead tomorrow?" I'm losing my voice but it doesn't make any difference; I don't think I have anything else to say.

Devin pushes more air out of his lungs and says, "You're going to be fine. The last thing you need is me in your life, fucking things up for you."

"So don't fuck things up." The words slice at my vocal cords.

"And they said I was the smart one." Devin smiles weakly. "Be good, Serena. I'm outta here." My brother disappears into the crowd of Yonge Street shoppers milling around us and I don't try to stop him. Morgan was absolutely right; Devin doesn't want our help. He's exactly where he wants to be. Somehow I thought I could change that. I thought the strength of my hopes for him could make him well, as though I'm living a fairy tale where wishes have magic properties.

I didn't even fully realize that's what I believed until Devin proved me wrong. It's so cold out on the street and I've been wrong about so many things, but I'm not sorry I came. I line my back up against the nearest wall and let it catch me, sadness choking up through my throat and demanding I recognize it for what it is. At last, I've let my brother go.

CHAPTER TWENTY-SIX

IT'S SPRING NOW. GREEN bits are poking through snow the colour of ashes. Stale snow always looks disgusting, unless you're in the country where it can remain a gleaming white. But it probably won't snow again until next winter so it's just a matter of time until the green wins.

For a while I wondered if I'd been wrong to tell my parents about my meeting with Devin. Mom hit bottom and went almost catatonic. There was one week where she called in sick to the museum three days in a row and never got out bed, just lay under the covers listening to her white noise machine. She wouldn't even go see Doctor Berkovich. In the end my father was the one who called for an appointment and escorted her there. The fifty-minute-long session cemented his opinion that Doctor Berkovich is a useless placebo, and Dad carted her back to the family doctor for a referral to another therapist.

Mom never wanted to take antidepressants but she's on one now, at least until she begins to feel a bit better. Her new therapist also wants her exercising, so I bought a yoga for beginners DVD and we've been contorting our bodies a few times a week. Dad and I are trying to be positive and encouraging with her, which can be tough because some days she's an energy drain and you just want to shake her and scream at her to snap out of it.

At one point Dad wanted to go downtown to find Devin for himself, but then Mom's problems took over and it started to seem like not such a good idea anyway. Of course, I can understand about wanting to see for yourself, refusing to believe that there's nothing you can do to change someone else. But I've had to stop my constant worrying over Devin, wondering how he's keeping himself alive and asking myself a hundred other questions about him that I have no answers for. I don't know how you make yourself stop asking those questions, but I'm trying. I miss him, but I need to believe that somehow the universe, Terry Fox, or God — whatever you want to call it — will look out for Devin. Maybe that's magical thinking too, but everyone needs to believe in something, which brings me back to my former twenty-nine pounds of chunk and the idea that people will always disappoint you.

That's just not true. People won't always disappoint you. People won't always surprise you either. There are no absolute rules to guide you through life.

One thing I *can* say is that my brother Morgan actually is almost as cool and wonderful as everyone seems to think. This still grates on me at times, but I have an appreciation for it now too. He and Jimmy picked up a calico kitten from the Toronto Humane Society and named her Ingrid. I'm going to cat-sit when they go to Regina to visit Jimmy's parents at the beginning of June.

Because it's my birthday today Morgan scored me six free concert tickets for a New Jersey band called Comet Down. I've only heard four of their songs online but Morgan promises they'll be awesome and Nicole's already crushing on their lead singer. I like that all the other members of the band are girls, which is the opposite of most coed bands. Normally if a band has *any* girl in it, she's the lead singer.

Anyway, six tickets means me, Genevieve, Nicole, Izzy, Marguerite, and Aya, but an even bigger group of us are heading out to dinner beforehand. Aside from the one or two times a week Gage and

I see each other we pretty much do our own things, but everyone wanted to celebrate my birthday together tonight so he'll be there along with Damien (whom I've met a few times now) and Joyeux. I swear, Joyeux and Aya look like cartoon characters walking next to each other — Joyeux's legs practically stretch up to her neck — but they're so amazing together that everyone has fallen in love with the idea of them as a couple.

Just last week I hung out with Gage and Akayla for the first time, and when Gage introduced me as his girlfriend Akayla reminded him that he said I was just a friend. She's as sharp as a tack and doesn't miss a thing. She's also a big goofball and made me sing and dance with her for ages and Gage was evil again and caught the whole thing on video. Because I sucked up to Akayla all night and did everything she wanted, I think she liked me, but Gage and I aren't going to complicate things by doing that too often.

Genevieve, Nicole, and I went ahead and started up an official school club three weeks ago. It took a while to get the materials together for it and we still don't have a name but we do have two co-advisors and fifteen members so far. My dad's happy that I'm in a school club because he says it will look good on university applications later, but when we got talking about the details I think it freaked him out to hear some of the things that have been going on at school. For example, one of our members is this really sweet freshman girl who a group of freshman female savages are playing hardcore mean girl with on the Internet. Then there's this new sophomore guy, Ruwan. He's only been at Laurier a few weeks, but two guys in his math class have been calling him a fag and pushing him around. Ruwan didn't want to join the club to begin with but Dina Manzoor made him come with her and now I think he's glad because we can all talk about these things without having to feel embarrassed, and we strategize about ways to deal with them too.

We have another meeting in two days, and I jot down a partially formed thought I have about the club before it can slip my mind. Gage will be here to pick me up any second now so I don't have time to flesh it out. I grab my brush and run it through my hair on my way downstairs. Because of Gage, turning sixteen has loomed large in my life over the past couple of months, but sixteen-year-old me isn't any different from the person I was yesterday and the day before that. Then again, I know I'm not exactly the same person I was when Devin left or when I started going out with Jacob or even when I broke up with him.

The doorbell rings. I slip my suede jacket out of our newly cleaned (I boxed all the old coats and put them in the basement) front closest and answer the door. Gage has told me his hair actually will be dirty blond by July, bleached by the sun, but at the moment it's still light brown. The low-hanging sun is making him squint, lighting up his eyes in a way that makes it difficult for me to breathe.

"Hey, birthday girl," Gage says, his dimples popping into place.

"Hi." I smile back and step outside, where I wrap my arms tightly around him and kiss him on the mouth. We've done that a lot over the past couple of months but no semi-nude make-out sessions on his couch, so I'm in a rush to get to Gage's place and pick up where we left off in February. I'm even wearing this cute pink plaid bra that I bought special for the occasion.

Gage and I don't get very far before starting to let loose — my driveway, to be exact. He reaches for me across the gear shift, one of his hands sliding under my open suede coat as he kisses me. His fingers skim across my left breast and then my right, massaging them both at one time. I dig my fingers under his shirt, scratching with my short nails.

Outside a car cruises by, reminding us that my parents will be home soon. Gage laughs under his breath and says, "I guess I better start driving." When we reach his house, a woman who I assume is Mrs. Cochrane is standing around in the front yard, chatting with an elderly woman in a white and orange pantsuit.

"Our neighbour," Gage explains. "My mom does her hair."

Gage and I get out of the car and amble towards them. "Hi, Mom," Gage says. "We don't want to interrupt. I just thought I'd introduce Serena. It's her birthday today."

Mrs. Cochrane peers down her glasses at me. Her burgundy-tinted hair is so thick and glossy that I'm tempted to ask what kind of shampoo she uses. "Happy birthday, Serena," Mrs. Cochrane says, pointing towards the woman next to her. "This is my friend, Elouise."

I say hello to them both and Elouise nods at me before switching her gaze to Gage. "Is this your girlfriend? She's a pretty thing."

"She is." Gage smiles politely at Elouise. "She's both those things." Gage's hand falls on the small of my back to rush us away. "Good to see you again, Elouise."

I glance at Elouise and Mrs. Cochrane over my shoulder as we're walking away. "Nice meeting you both."

Once we're inside I turn to Gage and say, "We shouldn't have left so quickly. Now what're they going to think?"

"They're too busy gossiping about other neighbours to think about us," Gage assures me. "Anyway, I want to give you your presents before we meet up with everyone else." He checks his watch. "We have just over an hour."

I already know my parents' gift will be a contribution to my baby blue scooter fund, but I don't have a clue what Gage has bought me. "Sit down," he tells me, motioning to the couch. "I'll get them."

Thirty seconds later he's back with a gift basket and two boxes — one tiny and one large. "I know you don't care about flowers and you're always drinking hot chocolate," he says as he hands me a basket full of gourmet hot chocolate.

He's right. I'm always drinking hot chocolate, even in summer.

"It's perfect!" I tell him. "Thanks." I read the labels on the packages — mocha, traditional, cinnamon spice — and begin to drool.

The large box turns out to be new Rollerblades, which I've needed for a while and mentioned a couple of weeks ago while we were talking about going blading this summer, and the small box contains a gorgeous Swarovski crystal aqua anklet, which immediately makes me think of my mother.

"Because you have such beautiful ankles," Gage says. "Do you want to try it on?" I whip my left shoe and sock off and stretch my bare foot out towards him so he can fasten the anklet on for me. "My hands are shaky," he admits as he undoes the clasp. "This feels like a first date."

"That's not good," I tease, my face heating up. "How're you going to unhook things?"

"I don't know," Gage says with a dirty look that makes me hornier than ever. "I guess you'll have to help me."

So much for wondering how the bracelet looks on my ankle. As soon as he fastens it on we're grasping for each other, crushing our lips together and stripping off clothes until I'm sitting on top of him on the couch with both our chests bare but our jeans on.

"So did they grow?" I joke as I wriggle against his pelvis underneath me.

Gage holds my breasts in his hands and pretends to think it over. His lips explode into a grin as he says, "I don't know. I'm in sensory overload." He reaches for my hips and adjusts my position on top of him slightly, his breathing heavy.

He thrusts and I shimmy. I make little noises of joy as he shows my boobs more appreciation. I know exactly what he means about sensory overload. I'm there now. This is part of the reason I had such trouble reining myself in on our first date. He gets me so hot. When it comes to Gage I'm definitely an addict, and I shift my weight on top of him, drop my hand down behind me, and begin to massage him through his jeans. "Is this okay?" I whisper.

"It's good," he tells me in a hushed voice. "It's good."

And by the end of it we're both better than good; we're amazing. And still wearing our jeans too. We lie on the couch together like we used to and Gage whispers in my ear, "Happy birthday, Serena. I'm glad I got up the guts to ask for your number. The last few months have been great, getting to know you."

I couldn't agree more. On one level I've been impatient because we've barely touched each other during the last couple of months, but on another level that hardly seems to matter. Just hanging out with Gage is great, and although I can't say for sure what we'll be to each other this time next year or the year after that, I think we're both ready to work through whatever complications are on the horizon.

My phone rings — the sound of Abba's "Waterloo" (I got hooked on it watching *Mamma Mia*) — pealing through the family room. "You better get that," Gage says, reaching over the arm of the couch to grab for my cell on the side table. "It's probably someone wanting to wish you a happy birthday."

I sit up on the couch and answer it without even bothering to look at who's calling. "Hello?"

"Serena?" A male voice asks.

"Yeah."

"I just wanted to wish you a happy birthday. It is today, right? The seventeenth?" I glance swiftly over at Gage, shocked to hear Devin's voice on the phone. As far as I know, he hasn't been in touch with any of my family (except me, when I tracked him down almost two months ago) since he left last June.

Gage stares back at me with wide eyes, wondering if something's the matter.

"It's today," I confirm. "Thanks, Devin."

Gage's eyes pop. He looks nearly as surprised as I feel.

"Sixteen," Devin declares. "I hope you're doing something special for it." He laughs dryly into the phone. "Remember how Mom used to make us all sing happy birthday to each other?" First thing in the morning my mother would gather us all around the kitchen table, stick a candle in the birthday boy's or girl's freshly baked muffin, and lead us in a loud and off-key rendition of "Happy Birthday." Of course I remember. Every time I smell warm muffins in the air it smells like somebody's birthday.

"So where's my song?" I kid. My heart's beating faster from just hearing Devin's voice on the phone. I don't expect anything from him anymore, but he's made me happier than he could ever know.

"You know I could never sing," Devin says. "But happy birthday anyway. Any sign of your old pal, Clara?"

A chuckle bursts up from my diaphragm, Clara's ghostly black and white image shimmering behind my eyes. Whether the picture comes from my own memory or Devin's description from last Christmas, I can't tell. It's all the same now, a shared story and vision from our past. "She's right here," I tell him. "Want to say hello?"

"You say hi for me."

I can't ask him any questions and spoil things. Everything now is up to him, but it's a good sign that he called, isn't it? I feel it in my bones.

"See you later, sis," he continues.

"Talk to you later," I say back. "And, thanks."

I disconnect and curl back into Gage's arms, my eyes wet. "I can't believe that," I mumble. "I can't believe he just called."

Devin called once, so he can call again, and I won't let myself obsess about exactly when that will happen, but I'm going to keep right on believing he'll work his way slowly back to all of us.

"Maybe he'll get in touch some other time," Gage says, broadcasting my thoughts.

"I really hope so." I plant a grateful kiss on Gage's chin. "How long do we have left?"

He holds his arm over our heads and scrunches up his eyes to read his watch. "About fifteen minutes. I guess I should clean myself up and get ready."

"In five minutes, okay?"

Gage strokes my hair and nestles his head into the crook of my shoulder. "Okay."

This is what it's like, starting over every day. Messy and gradual. Good and bad. Better and better and better. This is the very beginning of sixteen, and I can't wait to see what happens next.

ACKNOWLEDGEMENTS

A hundred thousand thanks to Deborah Kerbel and Barry Jowett for their grace and guidance. Without you this book wouldn't have been possible! Hearty thanks also to Courtney Summers, Monica Kulling and Margaret Buffie for their continuing support, and to the sensational team at Dancing Cat Books – Alessandra Ferreri, Bryan J. Ibeas, Angel Guerra, and Tannice Goddard.

Always and forever, special thanks go to my husband, Paddy, for being my trusty first reader and (in the words of Jim Croce), "the one I want to go through time with."